Also by Sharon Sala

come
Back to Me

SHARON
SALA

sourcebooks
casablanca

Published by Sourcebooks Casablanca, an imprint of Sourcebooks, Inc.
P.O. Box 4410, Naperville, Illinois 60567-4410
(630) 961-3900
Fax: (630) 961-2168
sourcebooks.com

Printed and bound in the United States of America.
OPM 10 9 8 7 6 5 4 3 2 1

Prologue

Blessings, Georgia

MOONLIGHT COMING THROUGH THE LEAD-GLASS PANES of an upstairs window left shadows on the wall behind George and Ruth Payne's bed. Without intention, the shadows resembling jail bars were now a valid representation of where life had taken them, because Ruth had been handed a sentence George couldn't fight.

Ruth was dying.

She had reached the end of available cancer treatments two months ago. There was nothing more modern medicine could do for her, so she'd chosen to stop everything but the pain meds and was just biding her time.

George slept facing the windows with Ruth curled up on the bed behind him, her arm around his waist to keep him close. Throughout their married lives, she had trusted him with all her troubles, and he'd never let her down. Knowing he could not stop what was happening to her now was about to break him. He just couldn't let her know.

Even asleep, George was hyperaware of her tiniest movement, of the softest breath coming out of rhythm, but the strident sound of a ringing phone was a rude awakening.

He woke with a gasp, reaching for the receiver before his eyes were open, trying to remember if their son,

Aidan, who was in his senior year of high school, was home from the basketball game and in bed. And then he saw the clock. Three fifteen a.m. It had to be bad news. At this time of the morning, it always was.

He answered, his heart pounding.

"Hello."

"George?"

"Yes, this is George. Who's this?"

"Your store is on fire!" the caller said and disconnected.

George leaped out of bed, turning on lights as he went, and began getting dressed.

Already pale and shaky, Ruth raised up on one elbow, concerned by the look on George's face.

"What's wrong? Is Aidan okay?" she asked.

"They said the store is on fire," he said and stepped into his loafers, then ran to the dresser for his wallet and keys. "Stay in bed. I'll call when I know something."

"Oh my God," Ruth moaned. "This can't be happening."

George knew what she meant. Because of her cancer, their savings had been depleted, and their checking account was down to spare change. They'd been living from one month to the next solely on the income from their auto supply store.

George was scared but wasn't going to let her know. "I know, sweetheart. We'll figure it out. Just rest. I'll be home as soon as I can."

And with that he was gone.

Down the hall, eighteen-year-old Aidan had also been awakened by the phone, but when he heard his dad running down the stairs then driving away from the house, he got up to go check on his mom.

Ruth heard her son's footsteps and turned on the light as Aidan knocked on the door.

"Come in," she said, and as always, put on a brave face for him as he entered.

He had his father's black hair and brown eyes, but he was tall like her father, Preston. It saddened her, knowing she'd never live to see her son grown.

"What's going on?" Aidan asked.

"Someone called and said the store was on fire," she said and then burst into tears.

Aidan rushed to her bedside and took her in his arms.

"It's okay, Mama. It's going to be okay," Aidan said, knowing full well nothing was ever going to be okay again.

———∾∾∾———

George drove through the neighborhood like a madman, shaking all the way to his bones. Life seemed determined to take them down, and no matter how hard he tried, he couldn't stop it.

He saw the flames above the rooftops before he hit Main Street but still wasn't prepared for seeing their livelihood going up in flames. It wasn't until he was speeding toward the fire that it dawned on him no one was there. No fire truck, no firemen, not even the police.

"What the hell?" he moaned as he made a U-turn and raced back down the middle of Main Street to the police station, coming to a sliding stop at the curb. He got out running and shouting, "Help! Somebody help me! I need help!"

Within seconds, the front door to the station opened, and Travis Welty, the night dispatcher, was silhouetted in the doorway.

"George Payne? What's going on?" he asked.

George pointed back toward his store. "Someone called to tell me my store is on fire! Why hasn't the fire department responded?"

"Oh lordy! No one called us!" Travis cried and ran back into the station. Within seconds, he had dispatched fire and rescue to the scene.

George sped back to the fire, unaware he was crying. He parked on the opposite side of the street and got out, but his legs were shaking too much to stand up, so he sat at the curb. By the time the fire truck arrived, his store was gone, and all of the focus was on the fire spreading to the bakery next door.

Even though it was hours before dawn, word of the fire had spread, and people were gathering. Someone noticed George and ran to him, asking what had happened.

"I don't know," George said. "Someone called me. I came here to this."

"Tough break, man. Are you insured?"

George drew a shaky breath and then frowned as he turned and looked up at the man staring down at him.

"I'm sorry. What did you say?" George asked.

"I asked if you were insured?"

"Oh. Yes," George said.

The man slapped George on the shoulder. "Then you'll be okay," he said.

George didn't respond, but the guy didn't know. He wouldn't be okay. He didn't think he'd ever feel okay again.

He was staring blankly at the flames coming out a window of the bakery when he heard a car coming up the street at a high rate of speed. He turned to look just as it skidded to a stop at the police barricade. The driver, a woman, got out screaming as she ran toward the fire.

George frowned. It was Sonja Ritter. She and her husband, Marty, owned the bakery, and Phoebe, their only child, was Aidan's girlfriend.

And then it hit him.

Marty! The bakery! Dear lord! What if Marty was already at work?

He saw the horror on Sonja's face as she pushed past the barricade, screaming her husband's name as she raced toward the fire.

"Marty! Marty!"

A police officer grabbed her. "No, Mrs. Ritter. You can't go any closer."

Sonja pointed to the flames now coming through the roof of the bakery. "Marty was in there! Did anyone see him come out?"

The news spread through the crowd as George ran toward her, shaking with every breath.

"Ma'am, are you sure he's in there?" the officer asked.

Sonja groaned. "Yes, I'm sure. We were talking on the phone when he said something exploded next door. He hurried to the window to look out. The last thing he said was that he saw some man running away. Then he said he could smell smoke and thought the man he'd seen was going for help. He said he was going to get the fire extinguisher, and I hung up. I waited and waited for him to call back, but he didn't."

George quickly interrupted. "Maybe he was the one who called and told me the store was on fire! Someone did. I still don't know who."

"I don't know about that," Sonja wailed. "What I do

know is that Marty goes to work at three every morning to start the dough. He was in the bakery. Did he get out? Please tell me he got out!"

"Not that we know of," the officer said.

Sonja looked toward the blaze and staggered.

George grabbed her before she collapsed, holding her close against him as he took a slow, shuddering breath. The loss of his business was no longer the worst thing happening.

It was just before daybreak when they got the fire under control. A couple of firemen remained on the scene to watch for hot spots, and it was midmorning before the debris had cooled enough to search for Marty. They found his body beneath the rubble near the back door and a fire extinguisher beneath him.

George left the scene a broken man. His feet were dragging as he walked back into his house and climbed the stairs to check on Ruth. He entered their bedroom just in time to witness Aidan giving her pain meds. George's heart sank. Her pain must be getting worse.

When she saw him, she patted the bed beside her, wanting him to come closer.

"Sweetheart! Thank God you're home. What happened? Did they save anything?"

He shook his head.

"The bakery caught fire as well. Marty was already at work. He didn't make it out."

Aidan gasped. Phoebe's dad! She and her mother were going to be devastated.

"Oh my God! I need to call Phoebe," he said and ran out of the room.

George sighed. Phoebe and Aidan had been a couple for so long that George thought of her as one of the family. He could not imagine how this was going to play out.

Ruth moaned. "They'll blame us," she said.

George frowned. "No, they won't, darling. We didn't start any fire. Sonja was on the phone with Marty when they heard some kind of explosion. She said Marty saw someone running from the fire. He thought they were going for help, but there was no one there when I arrived. I had to get the police and fire dispatched myself."

Ruth shook her head and covered her face.

George sighed. He'd thought nothing could be worse than learning Ruth wasn't going to survive cancer, but this was bad. The fact that he still had Ruth while Sonja was the grieving spouse was brutal irony but proof that life held no guarantees.

Across the hall, Aidan was sitting on the side of his bed, listening to the phone ring at the Ritter residence and waiting for someone to pick up.

"Ritter residence, this is Joe."

Aidan swallowed nervously. Marty's brother was a scary man.

"Mr. Ritter, this is Aidan. May I please speak to Phoebe?"

"They're not taking phone calls," he said. "I'll tell her you called. If she wants to call you back, she will."

"Oh, uh…thank you, sir. I am so sorry."

"Yeah. Thanks," Joe said and hung up.

Aidan was surprised by the tone of Joe's voice. If Aidan hadn't known better, he would have thought Joe was angry at him. He thought a moment, then shook it off. Phoebe would call soon and everything would be okay. He went downstairs to start making something for his mother's lunch. There was leftover chicken and noodles in the refrigerator, and he put it on the stove to heat. He was getting the tray ready to take upstairs when the phone rang.

He ran to answer.

"Hello?"

"Aidan, it's me. Daddy's dead."

He could hear her choking back tears as she tried to talk. "Oh, Bee, sweetheart…I heard. I'm so sorry about your dad. Is there anything I can do? Anything your family needs?"

"No, but thank you," Phoebe said.

The tone of her voice was weird, but then he reminded himself that her dad had just died in a horrible way. She was obviously upset.

"Okay. I love you, Bee. Can I come over…maybe tomorrow?"

The silence was startling and then, as it lengthened, scary. "Bee? What's wrong?" She was crying harder now, choking on sobs. Finally, she blurted it out, and it was the last thing he could have imagined she would say.

"Mom doesn't want you here."

His heart skipped a beat. "What? Why not?"

There was a long moment of silence, and then when she did start talking, it was barely above a whisper.

"Uncle Joe thinks the fire was suspicious. He thinks your dad might have set it for the insurance money because of your mom. He says y'all are going broke. He says it's your dad's fault that Daddy is dead."

Aidan froze, his voice suddenly low and gruff. "The hell you say."

"I'm sorry, but—"

Aidan interrupted. "The son of a bitch did not just call my dad an arsonist and a murderer?"

Phoebe was scared now. Daddy was gone, Mama couldn't stop crying, and Uncle Joe was so angry. Now Aidan was angry, too, and they'd never been mad at each other before. Her heart was breaking and she was drowning in tears.

"Please, Aidan, I'm—"

Aidan was so hurt he could barely breathe. It wasn't enough that he and his dad were watching his mother die before their eyes, but now they were maligning Dad? When they'd just lost everything, too? Tears were running down his face when he interrupted her again.

"You're what?" Aidan asked. "Sorry? Is this what you believe, too? Do you honestly believe my father could do something like that?"

She was crying hysterically. He could hear her, but he was too blindsided to care. And then she screamed in his ear.

"I don't know what to think. I know how sick your mother is, but my daddy is dead! My mother came home screaming. She hasn't stopped crying. What do you want me to do?"

"You. Don't. Know?" Aidan picked up a bowl and threw it across the room. It shattered, just like his heart. "Guess what. Neither do I. I thought you loved my family, but now you accuse Dad of your father's death! Of burning down his own business…the only way we had of putting food in our mouths…the only way we had of paying for Mom's medicine. You aren't the person I thought you were, but it's just as well that I found out now before I wasted another day of my life loving you. I can solve you and your mama's problem right now. I don't ever want to see your face again."

He hung up the phone and caught a glimpse of himself in the mirror near the back door. Shocked by his expression, he wiped away the tears, shoved a hand through his hair, and looked away. The betrayal he felt was nothing to the pain of a broken heart. He took a slow, shaky breath and thought of what still lay ahead for his family. His mama was still dying. Dad was officially bankrupt. And they both needed him.

To hell with Phoebe. To hell with her mother. To hell with all of them.

He went to get a broom and dustpan to clean up the broken glass, then finished his mother's food tray and carried it upstairs.

"Lunch," he said as he walked into the room.

"Oh, Son, that's so sweet of you," Ruth said and tried to sit up.

"Let me," George said and helped prop her up, then took the tray from Aidan and sat down to feed her. "I'll be down to eat with you in a little while," he told Aidan.

"I'm not hungry," Aidan said and left.

George frowned. This wasn't like Aidan. Something was wrong besides the fire, but whatever it was had to wait. Ruth came first.

Aidan wasn't sure how to process what had just happened. He wanted to cry, but he'd been told too many times that grown men didn't cry. He needed to talk to someone, but his dad was too wrapped up in taking care of his mother, and he now had the added loss of their business to deal with as well.

Aidan was on the way down the stairs when the doorbell rang. He went the rest of the way down in double time and then hurried to the door. It was Ralph Ames, the chief of police.

"Hello, Aidan. I need to talk to your father."

Aidan heard the words as physical blows. Was that son of a bitch Joe Ritter already spreading his lies?

"He's feeding Mom. If you'll take a seat in the living room, I'll go tell him."

Chief Ames nodded and stepped into the room on his right, but he couldn't sit. Today was one of those days when he hated his job.

Aidan was scared and sick to his stomach as he ran up the steps and into his parents' bedroom.

"Dad, Chief Ames is downstairs. He wants to talk to you. I'll help Mom."

George looked a bit startled and patted Ruth's arm. "I won't be long, darling."

"Why does he need to see you?" Ruth said.

"I'm sure it's just standard procedure," he said and left the room.

Aidan made himself smile and then scooped up a bite of chicken and noodles.

"What was it you used to say to me to get me to eat when I was little?" Aidan asked.

"Eat it before Daddy gets it," Ruth said.

"That's right, so open wide, Mom. Eat it before Dad gets back."

Ruth giggled.

Aidan smiled as he slipped the bite into her mouth.

But George wasn't nearly as lighthearted as he hurried down the stairs. He already knew Marty Ritter's death would be the only focus of this whole event. If Sonja was correct in saying Marty had seen someone running away from the auto supply store after the explosion, then the fire was very likely arson.

He hurried into the living room to find the chief pacing between the front windows.

"Chief Ames, can I offer you a cup of coffee?"

"No, but thank you. I just have a few questions, and then I'll let you get back to your wife."

"I have time. Aidan is feeding her. Take a seat," George said and dropped into the nearest chair before his legs went out from under him.

Ames sat in a chair across from where George was sitting.

"How is your wife doing?" he asked.

"She's dying," George said and swallowed past the lump in his throat.

Ames blinked. "I'm very sorry," he said.

"So am I," George said. "Now how can I help you?"

"I need your version of how the fire started," Ames said.

George's eyes narrowed angrily. "How the hell would I know that?"

Ames blinked again. "Let me rephrase that. How did you come to be at the fire?"

"We were all asleep when the phone rang. Scared the crap out of me. For a second, I couldn't remember if Aidan was home from the basketball game, and then I saw the clock as I answered. It was 3:15 a.m. A man said my name. I answered yes. He said 'Your store is on fire' and then hung up. I assumed firemen were already on the scene and someone had just called to inform me. I raced to get dressed and rushed downtown, only to find I was the only one there. I turned around and drove down to the police station and got out yelling for help. Travis came out, and I told him my store was on fire. He ran back inside as I drove back to the scene. By the time the fire truck arrived, the auto supply store was gone, and the fire was already spreading to the bakery. I sat on the curb and cried. I have no idea who called me, but it is patently obvious that whoever called me was likely the person who set the fire. I didn't think I had enemies in Blessings. Obviously I was wrong."

"Was the store insured?" Ames asked.

"Of course. Are there any business owners in Blessings that aren't?"

"Well, that's beside the point," Ames said.

George flinched. "Really? Then what, exactly, are you insinuating?"

"I've been given to understand that your wife's illness has depleted your finances."

At that moment, Aidan walked into the living room, angrily interrupting.

"By any chance did you get your information from Joe Ritter?" Aidan asked.

Chief Ames flushed. "That's none of your business."

George stood up. "Aidan? What's going on?"

Aidan was so angry he was shaking. "The Ritters are out for blood, that's what is going on. I'm banned from their house, and they think you set the fire for the insurance money. Phoebe said that's what her uncle thinks, and that it's your fault Marty died."

George paled. "You aren't serious."

"Yes, I am," Aidan said, then glared at the chief. "I live here, too, you know. The phone call also woke me. I heard Dad running down the stairs then driving away. I got up to stay with Mom. You find who made that call, you'll find who set the fire, but it damn sure wasn't my dad. Are you done here?"

Ames stood. "Listen here, boy. A man is dead and—"

George was proud of his son for speaking up, but this was his fight. He stepped in front of Aidan in a challenging manner.

"Chief Ames, are you taking the word of Joe Ritter over me?"

Chief Ames flushed again. "I'm not taking anyone's word. I'm here to get the truth."

George put his hand on Aidan's shoulder. "Well then, we're done here, because I already told you my truth. Now you go talk to Joe and Sonja, why don't you? She said Marty saw a man running away, but he didn't know who it was, right? And someone called me with the intent to lure me to the scene of the fire and incriminate me. So do your job. Check my phone records. They should show a call to my residence about 3:15 a.m. And yes, my business was insured, but four months ago I used the store for collateral to borrow money at the bank to help pay for Ruth's cancer treatments, so whatever money I get from the insurance company is going straight to the bank. I would have nothing to gain by burning down the store. In fact, the fire will bankrupt us. We were living month to month on income from the store. Everything else is gone. Now I'd like for you to leave my house. I need to go check on Ruth."

George walked out of the room as Aidan strode to the door, yanked it open, then stepped aside as the chief headed out. Ames had barely crossed the threshold before Aidan slammed the door behind him.

—∿∿—

Phoebe Ritter couldn't stop crying. Her daddy was dead. Her mother was in hysterics. Her uncle Joe's rage scared her, and Aidan hated her. She'd gone to bed last night so happy. How could a good life turn bad this fast? She was so wrapped up in her own misery that it didn't occur to her Aidan was feeling the same way. And even if it had, she could do nothing about it. Uncle Joe and Mama had forbidden her to talk to Aidan again, and Phoebe was a girl who never challenged rules.

So she cried alone, and so did Aidan, while the love they had for each other continued to crumble beneath the first real test of life.

—∿∿—

Within a week, Chief Ames had confirmation from the bank that all of the insurance money would go to cover George's loan. He also had proof from the phone company that a call was made to George Payne's number at 3:14 a.m. the morning of the fire. There was nothing to prove George'd had a reason to set the fire, and he gained nothing by it happening. Ames had nothing to charge George with, and with that kind of alibi, he'd been cleared of any wrongdoing.

But while the law was no longer interested in George and was now looking for an arsonist, Joe Ritter had riled the people of Blessings up so deeply that they had yet to clear George in their hearts.

Being shunned by people he'd known all his life was,

for George, the last straw. Early one morning, he called
Aidan into the bedroom for a family meeting.

"What's up, Dad?" Aidan asked as he came in and sat
on the bed beside his mom.

"I want to move away," George said. "We can't start
over here. Too many people still believe we had something to do with the fire."

Ruth nodded. "We started life together, and we'll end
it the same way, no matter where we are. Whatever you
two decide. The way I am now, I'm useless to help, but
I'm also sheltered from that hate, and I can't bear thinking of what you are experiencing."

Aidan's heart skipped a beat. Phoebe had broken
his heart, but he never thought about never seeing her
again. However, he knew his dad was right. Their life
here was over.

"I'm with you, Dad. I hate going to school because of
the snide looks and accusations. I'm all ready to find a
place where we aren't treated like criminals."

"Good," George said. "The only person I'm going to
miss is Preston."

Ruth's eyes welled at the thought of leaving her
father behind because she was so close to leaving all of
them behind when she died, but she had nothing to add.

"I'll tell him tomorrow," George said.

<hr />

Aidan went to bed that night torn between the urge to
tell Phoebe they were moving and letting her find out on
her own. If he talked to her again, he'd break—he knew
it. He missed her so badly he ached. They'd been caught
up in the mess between their parents, and her absence

through all of this was telling. He understood she'd lost her father, but his family had nothing to do with it, the Ritters now knew it for a fact, and the knowledge still seemed to make no difference.

He could hear the murmur of his parents' voices across the hall. The sound of their presence so close by was comforting. He rolled over and closed his eyes. The auto supply store and the bakery had already burned, and now what was left of their world was coming down around them.

George paid a visit to Preston the next morning and told him their plans. The devastated look on his father-in-law's face said it all. Then Preston pulled himself together, told George he completely understood, and asked how he could help.

Within a couple of days, the Payne family was temporarily camped out in Preston's big two-story house while George and Aidan were in the process of storing their belongings so they could get their house ready to sell.

A week into repainting the rooms, Ruth died in her sleep.

The final end to the tragedy that had become her life seemed to bring the residents of Blessings to their senses. But since they had been so blatant in shunning George, they didn't know how to break the ice to acknowledge her passing.

Unaware of the changing mood, George took the situation out of their hands by burying his wife graveside without a service or an invitation to anyone, save for a preacher's prayer. The hurt had gone too deep to fix.

———

Grieving his daughter's passing and at a loss as to how to help George and Aidan other than by making sure they had money to start over, Preston bought their house and added it to the rental properties he already owned. His heart was breaking, knowing he was losing the last of his family and that he'd been the one who'd made it possible for them to leave.

———

Phoebe woke slowly, knowing it was Saturday and she and Aidan could hang out. Then she remembered. Heartsick, she threw back the covers. Another day to face without him.

After a shower, she dressed in jeans and a pink short-sleeved T-shirt, then brushed the tangles out of her hair before going to eat breakfast.

As she neared the front of the house, she heard Uncle Joe's voice and frowned. Why was he here again, and so early? She listened and thought she heard a hint of a giggle in her mother's voice. She frowned, wondering what the heck was going on, and then she heard something that stopped her heart. George Payne and his son were moving today!

Panicked, she ran into the living room to find her mother sitting on the sofa beside Joe. They were drinking coffee, and their voices were so upbeat.

"Mom! Is it true? Is the Payne family leaving town today?"

Sonja's eyes narrowed defensively. "That's what Joe says. I could not care less."

Phoebe's voice began to shake. "I don't understand you, Mama. You love Aidan. You've said that for years, and all of a sudden you don't?"

"He's George Payne's son. That's enough for me," Sonja snapped.

Phoebe took a deep breath. "You already know that his daddy gained nothing by that fire. The bank got the insurance money. The fire ruined them. You used to be a kind woman, Mama. You were always fair. You taught me not to judge. And look at what you've done."

Sonja wouldn't look at her daughter, but the moment she went silent, Joe had plenty to say. He eyed Phoebe's T-shirt and frowned. "That shirt is too tight on you. You need to go change."

Phoebe gasped, glared at her uncle, and then looked at her mother, waiting for her to speak up. When she didn't, Phoebe lost it.

"You aren't my father! You don't tell me what to do," she screamed. Then she glared at her mother. "Why is he even here? Does he think he's going to take Daddy's place in our lives…or is that what you want? Is he already in your bed?"

Sonja was too shocked to answer, but Phoebe wasn't through. "For God's sake, Mom! Speak up for me! You bought this shirt for me! It was fine then."

Sonja's cheeks reddened, mostly with guilt, but instead of backing up her daughter, she took Joe's side. "Maybe it shrank in the wash," she said.

Phoebe's eyes widened as she looked from her mother to Joe, then she pivoted angrily and headed for the door.

Joe shouted. "Where do you think you are going, young lady?"

"I'm going to see Aidan," she said and was reaching for the knob when Joe came up behind her and grabbed her by the shoulders.

Phoebe spun and slapped him so hard it stung her hand.

"If you touch me again, I will scream bloody murder, and I won't stop until they haul you away in handcuffs!"

Sonja stood up, shocked by what her daughter had done but even more so about what she'd said. "What's the matter with you?" she cried.

"You're what's the matter," Phoebe screamed and then began to cry. "You and Uncle Joe told lies about George Payne, and everyone believed them. You ruined his life, and you made Aidan hate me. If Aidan leaves me, I will never forgive either one of you."

Then she opened the door and ran out, leaving her mother and uncle staring at each other in disbelief.

Phoebe ran down the street in a panic, fearing she would be too late to see Aidan, praying he wouldn't leave still hating her.

When she ran past the house where they used to live, she saw that the "for sale" sign was gone. It dawned on her then that they might have been waiting for the money from the sale and that's why they had stayed as long as they had.

She reached Main Street and ran across it, darting between cars and ignoring the drivers who honked in disapproval. She passed the courthouse and turned right at the next block, still running. Ignoring the pain in her side and the burning muscles in her legs, she lengthened her stride.

Finally, she reached the street where Preston Williams

lived, and when she turned the corner and saw George's car still in the driveway, she went weak with relief.

Thank you, Lord.

———

Aidan was carrying a suitcase to the car when he heard the sound of running footsteps. He looked up to see Phoebe coming toward him. Her face was red like she'd been crying, and her long brown hair was in wild disarray. Her appearance now, after all he and his family had endured alone, both hurt and angered him. He shoved the suitcase into the trunk and headed back inside.

"Wait! Aidan, wait."

He stopped, then slowly turned to face her.

"What are you doing here?"

Sunlight momentarily blinded her as she looked up. She blinked rapidly to clear her vision and looked up again, searching his face for a sign that he was glad to see her, and saw nothing but hate and disgust.

Her heart sank.

"Please don't go."

Aidan's body language was one of defiance. The tone of his voice held nothing but disdain.

"The only thing that matters to me here is that I'm leaving my mother behind. Her death broke what was left of my father's heart, and your family destroyed his reputation. We can't get out of Blessings soon enough for me. Go home."

Phoebe started to shake. This was really happening. She was losing Aidan forever.

"I'm sorry. I'm so sorry," she said. "Please don't be mad at me! I know your father is innocent."

Aidan turned his back and walked into the house.

Despite the sweat running down her back, she suddenly shivered. She'd never seen him like this—cold and shut down—but she couldn't leave. She stood on the sidewalk waiting, half-blind with tears as he and his father came out of Preston Williams's house together.

Preston gave each of them a last hug and then stood on the porch as they headed to the car.

Preston saw her but didn't acknowledge her.

George glanced at her, started to speak, but shook his head and slid into the driver's seat.

Aidan put the last of their things into the trunk and slammed it shut.

"I'm sorry, Aidan," Phoebe said.

He didn't look at her as he got into the car.

George started the engine.

"Please! You have to forgive me," Phoebe cried.

George put the car in gear and backed out of the drive.

Phoebe started running down the driveway after them. "Come back! Come back! Please, Aidan, come back to me!"

Aidan glanced in the side mirror outside his window, startled to see her running behind the car. But they were going faster, and her image was growing smaller and smaller. The last sight he had of her before they turned the corner, she was on her knees in the street, her hands covering her face. The pain in his chest was so great he thought he would die.

He took a slow, shaky breath and looked away.

———∿∿∿———

Phoebe cried until she was sick, then dragged herself to her feet and turned toward home, walking without cognizance of who she'd passed or where she was. It was instinct that got her there.

Her mother must have been watching for her because she ran out of the house as Phoebe started up the steps.

Phoebe didn't look at her and didn't speak.

Sonja was trying not to panic. She'd sent Joe home so she could patch things up with her daughter, but when Phoebe pushed past her without acknowledging her presence, her gut knotted.

"Phoebe?"

Phoebe turned around. "They're gone. They hate me. Don't talk to me. You have nothing to say that I want to hear."

Then she went down the hall to her room and shut the door.

Sonja was scared. She hadn't meant for this to happen. She followed Phoebe down the hall, knocked on her door, then tried to open it. It was locked.

"Phoebe Ritter, you open this door right now," Sonja shouted.

Silence.

She knocked on the door again and then pleaded.

"Phoebe, I'm sorry. Please let me in. We need to talk."

More silence.

"Phoebe Ann!"

Silence.

Sonja sighed and went back to the living room. Her gaze fell on Marty's recliner, then she looked away.

"Oh, Marty, what have I done?"

Chapter 1

New Orleans, Louisiana

IT HAD BEEN NEARLY TWENTY YEARS SINCE AIDAN PAYNE'S exit from Blessings, Georgia, yet here he was, loading up his truck and a U-Haul rental to go back.

He'd never planned this. He'd certainly never wanted it, although he'd never gotten over leaving Phoebe. His family's reason for leaving had left a bitter taste in his mouth, and now it had been such a long time that going back felt awkward, even wrong.

His dad had been gone for more than five years, but the news of his granddad's death had shocked him. The shock went deeper when he was told there would be no funeral, no memorial service whatsoever, and was given a message that his presence was not required.

It made Aidan feel guilty—almost as if his grand-father was saying, "Since you wouldn't come home to Blessings while I was alive, then you don't need to come back just to put me in the ground." So he'd honored his grandfather's wishes and stayed away. But Preston's passing had also left Aidan with the responsibility of liquidating the properties, and he couldn't do justice to that job long-distance.

The sun was just coming up when he finally left New Orleans. He drove without thought of where he was going, only that he had a journey to complete. It was later in the morning when he drove out of Louisiana and straight into a thunderstorm.

The windshield wipers were on high, swiping back and forth in a repetitive, hypnotic motion but not fast enough to give him a clear view of the highway. He finally yielded to the storm and pulled onto the shoulder to wait for it to pass.

But not all of the travelers were as cautious as Aidan. The thunderstorm and traffic were unsettling, especially when the 18-wheelers blasted past where he was parked, drenching his truck with spray from the road and rocking his vehicle and trailer from the draft of air as they passed.

Being insulated from the elements within the truck cab created a deceptive sense of being invisible to the outside world. And in that environment, he gave the anger of old memories a pass and let them in, which immediately took him back to Blessings and Phoebe Ritter.

He vividly remembered the last sight he'd had of her, down on her knees as they'd driven away. It had taken him a long time to deal with how they'd parted. He had never been able to make a connection with another woman that mattered to him they way she had, even though he assumed she was likely long gone from Blessings or already married and settled. He didn't know how it might feel, seeing her in a life without him. All he knew was that he didn't want to resurrect old heartache again.

A short while later, the strongest part of the thunderstorm had passed, so he got back on the road, stopping once for fuel, rejecting the food choices at the deli quick stop and grabbing a cold Coke and a bag of corn chips instead. He needed to eat, but the closer he got to Georgia, the tighter the knot grew in his belly. He finally opened the Coke, took a couple of sips, then dug into the chips, eating as he drove.

Another hour down the road, his phone, which was synced into Bluetooth in the dash, began ringing. He'd left his restaurant manager, Sam Bateman, in charge of Mimosa, his four-star restaurant just off Bourbon Street, with orders not to call unless there was an emergency. The fact that Sam *was* now calling made Aidan anxious as he answered.

"Hey, Sam. Please tell me nothing is wrong and this is a frivolous call."

"Sorry, Boss. Anything but."

"What's wrong?" Aidan asked.

"The freezer and the walk-in cooler are going out."

Aidan groaned. "Both of them? You can't be serious. What the heck is going on?"

"I called the company repair service. They were prompt, but the news is bad. It appears we had a serious power surge, and it damaged the motors in both. Probably from that thunderstorm last night. He's replacing one motor as we speak, but the freezer is an older model, and he's having a hard time finding a replacement."

Aidan's thoughts were all over the place. Who did he know who could help? And then it hit him.

"Hey, here's a thought. Unless someone has already purchased the building where Monty Byron's barbecue joint used to be, the industrial appliances are still there. I know because I looked at that location before I decided on the one I have now for Mimosa, and there was a freezer just like mine. If there's a workable motor in it, then it's possible it could be harvested. Contact the property manager for that location and see what you can make happen. Let me know if this works out."

"Absolutely, Boss," Sam said and disconnected.

Aidan rubbed the back of his neck in frustration. Pulling the U-Haul trailer with his tools and the clothing he would need for an extended stay to deal with all the real estate Preston had owned slowed his progress, and the thunderstorm had slowed him even more. He was still about an hour from Montgomery, but he'd already decided to stop there for the night and get an early start tomorrow.

He finally reached the city, then drove until he found a motel with a parking space large enough to accommodate both his truck and trailer. He was tired and hungry but not in the mood to eat out, so he ordered pizza from his room, then jumped in the shower.

By the time he got out and dressed in a pair of sweats and a T-shirt, he had a text from Sam informing him that he had the motor they needed and wishing him safe travels.

The relief of knowing that issue had been successfully dealt with made Aidan's large pepperoni pizza that much more inviting when it finally arrived. He ate more than half of it, drank a third of the liter of Coke he'd ordered with it, then stuck the leftovers in the minifridge and lay down to watch some television. Instead, he fell asleep dreaming about Blessings.

"Make love to me," Phoebe said as Aidan pulled her down into his arms.

The stars above were as thick in the sky as the blades of grass beneath them. The air was still, the night sultry with the scent of wisteria blooming nearby, while the buzz of cicadas droned in the background like radio static from a station far away.

The fall of her hair against his chest and throat felt like silk as she leaned over, brushing kisses up his neck, then on his mouth. This was not the first time they'd made love, but their love burned hard and hot, and tonight they threw caution to the wind.

When it was over and Phoebe could breathe without crying from the intensity of what they'd done, she looked up at him, his features shadowed by the night, and threw her arms around Aidan's neck.

"I love you…so much," she whispered.

Aidan pulled her close.

"I love you, too, Bee. Forever."

Aidan woke to the sound of his alarm going off.

"Six a.m. Ugh," he mumbled and stretched as he got out of bed.

There was a dull ache at the back of his head that matched the growing ache in his heart. Dreaming about that perfect time in their lives still hurt.

He took something for the headache and headed for the bathroom. After a quick shower and shave, he tossed the pizza he'd saved and was back on the road eating sausage-and-egg biscuits from a fast-food restaurant and washing them down with coffee. Once his hunger had been sated, he thought about the dream again. Going back to Blessings was resurrecting his past.

They'd been so young and rash—so in love. When he'd started college, he'd tried to forget her and began a relationship with a girl in one of his classes. But within six months, he'd done something unforgiveable. In the middle of making love to her, he'd called her Phoebe. There was no way to explain his way out of it, and she'd broken it off. He couldn't blame her. Through the years, he'd had the occasional relationship, but like the girl in college, it had gone nowhere. He'd never been able to connect with anyone else as deeply as he had with his Bee, and after a while, he'd quit trying.

He drove out of Alabama into Georgia with a blue sky overhead and no storm clouds in sight, finally making good time. He stopped at a gas station around noon to fuel up, bought himself a honey bun and a bottle of cold sweet tea, then ate as he drove, always with an eye on the traffic and the trailer he was pulling.

It was midafternoon when he exited the interstate for a smaller, two-lane highway. He was cruising along without issue when he realized things were beginning to look familiar. He saw the rocky ledge above the trees along the roadside a mile outside of Blessings. His gut knotted. It wasn't far now.

A car came toward him with streamers flying and *Just Married* written on the front bumper. He honked and waved as it passed and thought to himself the guy looked familiar, then shrugged it off. There was likely a host of people who were going to look familiar to him.

His dad had been a distant cousin to the Payne families who lived up in the hills around Blessings, but they'd never been close. He remembered one family who had three sons, Adam, Luke, and David Payne, who were fairly close to his age, but he wasn't sure he'd recognize them if he saw them again.

Then he passed the city limit sign, and as he entered

the town and started down Main Street, the skin suddenly crawled on the back of his neck.

Blessings, Georgia, had been caught in a time warp.

Except for a beauty shop on Main that hadn't been there before called the Curl Up and Dye, the town looked the same. The gas stations were in the same locations. The bank still rose a whole story higher than every other building on the street, and the police station was in the same place. The Piggly Wiggly had a new storefront but was in the same location. There was an empty lot where their auto supply store used to be. He went right by the lot where the bakery had been and kept driving.

Out of curiosity, he turned off Main, headed toward his old family home, and found it had been remodeled to the point he almost didn't recognize it. He kept driving through the residential neighborhoods until he came to the street where his granddad had lived. The big, two-story house looked the same. Well-kept, freshly painted, and the yard recently mowed.

He backed up into the drive and unhooked the trailer, then set blocks at the wheels to keep it from rolling. After one last check to make sure everything was secure, he grabbed his suitcase from the back seat and headed for the house.

The lawyer had mailed him keys and information regarding the property itself more than a week ago, including the code to the security system and phone numbers for the people responsible for keeping up the property after Preston died. At Aidan's request, all of the utilities had been left on, and the person who cleaned the house was still on the payroll.

It was hard for Aidan to believe his grandfather was

gone. He'd stayed active and in fairly good health and had visited Aidan often in New Orleans. Except for those distant cousins, Preston had been his last living relative. He felt very alone in the world.

He unlocked the door and walked in, quickly silenced the alarm, dropped his suitcase in the foyer, then stood in the silence, reacquainting himself with the layout.

He half-expected his granddad to come striding out of the library to greet him. Swallowing past the lump in his throat, he carried his bag up the stairs to the master suite, then wasted no time going to the kitchen to check out the food situation. There was nothing, but the room *had* been thoroughly cleaned.

He found a notepad and pen to make a list and began writing down food to buy, then checked out the downstairs powder room and the bathroom in the master suite, adding soap, shampoo, toilet paper, and laundry soap to the list. As soon as he had the basic necessities listed, he locked the house. But before he went shopping, he had a visit to make, and he drove toward the cemetery.

The sun was in his eyes when he turned off the street into the White Dove Cemetery, then drove to the south side and parked in the shade beneath two Georgia pines. He didn't hesitate as he got out because he knew where Preston Williams would be buried—right beside his wife. He started out across the green, grassy expanse toward a tall headstone in the figure of an angel. Aidan had come out here with his granddad every year on his grandma Ruth's birthday up until Aidan and his father had moved away.

He saw the pile of newly turned earth from a good distance away, then blinked rapidly to clear his vision.

It seemed so wrong that his granddad was beneath that pile of dirt. After reaching the family plot, he glanced at his grandmother's grave, then at where his mother's body had been laid to rest, and then finally, he looked down at Preston's. The monument company had yet to add a date of death.

"Hey, Granddad. How's it going? I know you and Grandma must be so happy to finally be together again."

Aidan cleared his throat and looked off across the hundreds and hundreds of tombstones. He used to know where the oldest ones were but not now. Too many years and too many headstones added since then to be sure.

He stood there for a few moments, wishing Preston was standing beside him waiting to offer some much-needed advice because he could use some.

"So, Granddad, I guess I'll go get settled in. I have a big job trying to decide what to do with the estate. You know I'm not going to live here, but I promise not to upset your renters. Whatever happens, I'll have their best interests at heart."

A blue jay scolded him from a nearby tree, and a jet plane flew over, far above where he was standing. It was so high he couldn't even hear the engines.

"So, I have something to confess. I almost didn't come back, because I didn't want to return and find Phoebe Ann Ritter happily married to someone else. Yes, that makes me a heel, because I'm also the one who left her behind. I couldn't let Dad leave alone, and I didn't know how to tell him I wanted Phoebe to go with us. She was a Ritter, part of the family that caused us to leave. Anyway, I'm here to deal with your properties, to tell you how much I love and miss you, and that I will honor your wishes."

The pain in his chest hurt like hell, and he was bordering on tears as he got into his truck and went back toward Main.

There were quite a few cars in the Piggly Wiggly lot as he parked, which made him a little nervous. He wondered if anyone would recognize him or if he'd recognize anyone he'd known. He'd finally quit growing in college, topping out at a little over six feet, four inches tall. His hair was still dark, but there were faint lines at the corners of his eyes now. He'd learned hard lessons at a young age and trusted few people, even those he knew. One of the waitresses at Mimosa called him Sir Henry, which made no sense to him until Sam told him it was a compliment and that she thought he looked like an English actor named Henry Cavill. Aidan had Googled the name and found hundreds of pictures of a man in a Superman costume, which confused him even more. He wasn't even close to a superman.

He got out, patting his pocket to make sure he had the grocery list. The air was hot and the sun was in his eyes as he walked toward the Piggly Wiggly. The cool blast from the air-conditioning that met him at the door was all the welcome he needed. He paused to pull a shopping cart out of the rack, then glanced around for a few moments to orient himself within the store. The layout was different, and the fixtures were all newer, but it was to be expected. He shook off the feeling of not belonging here, then took out the list and started shopping.

Chapter 2

PHOEBE RITTER WAS ON THE LATE SHIFT AT THE PIGGLY Wiggly this week and would work until nine. If she was lucky, she might pick up some extra hours from someone wanting time off. It was how she had money for life's little surprises, like a car that wouldn't start or an unexpected trip to the doctor.

She came in through the front entrance with her brown hair up in a ponytail, wearing a white Piggly Wiggly T-shirt like all the other employees, and hurried to the break room to lock up her things.

Wilson Turner was the store manager and Phoebe's boss. Although Wilson desperately wished for a relationship with Phoebe, she would have nothing to do with him, or any other man, and everyone in town knew why.

Wilson was in the office up front cashing a check for a customer when he saw her coming toward the registers. The customer walked away as Phoebe arrived.

"Afternoon, Phoebe."

"Afternoon, Wilson. Which register do you want me on today?"

He handed her a register key and a cash drawer with $250 in coins and bills.

"Take number three today."

"Yes, sir," she said, dropped the key into the cash drawer, and headed to work.

He eyed her pretty face and her trim shape as she

walked away, then shifted focus when another customer came in to return a purchase.

Today Phoebe would be stationed at the register in the middle of the other checkers. Millie Garner was on register two and about to become a grandmother again. Trisha Branson was on register four and five months pregnant. All they talked about these days were babies. Phoebe understood their fixations, but she had nothing to add.

They were both busy as she walked up, so she opened her register and slid in the cash drawer, then pulled the wristband with the register key over her hand, letting it dangle from her wrist as she turned on the light at her station. Within minutes, she was busy with her own customers, chatting as she worked.

—⁓—

Aidan tossed a couple of boxes of cereal into his cart and moved from the cereal aisle to canned goods, picking soups and cans of tuna, then moved to the fresh meat area for a couple of packages of ground beef before going to condiments and pickles.

He passed shoppers up and down the aisles, aware he was being watched. Either it was because he was a stranger in a small town or because they recognized him. He wasn't in the mood to strike up a conversation with anyone, so he chose not to make eye contact, and no one felt the need to speak to him.

He was halfway down the bread aisle when he saw an older woman coming toward him pushing a cart with stacks of juice boxes and bananas. He recognized her instantly and was surprised by how little she had changed. She glanced at him almost absentmindedly, then did a double take and broke into a huge smile.

"Oh my word! Aidan Payne! What a surprise! My stars, you sure took after your grandfather, Preston. My sympathies on his passing."

"Thank you, Miss Jane. I see by the juice boxes and fruit that you still have the day care."

Jane Farris rolled her eyes. "The Before and After is still in business, though some days I think I'm getting too old for the youngsters. Did you come to wind up Preston's affairs?"

"Yes, ma'am. I'm staying at his house for the time being. I'll likely be putting all of his rental properties up for sale. I live too far away to be an absentee landlord."

"Where do you live?" Jane asked.

"New Orleans. I own a four-star restaurant called Mimosa. If you're ever in the city, stop in and let me treat you to a meal."

Jane beamed. "That's so sweet of you," she said. "I'll be sure to do that if I ever get up that way. It's wonderful to see you."

Aidan smiled. "Thank you. I'm sure we'll see each other again before I leave."

"Absolutely," Jane said and gave his arm a pat as she moved on.

Aidan was still smiling as he grabbed a loaf of bread on the way to the checkout stand. He got in the shortest line, which happened to be at register two, and then took the time to recheck his list, making sure he hadn't missed anything. He glanced up just as a tall kid in his late teens walked into the store.

The boy paused long enough to shove the hair away

from his face and then moved toward the registers in a long, lanky stride. When he stopped at register three, Aidan watched him suddenly step behind the checker and put his hands over her eyes.

"Guess who," he said.

The woman's squeal of delight made Aidan and everyone around them smile. He was still grinning as the woman turned around. At that point, everything faded into the background as he watched an older version of his Phoebe Ritter throw her arms around the boy's neck.

Well, hell. That had to be her son.

Phoebe was ecstatic to see Lee. Her son was in college in Savannah, and because he had a part-time job there as well, she didn't often see him.

"Lee, you tease! I didn't know you were coming home!" Phoebe said.

"Aw, Mom, you know how it is. I ran out of clean clothes," he said, which made everyone around them laugh.

Everyone except Aidan.

When the woman at his register called out "next" and waved him forward, he began unloading his purchases onto the conveyor. He could still hear Phoebe and her son talking, but he couldn't bring himself to look up. His head was spinning. Less than two hours back and not only was Phoebe still here, but she was a parent. She'd definitely done a better job moving on than he had, but at least the initial fear of seeing her again was over and he had survived the experience. He didn't want to know who she'd married. All he wanted was to get out of the store before she saw him.

He loaded the sacks of groceries into his cart, paid, and walked out while Phoebe and her son were still talking.

———⁓———

Phoebe cupped Lee's cheek, feeling the burr of a day's growth of whiskers, and ached that his little-boy years were already behind him.

"I have to close tonight, honey. There are leftover ribs in the fridge and some coleslaw."

"I got this, Mom," Lee said. "I can take care of myself. See you at home, okay?"

"Okay," Phoebe said. "I'm off for the next two days. Perfect timing."

"Great," he said and gave her a quick kiss on the cheek before he left.

He jogged out of the store and was crossing the parking lot to where he had parked when he noticed a stranger loading groceries into his vehicle. There weren't many strangers in Blessings, and none of them drove a truck that sharp.

"Nice ride, man," Lee said.

Aidan looked up, startled that he was now face-to-face with Phoebe's boy.

"Uh…yeah, thanks," Aidan said and shut the door.

He walked a couple of cars up to leave the shopping cart in cart return, then headed back to his truck, unaware that the kid was not only looking at him in shock but had pulled out his phone and quickly snapped a picture before making a run for it.

When Aidan looked up, the boy was running across the parking lot. Ignoring a painful twinge of regret that Phoebe had a son that wasn't his, Aidan got in the truck, drove back to his grandfather's house, parked by the U-Haul, and then went inside with the groceries.

Although it had been a long time since he'd been here, he felt at home as he put everything away. He stowed the empty grocery bags and was about to go upstairs to unpack when the doorbell rang. He hurried into the foyer, but when he opened the door, he did not recognize the caller.

The old man smiling at him was sporting a mane of white hair and wearing white slacks and a flamboyant blue shirt with puffed sleeves. Aidan's first thought was that all he needed was a Mexican sombrero and a guitar.

And then the old man actually bowed.

"Pardon my rude intrusion into your day without calling ahead, but I am Elliot Graham, your neighbor across the street. I came to welcome you to Blessings and to extend my sympathies for your loss."

Aidan immediately liked him.

"Thank you, Mr. Graham. I'm Aidan. Come in."

"Elliot…please," he said as he stepped over the threshold. He followed Aidan into the living room and they both sat. "Preston and I were good friends. I don't mind admitting how much I miss him."

"I'm going to miss him, too," Aidan said. "He was a regular visitor at my house."

"Oh, I know. He talked about you all the time, so of course I asked why you never came here to visit, and when he explained, I immediately apologized. He assured me none of it was a secret."

"And that's true," Aidan said. "The whole town had a hand in the decision Dad made to leave. It was a betrayal we never saw coming."

Elliot nodded.

"I'm sure, especially since he had nothing to do with that fire. The truth will come out, and soon. You'll see. Well, I've intruded too much already on your privacy. I'll be going now, but my door is open to you anytime."

Aidan was reeling from what the old man had said when Elliot suddenly stood and headed for the door. Aidan hastily followed.

"It was nice to meet you," Aidan said.

"And my pleasure meeting you as well," Elliot said as he stepped out onto the porch.

Aidan was still struggling with what he'd said.

"Uh, sir…Elliot?"

"Yes?"

"What did you mean by 'the truth will come out soon'? It's been nearly twenty years with no suspects."

Elliot waved his hand, as if moving the question out of his space. "Oh…that's just me being me. Sorry. It popped out before I thought."

Aidan frowned. "I don't understand."

Elliot took a neat white square of handkerchief from his pocket, grabbed it by one corner, and opened it before mopping the sweat from his brow.

"I do not appreciate this heat," Elliot said, then smiled. "About what I said…it's nothing really. Sometimes I just know stuff."

And then he bolted from the porch and down the steps before Aidan could push for more answers.

Aidan watched him walking in a little march-step, his snow-white hair gleaming under the late-afternoon sun as he darted across the street, past the shade trees in front of his home, and into his house.

"Odd little fellow," Aidan muttered and closed the door before going into the kitchen to make something for his supper.

———

Lee pulled up into the driveway, parked beneath a tree, and sat for a few moments, looking at their little two-bedroom frame house. He had such admiration for how his mother had taken care of them on her own, never complaining about what they were doing without and making what they had seem special.

He'd known since he was old enough to understand why the woman who would have been his grandmother had moved away and why his father was missing. It hadn't made it easier to grow up without a father, but he hadn't held any resentment. Lee sighed, then picked up his duffel bag from the back seat and went inside.

He took his things to his room, then went across the hall to his mother's bedroom. The worn hardwood floors were clean, her bed was neatly made, and the wall facing the headboard was lined with thirteen framed school pictures of him—the first his kindergarten picture and the last a snapshot of him in his cap and gown at graduation.

Aidan sighed. He had just finished up his first year of college and knew his mom would be proud of his grades, but she was going to be surprised that he'd given up his apartment and job to spend the summer in Blessings. His plan was to get a part-time job here and save all the money he made instead of paying most of it in rent back in Savannah.

He walked to the side of her bed and sat down, picked

up the framed picture on the nightstand, and took out his phone to compare the photos.

His heart began pounding, his eyes welling with tears. He'd waited nineteen years for this moment, and now that it was facing him, he was scared. What if the story Lee had told himself turned out not to be true? What if Aidan Payne found out he had a son and didn't want him after all?

———

Phoebe was tired when she clocked out and headed home, but the knowledge that Lee was waiting for her lifted her heart. It had been so hard without him when he left Blessings to begin college, but she was proud of him and the full-ride scholarship he had earned. He was not only book smart but wise beyond his years. He had accepted her explanation of the absence of a father when he was a little boy with more compassion and understanding than she had for the situation.

Seeing the porch light on as she pulled up to the house was just like old times. He'd done that since he'd been old enough to stay home alone, and she'd missed it. She grabbed her things, ran up the steps, and let herself into the house.

"I'm home," she yelled.

"Me, too," he yelled back.

She laughed. Just like old times. She left her purse on a table as she hurried into the kitchen and found Lee at the stove, heating up food.

He gave her a big hug.

"I waited for you," he said. "Go change and get comfy. I'll set the table while you're gone."

"Wonderful!" Phoebe said and hurried down the hall to her room.

She changed out of her work clothes into a pair of shorts and an old T-shirt, swapped work shoes for sandals, washed up, and hurried back to the kitchen.

"You cooked," she said, eyeing the table and the inviting food.

"I just added some baked beans and fries to the ribs and slaw. Sit, Mom. Let me wait on you tonight."

"I won't argue," Phoebe said and smiled at him when he brought glasses of sweet tea, dripping with condensation, to the table, followed by the food.

After filling their plates, they began to talk as they ate.

"My grade point average for the year is 4.0, and I was accepted into an accelerated physics program next semester," Lee said.

Phoebe beamed. "Oh, Lee, congratulations. I'm so proud of you. I know you didn't get that from me."

Lee took a deep breath. "Did I get it from my father?"

Phoebe's smile slipped a little. The sorrow she lived with was once again evident on her face.

"Yes. He was very smart."

Lee ate a few more bites, then took his phone from his pocket, pulled up the picture, and pushed it toward her.

Phoebe smiled. "A new girlfriend?"

He shook his head, then waited as she looked down.

Her fork clattered onto the table. She pressed a hand over her mouth, but it didn't muffle the moan.

He grabbed her arm. "Mom. Are you okay?"

"Where did you…oh my God. That's the store parking lot." She looked up. "You took this today."

He nodded. "I saw him by accident. I wasn't sure, so I

took a picture, then came home and compared it to yours. He's older, but it's him, isn't it, Mom? That's my father."

She nodded, then started to cry.

"Don't cry, Mom. This is a good thing, right? You stayed in Blessings all this time waiting for him to come back."

"Yes, I did. But he didn't come back for me."

Lee frowned. "How do you know?"

She swiped angrily at the tears on her face. "Twenty years. I waited twenty years for him."

"But he's here now," Lee said.

Phoebe's eyes narrowed angrily. "But he's not *here*, is he?"

Lee was beginning to panic. "Maybe he just doesn't know where you are yet."

Phoebe wasn't having any excuses. "I've been here a long time. All he'd have to do is ask, but I can guess why he's here."

Lee needed answers but was afraid they would make him sad. "Why, Mom? Why is he here?"

Phoebe sighed. Her chest ached, and it hurt to breathe. Damn it. This might be the second-worst day of her life.

"He's probably here because of Preston's estate. Aidan is the heir, remember?" she said.

Lee nodded. "I know, but so were we. Granddad let us live here rent-free all these years and then gave us this house and enough money to pay insurance and taxes on it for years."

Phoebe heard Lee still talking, but in her mind, she was going back in time, remembering when Preston had stepped into the void Aidan should have filled. He had been her savior at the worst time in her life.

When Preston found out about her pregnancy and that her mother and Joe had moved away, leaving her behind, he'd been shocked. Then when they sold the family home out from under her, he stepped in like a fairy godfather and did all he could to help her survive.

It all began after Aidan left. She found out she was pregnant. She was shocked at first, but when her mother started telling her she had to get rid of the brat, that Sonja wouldn't have Payne blood in her family, Phoebe balked. The thought of destroying the baby she and Aidan had made from love was appalling. That wasn't happening.

Phoebe was eighteen, so Sonja couldn't force her to do anything. Her solution to Phoebe's rebellion was to leave her and the baby she was carrying behind when she and Joe left town.

At the time, Phoebe wouldn't let on how horrified she was that they had so casually abandoned her. But she still had faith that Aidan would come back for her, and that meant staying here where he could find her.

If she was going to be on her own, she needed a job. School was out, summer was upon her, and she'd been job hunting for days. When she finally got a call from the Piggly Wiggly to say she'd been hired, her elation had been short-lived. The real estate agent in charge of selling her family home waved her down on the street and told her the home had sold. Phoebe was devastated.

She had to vacate within the month, which meant she needed to find a very cheap place to live before she even had a paycheck. She was on her way to pick up a paper to check for rentals when Preston saw her walking and offered her a ride home.

His kindness was unexpected, and when he told her

that he knew about the baby and wanted to help her, she was so relieved that she cried all the way home. But when Preston suggested she tell Aidan about the baby, she told him the only way she wanted Aidan Payne back in her life was if he came back because he loved *her*, not because she was pregnant.

Preston accepted her decision, then offered her a place to live. Phoebe couldn't afford to stand on pride and willingly accepted. He helped her move her belongings into one of his smallest furnished rental properties and refused her offer of rent. He checked on her from time to time through the following seven months, satisfied that he was helping her the best way he could, and in doing so, he saved her.

Phoebe was still lost in thought when she realized Lee was speaking.

"I'm sorry, what did you say?" Phoebe asked.

"Aren't you going to talk to him?" he asked.

"I begged him once, Lee, on my knees, in the street… as they drove away. I'll never beg a man for anything again as long as I live."

Lee's shoulders slumped. "But he doesn't know about me."

When Phoebe heard the break in Lee's voice, she realized what she was doing. She was setting him up to have to choose between making her happy or realizing a lifelong dream of meeting Aidan Payne.

"You're right. I'm sorry. He doesn't know about you yet, but he will."

"I want to meet him, Mom. He's my father."

Phoebe lifted her chin. She was about to weather another one of life's blows and bring Aidan back into her world...but not for her, for Lee. She'd do anything for her son.

"And you should. I'm sorry, honey. I was so wrapped up in my hurt that I wasn't thinking. He'll likely be here in Blessings awhile. We'll make it happen."

Lee was torn. He was ecstatic at the prospect of finally meeting his father, but he could see how much this was hurting his mom. "Let's both sleep on it," he said.

Phoebe nodded, but she couldn't pull herself back together enough to regain the jubilance she'd felt when she'd come home. "You'll be going back Sunday night. We'll have to do it soon," she said.

"No, I'm home for the summer, Mom. I quit my job and let the apartment go. I'll get another one when it's time to go back. I planned on getting a job here so I could spend the summer with you."

Phoebe smiled. "Now that's news I love to hear."

"I'm going to job hunt tomorrow. There aren't that many part-time jobs in Blessings, and since school is out here, too, they'll go fast."

"You can always get a job at the Piggly Wiggly," she said.

"I know, but I worked there all through high school, so I'm considering it a last resort. Anyway, no worries tonight. I'll check out my options this weekend. Are you ready for dessert? I stopped by Granny's Country Kitchen for a piece of pie. It was so good that I bought a whole pie for us."

Phoebe grinned. "They have a new baker. She's Chief Pittman's wife, Mercy. Everybody raves about her biscuits and pies."

"With good reason," Lee said. "I'll get the pie. Do you want me to make you some coffee?"

"No, thanks, I'll just have a refill of iced tea. You get the pie, and I'll get the plates," she said.

He carried their dinner plates to the counter and then turned to face her. "I'm sorry this made you sad," he said.

Phoebe hugged him fiercely. "You do not apologize to me about this mess ever. You are the innocent party in all of it, and it's going to be okay. You'll see. Now let's get that pie cut."

He grinned when she popped his backside with the flat of her hand. That was her signal to hustle, so he did.

―――

It was after eleven p.m. when Lee went to his room for some down time. He wanted to check in with friends online and see if his girlfriend, Lola, had posted anything on Instagram or Snapchat. She and her family were in Cozumel on vacation, and then she was going to her older sister's home for the rest of the summer. He and Lola had reached a crossroads in their relationship and were using the time apart to see where it went. The situation was one of the reasons he'd opted to come home, but he wasn't going to tell his mom. He didn't want her to think she was his second choice. She would always be his touchstone.

―――

Phoebe walked past Lee's room, taking comfort from the narrow band of light shining beneath his door. She knew all was right with her world when her son was safe beneath her roof, and she had missed that feeling.

She stopped off in her room to get her nightgown,

and then went down the hall to the bathroom to get ready for bed. She turned on the shower so the water would be warm when she got in, then stripped off her shorts and T-shirt and clipped her hair on top of her head so it wouldn't get wet. After adjusting the water temperature, she stepped in, pulled the plastic curtain shut behind her, and reached for the soap.

The symbolic act of washing away the grime of the day got all mixed up in Phoebe's mind with wishing she could wash away how she'd betrayed Aidan's trust and love. Before she knew it, tears were running down her face. She pressed her hands over her mouth to stifle the sobs that followed.

Her eyes were red and swollen when she came out of the bathroom, and her legs were shaking as she hurried back to her room. The light was still on in Lee's room, and she didn't want him to see her this way, so she closed the door and turned off the light. If he came out into the hall, he'd think she was already asleep.

She paused a few moments for her eyes to adjust to the dark, then took advantage of the tiny slits of moonlight coming through the blinds to toss her dirty clothes in the hamper and turn back her bed.

She started to lie down and then impulsively dropped to her knees and began to pray. It had been a long time since she'd knelt before God, so she wasn't sure if He'd be listening, but she needed strength and direction, and He was all she had.

———

Across town, Aidan was already asleep, more at ease in this old house in Blessings than he was in his New

Orleans home, where he had the best security system money could buy. But there was no way to control where sleep took him or enough locks on a door to keep Phoebe out of his dreams.

He saw Phoebe running toward him. He'd been forbidden to see her. He'd done exactly what she asked… not to go over. Not to come around again. So he hadn't. Secretly, he'd been waiting for days and days for her to come to him and say she didn't mean it, or that her mother had a change of heart. Instead, she'd been part of the group of people at school who'd shunned him, and seeing her now, the pain in his heart hurt so much it was hard to draw breath.

"*I'm sorry,*" *she said.*

Too little, too late. They were leaving today. After what he and his dad had been through in Blessings, he could never betray him and take her back. So he hardened his heart and turned away.

"*Don't leave,*" *she cried.* "*I'm sorry, so sorry.*"

He remembered how soft her lips were against his mouth and how her body curled into his when they embraced and kept walking.

"*Aidan, please,*" *she begged.*

He wanted to bury his face in her hair and cry, but he didn't, and then the dream hit fast-forward and they were driving away and she was running behind the car, but this time she didn't stop. She was behind their car as they drove out of town. She was running right behind their car all the way to the interstate, and then all of a sudden she was gone. He turned around in the seat, searching for her, but she had disappeared.

He was screaming at his dad, "Turn around, turn around! We can't leave Phoebe behind!"

He woke up with tears on his face, almost angry that their parting still hurt. He had spent years believing this was all behind him, and yet the moment he was back in Blessings, it came rushing back. Seeing her today had been difficult. Maybe it was seeing her with her son and remembering all the times they'd talked about having their own family one day.

He wiped his hands across his face as he got up and headed downstairs. He turned off the alarm, grabbed a Coke from the refrigerator, and went outside.

The porch swing beckoned in the moonlight. He sat down before he took his first drink. The night air was still and sultry, but the Coke was cold as it slid down his throat. He took a second sip, then held the bottle against his forehead and closed his eyes. Maybe the reason this focus on Phoebe was coming back so strong was because he hadn't ended anything. He'd just run away.

Chapter 3

AIDAN NEVER WENT BACK TO BED. INSTEAD, HE GOT DRESSED and began unloading his tools from the U-Haul trailer and carrying them to the workshop in the backyard. After sunup, he would turn in the trailer at the U-Haul rental office by the feed store, then get back to the house and see what needed tweaking before he put it up for sale.

He planned to do the repairs himself and hire a helper to do the painting, so he poked around in the workshop until he found a can of black spray paint and a piece of plywood and lumber, then set about making a Help Wanted sign. As soon as the paint was dry, he took the sign to the front yard and hammered the stake into the ground. When he turned around to go back into the house, the sun was just coming up.

———

Phoebe's rest had been nothing but nightmares. Every time she closed her eyes, she relived some vignette from the past. Asleep, the memories were pure joy. Awake, they were painful. After hours of tossing and turning, she finally gave up and got out of bed. There was always laundry to do, and Lee had added to it by bringing home everything he owned. She began a load, then started the coffee. After that, she made waffle batter for breakfast. It would keep in the fridge until Lee woke up.

When the coffee was ready, she poured a cup and sat

down at the kitchen table to let it cool, still trying to decide how to handle what fate had delivered to their doorstep.

Normally, when Lee came home for a visit, Phoebe was elated. But Aidan Payne's presence in Blessings changed everything. Everyone in town knew he was Lee's father. It was only a matter of time before someone said something to Aidan, assuming he already knew. But it wasn't Aidan she needed to protect. It was Lee.

She didn't know Aidan anymore. He'd turned into a man she neither knew nor trusted. The last thing she wanted was a confrontation with him, but Lee had reminded her of something she'd spent years trying to ignore. Lee not only wanted to meet his father, he deserved to meet him. So she had to face Aidan to make that happen and do everything in her power to make sure Lee was not hurt by denial or rejection.

As she sat, her anxiety began to cool. She'd already lived through losing everything that had been dear to her. There wasn't a damn thing Aidan Payne could do to her that hadn't already been done.

Lee woke to the scent of fresh coffee and bacon frying. He rolled over to the side of the bed and sat up, happy to be home. He was thinking about his mother's cooking when he remembered today he would finally meet his father!

There were no words to express how he felt. The one thing he wouldn't give in to was fear. He wasn't stupid. There was every possibility he would be rejected. If that happened, it would hurt. But he'd already scored the best mother in the world, so he wouldn't let disappointment show. When push came to shove, she'd been both father and mother, and with Granddad for backup, he'd never once felt like something was missing. Still, he dressed with care before going to breakfast—just in case a good impression mattered.

Phoebe was keyed in to every sound in her house, and when she heard a hinge squeak on Lee's bedroom door, she knew he was up and on his way to breakfast. Perfect timing. The first waffles were almost ready.

He came in with his usual grin, snatched a piece of bacon from the plate like he always did, and then planted a good-morning kiss on the top of her head, which only highlighted the difference in their heights.

"Morning, Mom. Something sure smells good. Oh wow. Waffles?"

"You know it," she said. "Pour yourself some coffee and take a seat. First ones out are yours."

"Yum," he said, stuffed the piece of bacon into his mouth in one bite, and poured himself a cup of coffee.

Phoebe handed him a plate and then eyed what he was wearing. It was definitely a dressier version of his normal jeans and T-shirt.

"You look nice this morning," Phoebe said as she poured more batter into the waffle iron.

He shrugged as he dropped a slab of butter on the hot waffles. "It's out of respect, Mom. It's not to impress my father. It's for you. I want him to see how you raised me."

Phoebe's eyes welled. "Oh, Lee, you have always made me proud, but thank you."

He nodded, stuffed a bite of waffle into his mouth,

then rolled his eyes. "These are so good. Nobody makes waffles like you."

She grinned. "And the taller you get, the more of them it takes to fill you up."

He waved his fork toward the waffle iron. "You can have that one. I'll take the ones after."

"Deal," Phoebe said, carried the plate of bacon to the table, and kissed his cheek as she snagged a piece of bacon for herself.

He wiggled his eyebrows at her, then poured a little more syrup onto his plate.

Phoebe laughed. The panic she'd felt yesterday had settled. Whatever happened, they'd figure it out like they always did.

Aidan had already returned the U-Haul trailer and was back at the house going room to room, checking the caulk on the windows and looking for any wood rot or signs of termites. He was down on his knees beneath a living room window when he heard a car slowing down on the street. He looked out just as it turned into the driveway of the house.

He recognized the driver as Phoebe's son and thought he was likely here about the Help Wanted sign, but when the car parked, the passenger got out first.

"Well, hell," Aidan muttered.

It was Phoebe. Her hair was no longer in the ponytail she'd worn at work but hanging loose just below her shoulders. The pink shirt she was wearing had ruffles around the V-neck, and her jeans accentuated a curvy body that was almost too thin.

He glanced at the boy. He was clean-cut, neatly dressed, and obviously deferential to his mother because he clasped her elbow as they started up the steps. Then the doorbell rang, and before Aidan knew it, he was running to answer it.

———

Lee glanced down at his mother. There was a muscle tic at the corner of her eye and a jut to her chin he recognized all too well. He slid an arm around her shoulders and gave her a quick squeeze.

"Are you alright, Mom?"

Phoebe made herself smile. "I'm fine. Are you okay?"

"Yes, ma'am."

"I won't let him hurt you," she said.

"That won't happen," Lee said.

"How can you be so sure?" Phoebe asked.

"Because you loved him, and you wouldn't love a jerk."

She laughed.

And that's what Aidan heard as he opened the door. She was laughing, and he felt like a hole had opened up between him and hell that he could fall in at any moment.

"Hello, Phoebe," Aidan said, then glanced at the boy.

The laugh was gone as Phoebe lifted her chin.

"This is my son, Lee."

"Nice to meet you," Aidan said. "Are you here about the Help Wanted sign I put out?"

"No, he's not here about that. May we come in? We need to talk," Phoebe said.

The tremor in her voice was startling. Why would she be scared?

"Of course," Aidan said and stepped aside. When Lee glanced at him and then quickly looked away, it made Aidan wonder why she'd dragged her son along to this very awkward reunion. "The living room is just to your right," he said, but they were already halfway there. Instead of escorting them, he wound up following.

Phoebe and Lee sat down on the dark leather sofa together. When Phoebe gave her son a brief pat on the knee, Aidan frowned and took his grandfather's chair.

"I know this visit is unexpected, but I didn't want this news coming from anyone but me," Phoebe said. "Everyone in Blessings knows it. They've always known. Lee has known since he was big enough to talk. Your grandfather knew as well."

"What news?" Aidan asked.

Phoebe took a deep breath, and this time, it was Lee who was comforting her as he took her hand. Phoebe met Aidan's gaze with a straightforward look while hating the tremor in her voice.

"A short while after you and your dad left Blessings, I found out I was pregnant."

Aidan gasped, and then his gaze went straight to Lee—to the dark hair, brown eyes, and long legs. He looked back at Phoebe in dismay.

"I have a son? This boy is my son?"

She nodded.

Lee stood abruptly, as if willing to be inspected. "Yes, sir. I've never been in trouble. I graduated valedictorian of my high school class. I have a full-ride scholarship at Armstrong University in Savannah, and I earned a 4.0 grade point average my first year of college. I had a part-time job all year, but I don't like Mom being alone all the time, so I quit and came home to spend the summer here. I'll get another job when I go back in the fall."

Aidan stood, too, his voice shaking. "That's a very impressive résumé, which I don't really need. What I do require is a hug."

The smile that spread across Lee's face broke Phoebe's heart. She watched in silence as they embraced, remembering a time when she'd been the one in Aidan's arms.

The moment Lee hugged him, Aidan felt the loss of every moment in this young man's life that he should have been a part of and looked straight at Phoebe, needing someone to blame. But there were tears on her face, and so he said nothing.

"I've been dreaming of this moment all my life," Lee said, a little tearful but obviously overjoyed.

"I didn't know," Aidan said. "I wouldn't have let you grow up without a father if I had."

"Oh, but I didn't," Lee said. "I always knew who you were. Mom told me plenty about you, and Granddad told me even more."

Aidan was shocked. Preston had known, too? What he couldn't understand was why he hadn't told him.

Aidan didn't know it, but the frustration and anger he was feeling were evident on his face, and when he spoke, Phoebe got the brunt of them.

"Why the hell didn't you tell me? Why didn't my granddad?"

This time, Phoebe was the one who got up. When she did, Lee moved to stand with her as she unloaded her own anger.

"Oh no, Aidan Payne. Don't you dare go there! You do not get to be indignant! You do not get to feel left out! You told me over the phone that you never wanted to see my face again, and then the day you left, you left me on my knees...in the street...begging you to come back. But you didn't. I had to accept the truth of what you'd said and done. You didn't want me anymore. You hated me. You hated my whole family. Why would I assume you'd want our child?"

Aidan groaned, combing his fingers through his hair in frustration. "Why didn't Granddad tell me?" he asked.

Her eyes narrowed warningly. "Because I made him promise that he couldn't say a word unless you asked about me. Didn't you care, Aidan? Did you really flush me out of your system that fast?"

"Hell yes, I cared, but—"

Phoebe pointed a finger straight at him as she interrupted. "There are no 'buts' in this situation. Every time Preston went to see you, I waited for him to come back and tell me you had asked about me. And every time he came back, all he could do was shake his head. After a while, I quit asking."

"I'm here now!" Aidan said.

Tears started running down her face. "But you didn't come back for me. You came back because Preston died. He didn't have a funeral. He didn't want a service. He just wanted to be put to rest beside his wife. When you didn't come back then, I decided you had turned into someone I probably wouldn't like anymore. And now here you are, and out of respect for you, we're giving you the news of your fatherhood so you don't hear it on the streets. I hope you want a relationship with Lee. He is an awesome young man. But I don't want anything to do with you, Aidan." She swiped her hands across her cheeks and laughed, but it was not a happy sound. "God! I never thought I'd hear those words come out of my mouth!"

"I didn't come back because Granddad asked me not to," Aidan muttered, but he was in shock. Within the space of a few minutes, he'd gone from dismay to euphoria. He'd been given the ultimate gift and, at the same time, a well-earned rejection from the only girl he'd ever loved.

Lee was torn, but his allegiance was to the only parent he'd ever known.

"It's okay, Mom," Lee said. "Let me take you home now." Then Lee glanced at Aidan, afraid of how this was going down. "I really need to take her home."

Aidan felt guilt, regret, and a horrible loss of something he'd never known he had. And there was no argument to be made about what Phoebe had said because it was all true.

"Phoebe, wait. You are absolutely right. You had no expectation whatsoever of me accepting this news. Please forgive me. All I can say about this tragic situation is that we became the other victims of that fire. We were too young, and our love hadn't been tested. We both failed each other.

"I tried to help you, remember? I called asking when I could come over…to help…to do anything you needed me to do because I loved you so much, and I was rejected in the harshest way. I was no longer welcome in your house. So, while you were grieving your father's death, we were being ostracized by the entire town of Blessings because of the lies your mother and uncle told. We lost everything—business, friends, our good name, and then my mother died. I called you when your father died, but you didn't call me. I assumed you still hated my guts. If I had known about the pregnancy, I would have come back. But no one saw fit to tell me.

"We let each other down. I would give anything to change what happened, but I would never change having loved you…or finding out that we made a baby with that love."

Phoebe had no comeback for that. She remembered all too well how she'd treated Aidan when her father died. She'd let her mother and her uncle sway her against Aidan's father and wound up hurting Aidan too. But she had no idea their troubles would never be worked out. And then they'd moved. She'd waited too long to try and work it out. She'd waited until the day they were leaving town to go see Aidan. That was a mistake—her mistake—and nothing could change that.

She sighed. She'd said what she'd come to say, and Aidan had said his piece. And she could tell from the look on Lee's face that he wasn't going to let go of either of them now.

"Sir, about that Help Wanted sign…I don't know what you're needing, but I would like the job and the chance to get to know you better before you leave," Lee said.

And just like that, Aidan realized they both considered him a temporary father and that when he left, that would be that. He had to find a way to prove that would never be the case.

"Can you paint?" Aidan asked.

Lee smiled. "As in houses and rooms? Yes, sir! I've been doing that for Granddad's rental properties since my freshman year of high school. I'm also a pretty good plumber, too, but I got too big to crawl under houses."

Aidan was stunned. There was a whole other world going on here in Blessings that he'd discarded like outgrown clothing.

"I'd like to get to know you, too, so if it's okay with Phoebe, you're hired."

"It's okay," she said. "But don't hurt him, Aidan. Don't you dare break his heart."

Aidan heard "too" even though she hadn't said it, and the idea that she'd even think he would do that hurt.

"Damn it, Bee. Why would you think I'd hurt my own son?"

She shrugged. "I guess because you hurt his mother. If you want him to start work today, then I need him to take me home first. It won't take long."

Aidan was shaking and didn't even know it. "Yes, I'd like for him to come back."

Lee was beaming. "I'll hurry right back, sir."

Aidan sighed. "For the love of God, stop calling me 'sir.'"

Lee's smile widened. "Then it's okay to call you 'Dad'?"

Aidan nodded. "It is very okay to call me 'Dad.'"

"Great!" Lee said.

Phoebe wouldn't look at Aidan again, and as he watched them leave, the weight in his chest grew heavier and heavier. Finally, he turned around to face the empty house in disbelief.

"Damn it, Granddad! You should have told me," he shouted. A sob came up his throat, but he swallowed it back. Tears welled as his voice broke. "Why didn't you tell me?"

Lee was ecstatic as he drove back to their house.

"Mom, this is the coolest day ever! Thank you! Thank you so much for making this happen."

Phoebe sighed. "Oh, honey, I would never keep you from building a relationship with Aidan. He was the best friend I ever had, and I loved him so much. I'm positive you two will form a really great bond."

Lee sighed. This wasn't exactly how he'd planned this meeting. In his fantasy, Aidan came back for both of them. Lee didn't want to form a relationship with anyone who would drive a wedge between him and his mom.

"Do you really hate him, Mom?"

Phoebe shivered. Regardless of what she'd just told Aidan, she couldn't bring herself to say it again.

"Hate is too strong a word, Lee. Let's just say my last bubble of hope has burst, and the disappointment is extremely painful."

"If this is going to hurt you, I won't do it."

Phoebe frowned. "Yes, you are going to do it. What I'm experiencing is nothing new. It was just a shock to see him after all these years. I wanted him to know I wouldn't stand for anything but respect for you."

"Okay," Lee said. "But I want you to know I'm not going to abandon you for this new relationship. You're still the light in my world."

"One of these days you'll find the girl of your dreams, and I will gladly give up that honor to her. There's nothing more precious than that kind of love."

As always, Lee heeded her advice and thought of Lola, wondering what was going on with her, wondering if this summer was the end of them.

When they got home, Lee changed into older clothes,

promised to return in plenty of time for supper together, then drove his old truck back to his granddad's house.

Phoebe knew he was excited, and in the deepest part of her heart, she was glad Aidan had finally come back, even if it wasn't for her.

Chapter 4

AIDAN'S HEART WAS POUNDING AS HE STOOD AT THE LIVING room window, watching for Lee's return. He was still in a state of shock. The ache in his chest was the same one he'd had when his mother had died and then, in later years, his dad. Even though the ache this time had to do with birth, the loss still felt the same. Today, he'd met a grown man who happened to be his son, and while the joy of knowing he existed was huge, he was grieving the loss of the child he'd never known he had.

He kept remembering the broken sound of Phoebe's voice. *"Yes, you came back, but you didn't come back for me."*

He couldn't quit thinking how different his life would have been if he had come back. Saddened by today, he quietly accepted that from this day forward, his life would never be the same.

———

Lee came back less than thirty minutes later—this time driving an older-model red Ford pickup.

Aidan had moved to the front porch to wait, and when he saw Lee driving up, he stood to greet him. Lee got out on the run, loping toward the house with a big smile on his face. Aidan responded in kind and swallowed past the lump in his throat. Regretting what he'd lost gained him nothing. He had to be grateful that there was a future for them to build.

Aidan thumped Lee on the shoulder and then led the way back inside. Lee followed, still smiling as he bounced across the threshold.

"Is Phoebe okay?" Aidan asked as he closed the door behind them.

"If she's not, she will be," Lee said. "That's how we roll. What are your plans for Granddad's house? It's awesome, isn't it?" Then, without waiting for an answer, he stepped into the library to the left of the foyer. "I used to play in here when it was too cold to play outside. Granddad always put the Christmas tree in that window facing the street."

Once again, Aidan was struggling with the fact that his grandfather had watched Lee grow up but he hadn't been given the chance.

"Uh, Lee, can I ask you something? And I want an honest answer, not just what you think you should say."

"Sure," Lee said and sat down on the arm of a big overstuffed chair.

"Did you ever think about coming to look for me?" Aidan asked.

"Oh, no way," Lee said.

Aidan was stunned. "Whyever not?"

"Keep in mind I know all this as part of the story of my life. Mom talked about you from as far back as I can remember. She never once said a bad word about you, either. Think of it from Mom's point of view. You and your dad left Blessings in anger for how you'd been treated, and Mom's family was part of the reason, right?"

Aidan nodded, so Lee continued.

"And you told her you never wanted to see her again, then you rejected her one more time on the day you and your dad left Blessings. Is that right?"

Aidan's heart was sinking. Seeing this through Phoebe's eyes was suddenly making horrible sense. "Yes, I did," he said.

Lee didn't want to come across as angry or judgmental, but he had to be honest. "So, I was raised knowing what happened. She taught me from day one that it was her family's fault you all were hurt in that way. So I understood my existence would likely be an unwelcome one, and from my point of view, if you didn't want Mom, I didn't want you."

Aidan flinched. Lee's genuine honesty, without a sense of anger or blame, hurt like hell.

"That's fair enough," Aidan said. "But I need for you to know that I would never have rejected you or, for that matter, would not have rejected her either. We were both so young. We didn't know how to get past what had happened to the both of us without getting pulled into the bigger picture."

Lee's heart skipped. He wasn't about to let on, but there was a tiny place in his heart where his dream of them together still lived.

"So, you're not married?" Lee asked.

"No, never have been," Aidan said.

Lee looked straight at his father. "Is there anyone special in your life?"

"No," Aidan said and then had to ask. "What about your mom?"

"Oh man...no way," Lee said. "Wilson Turner, her boss at the Piggly Wiggly, would date her in a heartbeat, as would a dozen other men in town, but she wasn't ever interested and made it known."

"Why?" Aidan asked.

"For Mom, it's always been you. For as long as I can remember, your picture has been on her nightstand. That's why."

The words hit Aidan like physical blows. "Damn it," he whispered and then covered his face.

Before he knew it, Lee's arms were around him. "I'm sorry, Dad. We can't change the past, but we *can* include each other in our futures."

Aidan gave him a quick hug. "You're too young to be this smart," he said.

Lee grinned. "Mom says I'm smart like you."

Aidan shook his head. "No. If I'd had the good sense you do at your age, I would never have left your mother behind. But as you said, it's all about today and tomorrow, not what's already over. So…walk with me through the house and help me find the things needing repair."

"I'd be surprised to find much of anything," Lee said. "Granddad was always fixing and painting here. In fact, I repainted the whole downstairs last Christmas when I was home on break. I'm thinking the rental properties are the most likely to need some attention."

Aidan was impressed and didn't bother to hide it. "Really?"

Lee nodded. "Yes. We always repaired and repainted when a renter moved, but there are a few renters who've lived in the same house for more than twenty years. We always repaired what broke, but they probably all need updates and painting…if you're interested in doing that.

If you're planning on selling everything, then you might not—"

Aidan stopped him. "Look, Lee, the plan I came here with has taken a turn I didn't expect, but here's what I think. You know all this far better than I do, so I want you to take the lead. Guide me through the renters, and point out the deadbeats Granddad let slide and which houses you know are in the most need of repair."

Lee beamed. "Sure, I can do that, but he didn't have any deadbeats. He referred to the ones who paid late or who were always a month or two behind as the ones with lives in upheaval. And they loved him just like the rest of us did." Lee took a breath and then looked away. "I'm sure going to miss him."

"Me, too," Aidan said. "Until today, except for some very distant cousins, I thought my last family member was gone. You are a gift, Lee. The best gift I ever received. So take me on a tour of the house through your eyes. Show me what you love most about it and why."

"Then we start in the kitchen," Lee said.

"Why's that?" Aidan asked, as Lee led the way.

"Because it's where the holidays always started. We made holiday dinners together in here. Mom baked her first turkey here when I was two. I don't remember it, but I've heard the story often enough that it feels like I do."

"Tell me," Aidan said.

Lee grinned. "She thought she was buying a small turkey for just the three of us, but in reality, it was a turkey breast. When she opened the packaging and realized there were no drumsticks or wings, she panicked, reread the packaging, and burst into tears. Granddad laughed, told her he liked white meat best anyway, and praised her for being smart enough not to buy one that was too big."

"That's an awesome story," Aidan said as they moved through the rest of the house. Each room evoked a different memory for Lee, and as he shared the stories, their laughter began to ease Aidan's heart. By the time they headed up the stairs, Aidan was looking forward to the next story.

This was not the day Phoebe had imagined when Lee surprised her at work yesterday, but it was what had played out, and she wasn't one to dwell. Knowing Lee would be sidetracked for most of the day, she fell back on the routine she always had on her days off. She changed the sheets on her bed, then headed downtown. She needed a new filter for the central air unit and the oil changed in her car, but the oil change would take time, so her first stop was the pharmacy.

LilyAnn Dalton was at the register checking out a customer when Phoebe entered.

"Morning, Phoebe," LilyAnn said, ringing up Laurel Lorde's order while her daughter, Bonnie Carol, danced from one foot to the other.

"Mama, I need to use the bathroom," Bonnie said.

Laurel rolled her eyes. "Can't you wait a minute?"

Bonnie looked a little anxious. "I can wait, but I don't know if the pee can wait."

Phoebe headed to the register with a smile on her face. "Hey Laurel, I'll take her," Phoebe said.

"Oh, thank you," Laurel said.

Phoebe held out her hand. "Come on, wiggle britches."

"My britches are wiggling 'cause I need to pee," Bonnie said, grabbed Phoebe's hand, and led the way in short, hurried strides.

Phoebe took her into the public restroom, then waited with her. As soon as Bonnie was finished, Phoebe had the water running in the sink.

"Wash here, honey."

Bonnie was fascinated enough by the liquid soap that turned into foam that she used more than she needed.

Better that than none at all, Phoebe thought, then pulled a handful of paper towels from the dispenser and helped her dry.

"Thank you, Miss Bee," Bonnie said.

"You're welcome," Phoebe said and held the door open for her as they exited the bathroom.

Laurel was loaded down with bags and waiting at the front of the store. "I can't thank you enough," Laurel said.

"It was totally my pleasure," Phoebe said.

"Bonnie, did you tell Miss Phoebe thank you?"

Bonnie nodded and then looked up at Phoebe and grinned. "My britches aren't wiggling anymore," she said.

Phoebe chuckled. "That's good news, right?"

Laurel smiled and handed Bonnie a small bag. "Here, Bonnie. You can carry this. It has your little bottle of nail polish in it, so don't drop it or it will break."

Bonnie latched on to her sack with both hands, and out the door they went.

Phoebe smiled and waved, then grabbed a shopping basket and headed down the shampoo aisle to begin gathering up what she'd come for.

Other customers came in to pick up prescriptions and left soon afterward, leaving Phoebe in the aisles on her own, which was fine with her. She assumed the news of Aidan's return was common knowledge by now and it was just a matter of time before someone would say something.

Finally, she had everything she needed and started up front to pay. When she reached the register, two customers were in line ahead of her, so she settled in to wait. It wasn't until the man in front of her turned around and spoke that she recognized him. Moe Randall had been the manager at George Payne's auto supply store the entire time she and Aidan were in high school. But after the fire, he went to work as a mechanic in Savannah, making the hour-long drive morning and night. Now that he had retired, she rarely saw him around town.

"Hello, Phoebe."

"Hello, Moe. How have you been?"

Moe Randall had been a stocky man with a ruddy complexion, but now he was terribly thin with hair as gray as his face.

"As you can tell, I'm not doing well. I have cancer. They operated a couple of months ago but couldn't get it all."

Phoebe reached out in empathy, but when she patted his shoulder, all she felt was skin and bone.

"I'm so sorry. Is there anything I can do? Are you able to cope at home? Oh wait! What am I thinking? Corey is probably all over this."

Moe shrugged. "Corey lives in Savannah, when he's not in jail. I have everything set up for hospice when the time comes, but thank you for the offer."

The defeated sound in Moe's voice hurt her heart, and on impulse, Phoebe hugged him. "I'll say prayers," she whispered against his ear.

Moe shrugged. "Everyone dies," he said, then shifted the subject of the conversation. "I heard Aidan Payne came back to Blessings. Is that true?"

Phoebe nodded.

"Did you talk to him?"

"Yes, I talked to him, why?"

Moe shrugged. "Just being nosy, I guess. I always liked the kid. And George was the best boss I ever had."

Phoebe nodded again. "Yes, Mr. Payne was a kind man."

"Moe, are you ready to check out now?" LilyAnn asked, interrupting the conversation.

"Oh, yes, sorry," Moe said and quickly paid for his things and left.

LilyAnn shook her head sadly as Phoebe set the shopping basket on the counter.

"Poor Moe. His son is a total loser, and he told me last week that at his last doctor visit they gave him six weeks."

Phoebe glanced out the glass front of the pharmacy, watching as Moe backed away from the curb and drove away.

"That would be a hard thing to face," Phoebe said. "Knowing when you're likely to die. As for Corey, I'm sorry to hear he hasn't changed all that much from school. Poor Moe."

LilyAnn began ringing up Phoebe's purchases. "I heard you tell Moe that you'd talked to Aidan."

Phoebe lifted her chin. "Of course I talked to him. Why wouldn't I?"

"I don't know. I guess I thought since it had been so long and all," LilyAnn said and then sighed. "Never mind. None of my business. That will be forty-three dollars and twelve cents."

Phoebe slipped her credit card into the chip reader and then signed her name and gathered her purchases.

"Take care," LilyAnn said.

"You, too," Phoebe countered, and out the door she went. She had the car running and was adjusting the air conditioner when the weight of her situation finally became a reality. All these years, living life as the unwed mother who'd raised her son all on her own was her story, but her life was already changing. Even as she backed away from the curb, a new chapter was being written. She had only ever wanted one man in her life. And even though that dream didn't come true, she would have a part of him forever. Ignoring the ever-present disappointment that was her life, she headed to Bloomer's Hardware to get the filters for her air conditioner.

Fred Bloomer was up on a ladder at the back of the store when she walked in, but the pretty young woman at the register immediately came to meet her.

"Hello, Phoebe, can I help you find something?"

"Hi, Alice. How are the kids?"

"Fine. Growing. Loving summer vacation."

"I remember those days," Phoebe said. "So, I came to get a filter for my air-conditioning unit. The size is thirty-six by fourteen, and while you're at it, I'll take a couple of them."

"Are you particular about brands?" Alice asked as she led the way to where the air filters were shelved.

"I think those are the ones I've been buying," Phoebe said, pointing to the filters with a light-blue border.

"Got 'em," Alice said. "Anything else while you're here? Light bulbs?"

"Oh, yes! I'm so glad you asked. I am out of bulbs. I need one three-way for my reading lamp and a package of sixty-watt soft lights."

"I've got them right here," Alice said. "Anything else?"

"No, that's it," Phoebe said and followed her back to the register to pay.

Phoebe was already out of the store when Fred Bloomer came up to Alice.

"Good job adding the bulbs to her purchase," he said.

"Thank you," Alice said, grabbed her feather duster, and headed for the display shelves up front. This job was a godsend, and she didn't intend to disappoint her boss.

Phoebe's next stop was at the gas station to get her oil changed. She gave her car keys to the owner, Manly Jones, and went inside to wait where it was cooler. But when she saw an old classmate out in the garage area waiting for his vehicle, she groaned. It would have to be Ace James. He was always a royal pain in the ass. When he came into the waiting area, she tried to ignore him.

"Hey, Bee, how about a cool one?" Ace said, waving his open beer can at her.

Phoebe gave him a look. "Ace James, it is eleven in the morning, and you already know the answer to that."

The stocky blond shoved his cap to the back of his head and toasted her with a drink.

Phoebe rolled her eyes and looked away. Unfortunately, that did not deter Ace, who started in on her again.

"I heard your old lover finally drag-assed back to town. Is he pissed about the kid, or are all of you gonna finally live happy ever after?"

It was the sneer on his face that did it. She set her purse down by her chair, strode across the waiting room to where Ace was sitting, yanked the can of beer out of his hand, and poured it over his head.

Ace gasped, then jumped up and staggered out of her reach, but it was too late. She ended by throwing the empty can at him.

"What the hell did you do that for?" he yelled.

"I didn't like the question or the tone of your voice. That was a horrible thing to say to me. Don't talk to me again."

Ace grabbed the hem of his T-shirt and began wiping his face with it. "Geez, Bee. You're getting touchy. You need to get laid."

Phoebe doubled up her fist and punched him square in the nose. Blood spurted. Ace yelped.

Phoebe returned to her chair and took a little bottle of hand sanitizer from her purse, but when she tried to clean her hands, two of the fingers were throbbing something awful and didn't want to bend. It was all she could do to spot-clean a couple of blood splatters from her blouse.

Manly walked in whistling absently, then stopped. Ace had a bloody nose and was standing in a puddle of beer on one side of the room, and Phoebe was sitting in a chair on the other side of the room using hand sanitizer.

"What happened here?" he asked.

Phoebe looked up. "You mean Ace? He spilled his beer and then slipped and fell. Right, Ace?"

Ace wasn't about to admit a female had bloodied his nose. "Yeah, that's what happened, alright," he mumbled.

Manly sighed. Now he was going to have to mop up the mess.

"Your flat is fixed, Ace. That will be twenty-five dollars."

Ace counted out the cash, slapped it on the counter, picked up his car keys, and strode out of the waiting room with his handkerchief shoved up his nostrils.

Manly's eyes narrowed as he looked at Phoebe. "Are you okay?" he asked.

She frowned. "Do I look like something is wrong?"

"Uh…no, ma'am. Arlo is changing your oil. It won't be long."

She smiled. "Thank you very much."

"Would you like a cold drink? I have some bottles of water."

Her smile widened. "Cold water would be wonderful," she said.

He got a bottle from the mini-fridge behind the counter, turned the lid to break the seal, then handed it to her.

"Here you go, Phoebe. I saw Lee in town yesterday. He's growing into quite a man. You should be proud."

Phoebe winced as she reached for the water, then took it with her other hand. "Thank you, and yes, I am proud of the man he is becoming."

"Well then, I need to get the mop and clean up Ace's mess before someone else slips and falls."

The condensation on the outside of the plastic bottle was instantaneous. Phoebe resisted the urge to press it into the valley between her breasts as she removed the lid. She took a drink, then sat back to watch Manly mopping up the spilled beer before he went back into the garage to check on her lube job.

Phoebe stifled a moan. Her hand was throbbing. It looked kind of weird and was beginning to swell. Surely she didn't break a bone. That's just what she needed. She took another drink, leaned back in her chair, and looked up, trying to will the pain away.

The first thing she saw was a security camera in the corner of the room. Startled, she turned and looked behind her. There was another just like it in that corner. If they were on, there was a really good chance that her encounter with Ace would be the latest buzz in Blessings before sundown. She decided she didn't care. A few moments later, she got a text from Lee.

> Mom. Dad and I are going to Granny's for lunch in about an hour. He wants you to join us. He would have asked you himself, but he didn't have your number, so I'll take care of that ASAP and give it to him. In the meantime, want to go? Please?

Phoebe sighed. Showing up at Granny's like one big happy family would surely set the tongues wagging. And maybe that's what needed to happen. She didn't want to go, but she'd be damned before she let Aidan think she was cowed by his presence. So, with Ace James still on her mind, she answered.

> I would be delighted. I'm at the station getting my oil changed. Meet you there.

"So much for keeping my distance," she muttered and then pressed the cold bottle against her aching hand.

Chapter 5

LEE AND AIDAN WERE TOURING PRESTON'S RENTAL PROPER-
ties. At each house, Lee introduced Aidan to the tenants
and explained they were just checking the condition of
the buildings. Some of the renters remembered Aidan,
but a lot of them didn't know him, and it was obvious
they were all uneasy and afraid of where they now
stood. Was he going to sell all the properties, or was he
going to keep them and raise their rent? Would he be as
understanding as Preston about late payments?

Lee knew them all and could see that they were worried. He tried his best at each stop to calm their fears, but
without an explanation from Aidan, they didn't know
where he stood.

The problem with that was Aidan didn't know either.
Everything he'd had planned when he'd left New Orleans
was now up in the air. By the time they came out of the
third home, it was almost noon, and Aidan was stressed by
both the renters' uneasiness and questions and knowing he
was going to have lunch with Phoebe and Lee at Granny's.
He remembered the little restaurant as a gathering place
for good food and news, which translated to gossip.

"I guess it's about that time," Aidan said as he drove
toward Main. "Are you hungry, Lee?"

Lee grinned. "I'm always hungry."

Aidan chuckled. "Yeah, I'd forgotten how hollow-
legged guys your age are."

"Mom calls me the bottomless pit."

Aidan wanted to know more about Phoebe's life, and hearing Lee talk about her with such love told him more than any stories ever could. The bond between them was obvious.

Aidan braked at a stop sign, then waited for a trio of giggling teenagers to cross the street. When they saw Lee sitting in the truck, they all yelled and waved.

"Lee, glad you're home!"

"Welcome home, Lee. Call me!"

"Lookin' good, cutie! Don't call her! Call me!"

Lee grinned and waved at all of them without committing himself to anything.

Aidan laughed. "You are definitely on their radar," he said.

Lee just shook his head. "They're not on mine."

Aidan gave him a more careful glance. "You sound pretty sure about that, which usually means you already have a girl. Is that so?"

Lee shrugged. "Yeah, I have a girl. Her name is Lola."

"Is she a student at your college, too?"

Lee nodded. "She and her family are on vacation in Mexico now. It remains to be seen if we'll still be dating when summer is over. If we aren't, it won't kill me, you know? I like her…but I don't think I love her like a forever love. Mom always reminds me there's a difference, and I get it."

Aidan nodded. Phoebe was right. There was a hell of a difference between lust and love. One eventually cooled off. The other never died. He was still thinking about Phoebe as he pulled into the lot at Granny's and parked.

Lee pointed. "There's Mom's car. This is going to be the best meal ever."

"Why's that?" Aidan asked. "Is the cooking that good?"

"Yes, it's good, but that's not what I meant. It's going to be the first time I get to have a meal with both my parents! Come on! Let's get inside before all the chocolate pie is gone. The baker here makes the best biscuits and desserts you've ever eaten. Except Mom's pumpkin pies. No one makes better pumpkin pies than Mom," he said and got out of the truck with a spring in his step.

Aidan took a deep breath and joined him. Uncertain how welcome he was here in Blessings, he didn't know what to expect, but it was obvious what the meal meant to his son, so he gave Lee a quick pat on the back as they went inside.

Phoebe was in serious pain and anxious to the point of being sick to her stomach as she drove toward Granny's. The very last thing she wanted to do was share a meal with Aidan Payne. Right now, she didn't even want to talk to him, but it was no longer about what she wanted. She'd set a rule for herself and her son years ago that had deprived him of a father in his life. At the time, she'd been positive she was protecting him from heartache. Now she wasn't so sure.

If that wasn't enough to worry about, she was about to parade her past in front of God and everyone by having a cordial meal with the father of her son while knowing he didn't want anything to do with her.

She groaned just thinking about it. She'd spent so many years facing subtle judgment and outright criticism from the good people of Blessings that she didn't know what to expect.

Then this happened. The long-missing parent was suddenly on the scene.

She knew within moments of pulling into the parking lot that she had beaten them to the restaurant. She parked and checked out her hand again. It looked awful and felt worse. She'd ice it good when she got this lunch over with, and instead of waiting for them to show, she went inside to get a table in hopes she could control the seating. She had no intention of being seated out in the middle of the dining room and becoming fair game for the gossip.

Lovey was manning the cash register at the door when Phoebe entered. She smiled at Phoebe as a group of diners departed.

"Hey girl, I saw your boy yesterday. He's grown a bunch since he went away to college, hasn't he?"

"Yes," Phoebe said. "He's spending the summer here with me, and I won't object. Uh…is it okay if I seat myself? A couple more people are joining me in a few minutes, and I don't want to be out in the middle of the floor."

Lovey leaned forward and lowered her voice.

"It's Aidan, isn't it? I heard he was back."

Phoebe sighed. Why did she think she could handle this lunch? It was going to be hell.

"Yes, he and Lee are joining me. I'm going to take that booth in the back if that's okay."

"I'll seat you myself," Lovey said and grabbed three menus. "Follow me."

So Phoebe did.

Lovey left three menus just as Lila appeared.

"Hi, Phoebe, I'll be your waitress today. I see from the menus that you have people joining you. Can I get you something cold to drink while you wait?"

"I'd love some iced tea—sweet, of course."

Lila giggled. "Is there any other kind? I'll be back with some of Mercy's biscuits, too."

"Yum," Phoebe said and began to relax. This was Granny's Country Kitchen. The second-best place to home. Nothing to worry about, no matter who was sitting with her.

As she reached for one of the menus, she winced. At this point, her hand was beginning to freak her out. She could never put anything over on Lee. He didn't miss a thing, which meant she would have to confess what she'd done. They had a long-standing rule between them that they never lied to each other or misled each other in any way.

Lila came back with Phoebe's iced tea and the biscuits.

"Enjoy," she said and moved on to the next table to refill coffee cups.

Phoebe wanted butter, but she couldn't get a good enough grip to open one of the packets. Then she thought of her job and being able to use the keys on the checkout register at the Piggly Wiggly and tried not to panic. She couldn't afford to miss work.

Lila was coming back by the table, saw Phoebe having trouble, and stopped. "Need some help?" she asked.

"I do. Would you mind opening a couple of the butter packets?"

"Of course I will. What happened to your hand? It's really swollen."

"I, uh…jammed it."

"Bless your heart," Lila said and put the opened packets on Phoebe's bread plate. "Want some honey opened, too?"

"No, this is good," Phoebe said. "And thank you. I really appreciate it."

"No problem," Lila said and headed to the kitchen to turn in an order.

A couple of minutes later, Arlo, the man who'd changed her oil at the garage, came in on his lunch break, saw Phoebe, grinned, and gave her a thumbs-up.

A little puzzled by his behavior, she smiled back without understanding the thumbs-up business. She managed to get the butter out of the packet and onto her biscuit, and she took a bite, rolling her eyes at the melt-in-your-mouth goodness of one of Mercy Pittman's creations. Phoebe had finished half and was reaching for her napkin when Lee and Aidan walked in.

And here we go, she thought and smiled her biggest, happiest smile, daring any of the gossipmongers to start a story about being upset Aidan was in Blessings.

Aidan saw the smile at the same time an ache started in his chest. *There was a time when she smiled like that for me*.

"There's Mom," Lee said and led the way to the table. "Thanks, Mom," he whispered as he slid into the seat beside her, leaving the other side of the booth for his dad.

"For you…anything," Phoebe said and winked, then looked up at Aidan. "Has he talked your ear off yet?"

Aidan was relieved she was going to play this nice and easy for the public, whether she felt it or not.

"He's been amazing," he said, then shifted his feet to keep from stepping on her toes. "I'm impressed by how much he knows about Preston's holdings."

"Lee's been Preston's shadow since he learned to walk," Phoebe said and then saw a flash of sadness move across Aidan's face so quickly she might have thought she'd imagined it. Except she knew Aidan.

"Dad, you have to try one of these biscuits," Lee said and promptly put a biscuit on Aidan's bread plate and grinned.

Aidan chuckled. "Since you put it that way," he said.

"Butter?" Lee said.

"I'm not gonna argue," Aidan said, then glanced at Phoebe. "He's been talking about the woman who does the baking here. Said she's something special."

Phoebe nodded. "Her pies are to die for, too."

"Lee said your pumpkin pies are better," Aidan said and popped a bite of biscuit into his mouth.

Phoebe was caught between the way his eyes widened as the taste of the biscuit surprised him and the fact that Lee was bragging about her cooking.

"Well…thank you, Lee."

He shrugged. "Just stating a fact. So, Dad, what do you think about the biscuits?"

"You're right. They're pretty amazing," Aidan said.

Then Lila came sweeping past the table. "Hello, Lee. What do you want to drink?"

"Sweet tea," he said. "Dad, what about you?"

"Same, please," Aidan said and picked up a menu.

Lila was staring at Aidan with her mouth slightly parted, and then she glanced at Phoebe and winked.

Phoebe shook her head slightly, but it did no good.

Lila wiggled her eyebrows at Phoebe and rolled her eyes. Phoebe sighed. Yes, she knew Aidan was good-looking, but she refused to acknowledge it.

"I'll be back in a few," Lila said.

Silence continued as Lee and Aidan studied their menus, but since Phoebe already knew what she wanted, she took that time to check out the other diners.

A group of men at a table on the other side of the dining room suddenly began to laugh, one slapping his leg, another one wiping his eyes with his napkin. Their mirth, of course, caught the attention of most of the other diners, including Phoebe. Lila was at their table refilling their coffee cups when they laughed, so Phoebe assumed it was something Lila had said.

But when Phoebe realized Arlo was sitting there and that he was pointing at her, she tried not to panic. She had purposefully kept her swollen hand in her lap and hoped she was wrong about why they were laughing, but since Manly Jones had to mop up the beer she'd poured on Ace's head, Manly might have decided to look at the security footage just to see Ace taking a tumble.

Only that's not what he would have seen. She could only imagine how the whole thing played out from a bystander's point of view and couldn't blame Manly for sharing it with the guys he worked with, like Arlo. And Arlo might be sharing it with his lunch buddies, which meant it would be all over town in hours.

She glanced nervously at Lee and Aidan, but they seem preoccupied with the menus.

Then Lila returned to take their orders.

"Lord, girl! No wonder your hand is swollen," Lila said. "Arlo took a video of the security footage from

Manly's garage with his phone. He'll be showing that to everyone."

Phoebe frowned. "I'm having fried shrimp, coleslaw, no fries, and yes to the hush puppies."

Lila blinked. "Uh…oh, okay, sure thing," she said, wrote down the order, then glanced at Aidan. "How about you, sir? What are you having?"

Aidan was looking straight at Phoebe as he gave Lila his order.

"Chicken-fried steak, mashed potatoes, green beans, more biscuits, and Phoebe Ann, why is your hand swollen?"

The stern sound in his dad's voice caught Lee's attention. He looked up, suddenly aware there was more going on than ordering dinner.

"What? What's wrong with your hand, Mom?"

"Lila is waiting for your order," Phoebe said.

"I'll have what Dad's having," Lee said.

Aware she'd spilled the beans, Lila mouthed an *I'm sorry* and went to turn in their orders.

Lee leaned across the table. "We don't lie to each other, Mom."

Phoebe sighed. "I didn't lie about a thing. You just got here. I haven't had time to do more than say hello to either one of you."

Lee held out his hand. "Let me see, please."

Phoebe extended her hand and was a little startled to see that it was even more swollen than when she first sat down.

Aidan flinched.

Lee gasped. "Mama…what on earth did you do?"

"Better yet, explain what the waitress meant by seeing the video."

Phoebe's chin came up. "Don't use that tone with me."

"Please?" Aidan added.

She sighed. "Ace James popped off at me. Asked me if I wanted a beer, then made some remarks to which I took offense, so I poured the beer he was drinking on his head. That did not sit well with him, and when he told me I needed to get laid, I punched him in the nose. Probably broke it. Hope I didn't break my hand in the process."

Aidan was speechless.

Lee was furious. "Damn it, Mom. I'll make him—"

"You'll do nothing," Phoebe said. "I have already taken care of business, and unfortunately, it appears it was all caught on the security footage at Manly's garage. Ace already made a fool of himself, and not only is everyone going to hear about it, but considering how everything gets copied and shared, I'd lay odds they're going to see it, too. Promise me you'll do nothing."

Lee sighed. "I promise."

Phoebe glanced at Aidan. His face was flushed with anger.

"Although this ticks me off like you cannot believe, I accept I don't have the right," he said.

"Thank you," Phoebe said.

"Do you think anything is broken?" Aidan asked.

"I don't know. I can't afford to be off work, so I'll ice it for the next two days, and hopefully it'll be fine when it's time for me to go back to work."

Aidan didn't know what bothered him most—that she was hurt, that she had to worry about her financial situation before she sought medical treatment, or that a man in this town thought she was fair game for a remark like that. Something told him she'd dealt with this shit for years.

It was obvious to Phoebe that both Aidan and Lee were bothered, so she changed the subject.

"What have you two been doing all morning?" she asked.

They knew she was purposefully changing the subject and rallied in her defense. Aidan was spreading butter on another biscuit and, without thinking, put half of it on Phoebe's bread plate, like he used to do when they shared everything, including food.

"Lee is taking me on a tour of Granddad's rental properties. I've met three different families, and they all look at me like I'm going to evict them into the streets or something. He has an amazing grasp of the business. I'm thinking Granddad was grooming him to take over. If he was older, I'd just dump the whole lot into his lap and turn him into the manager."

Lee's eyes widened.

"I could—"

Aidan and Phoebe spoke up at once. "No," they said in unison.

"I shouldn't have said that. It was just a thought," Aidan said. "You have that scholarship. Not many kids' college educations are paid for before they get there. Besides, you'll have the whole rest of your life to work a nine-to-five job. Enjoy your youth. Ours was cut short by no fault of our own," he added.

Phoebe glanced at him and then looked away. That sad look was back on his face again.

Lila brought their food. Lee cut up the food on Phoebe's plate without comment, and the conversation shifted to passing the salt and talking about rental properties.

They had finished their entrees and were considering

dessert when Hope and Johnny Talbot came in and were seated at the booth in front of them.

Hope smiled and waved.

Without thinking, Phoebe waved back—with her swollen hand.

Hope's eyes widened, and she was out of her seat within seconds.

"What happened to your hand?" Hope asked.

"I jammed it," Phoebe said.

"On Ace James's face," Lee muttered.

Hope gasped. "Honey! You need to get it x-rayed. It's pretty easy to break bones in a hand because they're not very big." Then she saw Aidan, realized she didn't know him, and began apologizing. "I'm so sorry. I didn't mean to interrupt your meal like this."

"It's okay. Hope, this is Lee's father, Aidan Payne. Aidan, Hope Talbot is a nurse at the hospital here and just happens to be the sister of the woman who makes these great biscuits."

"Nice to meet you," Aidan said. "Your sister's skill at baking is amazing."

"A pleasure to meet you, too, and I can certainly see the resemblance between you and Lee," Hope said, then felt Phoebe's hand. "I think you've dislocated a couple knuckles. Go get that hand x-rayed. Nurse's orders."

Phoebe sighed, thinking about the cost of losing her temper. "I will, and thank you."

Hope returned to her seat as Lila came back to their table. "Anyone want dessert?" she asked.

"No. We're taking Phoebe to get her hand x-rayed, and I get the check," Aidan said.

Lila laid the check facedown at his place. "I'm so sorry, Phoebe. I hope you get better soon."

"It's okay, Lila…all of it…and thank you."

Lila gave her a thumbs-up and hurried off to another table.

Aidan picked up the check and slid out of the booth. Lee also got up, then turned around and helped Phoebe stand.

Leaving Granny's was more of a spectacle for Phoebe than going in had been, but it was to be expected. The diners must have been confused. She'd spent the past twenty years having absolutely nothing to do with the men in Blessings, and now in the space of a day, she'd shown up with the missing father of her son and broken another man's nose. She should be humiliated, but her hand hurt too much for her to care.

As soon as they were outside, Lee hugged her. "I'm so sorry you're hurt, Mom. I'm driving you to the ER."

"And I'll follow," Aidan said.

Phoebe started to argue. "Oh, you don't have to," she said, but Aidan had already turned his back and was walking to his truck.

"I need your keys," Lee said.

Phoebe handed him her purse. He dug them out, unlocked the door, helped her inside, then buckled her in before getting into the car.

"Wow! Let's get this car started up so we can cool it off," he said. "Today is gonna be a scorcher."

"It already is," Phoebe mumbled and closed her eyes as Lee backed up and then led the way from the parking lot, with his father right behind them.

As karma would have it, they were walking into the ER at the same time Ace James and his wife, Yvonne, were walking out. Ace ducked his head and started walking faster, but Yvonne grabbed him by the arm and hauled him back.

"Ace! I believe you have something to say to Phoebe."

"Mmmmsrry."

Yvonne gave his wrist a quick squeeze. "I'm pretty sure she didn't hear you," she drawled. "This time, say it like a man, not like the stupid teenager you were today."

Ace was ashamed to face Phoebe, but he was more afraid of Yvonne when she was mad, and she was as mad at him today as she'd ever been. He looked up, straight into Phoebe's eyes.

"I'm really sorry, Phoebe. Please forgive me." Then as he was about to apologize to Lee, too, he suddenly realized who was standing behind him. "Uh...oh... uh, shit. I'm sorry, Lee. Long time, no see, Aidan. My apologies all around."

Lee glared. "You do know who owns your rental house now, right?"

Ace was suddenly light-headed.

Aidan didn't say a word, which made Ace's belly roll.

"What do I have to do to stay in residence?" Ace asked.

Aidan's eyes narrowed. "I remember your daddy being one of the first ones to start calling my dad a killer...and now you go and insult a woman we both grew up with for no reason other than you're a jackass, and then insult me by assuming I'd disrupt your family and kick them out of their home out of spite. Your problem seems to be genetic. You don't have any more sense than your father. Yvonne, you have my sympathies."

Yvonne rolled her eyes. "Thank you, Aidan, but too late for that. We've already added to that gene pool with three more James boys, but I appreciate your sensitivity to my current situation. Phoebe Ann, we've known each other since grade school, and I am embarrassed beyond belief that the man to whom I am married talked to you in such a fashion. Rest assured it will not happen again." Then she glanced at Aidan again. "As for you, it's about time you showed up. Totally none of my business, but today I am not feeling kindly toward men in general."

She dragged Ace with her as she stormed off, leaving what was left of Aidan's ego in tatters.

Phoebe sighed. "I have managed to live under the radar here in Blessings for a long time until now. I can't believe this is happening, so can we please go inside and get this over with? I'm not through doing laundry."

———

A little more than an hour later, Dr. Quick brought Phoebe's X-rays into the exam room where she was sitting. He was followed by a nurse who was pushing a cart loaded with first aid supplies.

Dr. Quick slid the X-rays onto the light screen and then turned it on.

"Here's the reason for the swelling. Nothing broken, but you have two knuckles out of place. Who did you hit?" he joked.

"Ace James," Phoebe said.

Paul Quick's smirk quickly faded. "Seriously? As in Ace James with the broken nose who left earlier?"

"As in," Phoebe said. "Is it going to hurt putting them back into place?"

"Yes, ma'am, and I'm so sorry," Dr. Quick said.

Phoebe's shoulders slumped. There was a look of resignation on her face that made Aidan long to hold her.

"It's no more than I deserve for losing my temper. Do what you have to do, please, and get it over with," Phoebe said.

Lee sat down on the exam table beside her and put his arm around her waist. He'd dislocated his shoulder playing football his junior year of high school and remembered all too well how badly it had hurt when they popped the joint back into place.

"I'm so sorry, Mom," he said.

Then Phoebe felt a hand slide up beneath her hair and cup the back of her neck. She knew it was Aidan. The last time he'd touched her was the day before their world imploded.

"I'm sorry, too, Bee," he said.

She nodded but couldn't answer either one because Dr. Quick was already at work. Every spot he touched on her hand increased the pain. She didn't want to watch, so she closed her eyes. As the pain grew worse, the tears behind her eyelids began to roll. The first time she moaned, Lee's grip tightened around her waist. She moaned again, then exhaled through the wave of pain washing through her.

"I'm here, Mom, I'm here," Lee whispered.

"It's okay, honey. Compared to childbirth, this is nothing," Phoebe said.

Once again, Aidan was reminded of what she'd gone through alone and what he'd missed. Then he made himself focus. It wasn't about the past. This was now, and the tears on her cheeks hurt his heart.

Dr. Quick knew she was suffering, but he also knew that in a couple of seconds it was going to be shockingly worse.

"Deep breath, Phoebe," he said and then pushed as hard as he could.

Phoebe cried out, then went limp in Lee's arms. He caught her before she slid off the bed.

"Dang it," Dr. Quick said. "Lay her down gently while I get the other one in place and stabilize the fingers."

A nurse had pieces of tape waiting and handed them over one at a time as Dr. Quick taped her little finger to the ring finger.

"She needs to keep some ice on her hand for a couple of days until the swelling goes down." Then he added, "She's coming to," and she was.

Chapter 6

PHOEBE HEARD VOICES AS SHE WOKE UP, BUT DIDN'T recognize them. Then she opened her eyes, and the first person she saw was Aidan.

"Hey," he said.

"What happened?" she said and tried to sit up, but when she put her hand down, pain shot up her arm. That's when she remembered. "Oh, I hurt my hand. Could someone please help me sit up?"

Before Lee could get to her, Aidan slid an arm beneath her shoulders and lifted her to a sitting position. Being that close to her knocked him for a loop. He hadn't expected such a physical attraction. The way he felt at this moment, it was as if the past twenty years had never happened.

Phoebe inhaled the scent of his aftershave and sighed. Looked good. Smelled good. Dammit.

"Keep the fingers taped for at least a month," Dr. Quick said.

Phoebe groaned. "Oh great. That's going to be a trick at work. Oh well, I'll figure it out."

Dr. Quick gave her a pat on the shoulder. "I'll write you a prescription for a few pain pills. You won't need them for long, and for a day or two keep ice on your hand to help with the swelling."

Feeling defeated by the whole event, she nodded without commenting, and by the time the doctor left, she was crying.

"I'm sorry. This all happened because I lost my temper."

Lee hugged her gently. "You had a right to be angry, Mom. No one should tell a woman she needs to get laid. That's an insult. I'm angry for you, too."

Aidan was choked with emotion he couldn't name, but he felt like hitting something...or someone, too.

"I don't even want to think about how many other insults you've borne over the years. I wish I could change what happened. I wish they'd found out who set that fire. I wish your dad hadn't died in it. I wish with all my heart that I'd come back for you. I thought about it, but going back felt like I'd be betraying my father, and instead, I betrayed you. I'm sorry. I'm so sorry." Then Aidan turned to his son. "Lee, I'm going to wait in my car. I'll follow you as you take your mother home and then take you back to my house to get your truck. We've done enough for one day, and I want you to stay home with Phoebe for the rest of the day. She needs the help. I don't."

He reached out as if to touch Phoebe's face and then dropped his hand and walked away.

Phoebe's hand was hurting, but now her heart was hurting, too. What a mess they'd made, and yet she'd do it over again because her son was worth a thousand heartaches.

Lee looked anxious. "Dad's really sad."

"So am I," Phoebe said, wiping away tears. "It's a sad situation, but it will be better soon. You'll see. We'll both find our footing with where we are now, because you are what matters between us."

Lee sighed. He didn't feel all that confident this would be solved without some kind of showdown. Still, he'd met his father today, and that was the one thing he'd wanted more than anything.

A few minutes later, a nurse returned with the doctor's prescription and instructions for caring for her hand. Lee signed the checkout papers for her, and they left.

Phoebe was angry with herself for letting Ace get to her. She wouldn't be in this fix now if she'd just ignored him. She'd always ignored being hassled before, so why had she done this? Then she saw Aidan parked a distance away and knew. Because of him. She was hurt and angry that she'd waited for a man who had long ago quit loving her. She looked away as Lee helped her into the car and buckled her into her seat.

"Thank you, honey," Phoebe said.

Lee grinned. "You're welcome, Mom. I'm sorry you're hurt, but the truth is you're kind of awesome for punching that guy. I didn't know you had that in you."

Phoebe rolled her eyes. "Shut up and take me home, okay?"

He laughed as he shut the door and circled the car. As soon as he started the engine, he turned on the air-conditioning.

The cool air blasted Phoebe's face, cooling her flushed cheeks. Emotionally exhausted and aching all the way up the side of her neck, she lay back against the headrest and closed her eyes, waiting for the pain shot the nurse had given her to take effect.

--~~~--

Right now, Aidan Payne couldn't feel much lower. He'd walked out on the only girl he'd really loved instead of staying and fighting for her. He'd let her family's behavior color his opinion of her and lost a lifetime he'd never get back. He'd had a decent opinion of himself before his return to Blessings, but that was no longer the truth. He was ashamed of himself. He hurt for the boy who'd grown up without him. He hurt for all the discord and hardships Phoebe had to bear on her own, and he hurt for himself. Right now, it didn't feel like he would ever be happy again. When he saw Lee and Phoebe walking toward the car, he couldn't help but admire the woman she'd become.

Strong, courageous, self-sufficient, and honorable because she'd raised their son to love, not hate. She'd taught Lee to love a man who didn't know he existed, and she'd taught him what true love meant. Even though Aidan had had relationships, Phoebe had stayed faithful to him. Knowing his picture was on her nightstand was humbling and painful. He wanted a do-over for the past twenty years, but that wasn't going to happen.

He watched Lee helping her into the car and then noticed he stayed to buckle her in before he shut the door.

"So, Lee, even at the age of nineteen you are a better man than I am," he said to himself then looked away, pretending the sun was in his eyes instead of tears.

As Lee and Phoebe drove out of the parking lot, Aidan followed, and when they pulled up to a small, white frame house with a metal carport on the side, he parked behind them, gazing upon the accumulation of twenty years of Phoebe Ritter's life. If he compared the grand scale of his life in New Orleans with the big house, the sports car in the garage, and the four-star restaurant he owned to this small frame house, the older car, the job she had, and the handsome son helping her out of the car, it was obvious her struggles netted her the grander prize.

Aidan sighed. He wanted to be invited into that world, into that house. He wanted to be present at the holiday dinner when the turkey was in the oven and pies were cooling on the sideboard. He wanted to be a part of the laughter and jests—the stories of "remember when." But life had already proven to him that you don't always get what you want.

As Lee helped Phoebe up the steps, even though Aidan couldn't see her face, he knew she was in pain by the way she was holding her arm up against her body. He shook his head, thinking of her drawing back and busting Ace James's nose. The thought made him grin. Damn but she was one awesome woman.

But then they walked inside, and he watched the door closing behind them, thinking it was all too symbolic of the wall between their worlds. The only thing they shared now was Lee.

Tough little thing, aren't you, Bee? You weren't, but I guess life taught you the hard way to stand up for yourself. My apologies for not being there to do it for you. It would have been my honor.

A few minutes later, Lee came out the door with a smile on his face, leaped down the steps, and bounded toward Aidan's truck.

"Thanks for giving me a lift back to my truck," Lee said as he slid onto the seat and slammed the door.

"My pleasure," Aidan said. "Is your mom okay?"

"She will be," Lee said. "The shot they gave her for pain is beginning to take effect, and I have the prescription for pain pills to get filled. She's already in bed, ready to nap."

Aidan nodded. He wanted to ask more but didn't want Lee to think he was being nosy.

"You stay home with Phoebe this weekend. If she goes back to work and you have free time, just show up at the house. You don't need to call, which reminds me—put your number in my phone for me, will you? And then put my number in your cell, too."

"Really?" Lee asked.

Aidan frowned as he dropped his phone into Lee's outstretched hand.

"Lee. Son. I didn't know you existed until this morning. I am teetering between so sad I didn't get to help raise you and very proud of the man you are." Aidan reached across the seat and put his hand on Lee's shoulder. "The last thing I want on this earth is to lose track of you, and I hope one day you'll think to call me as easily as you would your mom."

Lee was beaming. "Thanks, Dad."

Aidan shook his head. "See what I mean? Today I became a father, and you're welcome."

Lee laughed.

Aidan backed out of the drive and then accelerated.

Inside the house, Phoebe had been listening for the sound of their exit before she relaxed enough to close her eyes. Falling asleep, she was still remembering the meal they'd just shared and the tenderness of Aidan's touch at the hospital. He might not love her anymore, but he cared what happened to her. She'd heard that much in his voice, and today it was enough.

Moe Randall carried his groceries into the house, then took out the sack with his prescription and tore into it with shaking hands. He opened the pain meds and washed down a dose with a big drink of water.

"God help me," Moe said softly, then put away all of the things that needed refrigeration before stumbling into the living room to his recliner.

He dropped into it with a thump, pulled the afghan off the arm and covered himself up, then leaned back and closed his eyes. He was so tired of the pain and nausea. So tired of everything…including life. He'd been living with a secret for the past twenty years, and this was the end result. His silence was killing him, and considering what his silence had cost, the end result was exactly what he had coming.

—◆◆◆—

Corey Randall robbed a liquor store in Savannah and left town the next morning in a stolen car. But this wasn't his first rodeo. He'd already switched license plates, lifting one from a parked car outside the city, and was heading straight to Blessings. He needed a place to lay low, and considering his old man was about to kick the bucket from cancer, no one would think twice about seeing him in town. The only person he had to worry about was his dad. Ever since the old man figured out he was dying, he'd been on Corey's back to change his life. But he and his dad had already had that conversation too many times in the past for it to suddenly make sense now. And while he was there, he intended to scope out what he would inherit. Knowing he was the only heir did make life simple.

Corey was about halfway to his destination when he

noticed the gas gauge. He'd thought he'd had enough fuel to get him to Blessings, but it didn't look like it now. His only options were to keep driving and hope he made it to Blessings or pull into the next station and refuel. He wasn't into walking anywhere if he could help it, and he was coming up on a two-pump bait shop: one for diesel, one for gas, and all kinds of bait for bayou fishing. It was the kind of low-key place a fugitive could feel safe in…and he'd gone to school with the guy who owned it. Time to stop in and say hello to an old friend.

Corey slowed down, then eased off the highway onto the gravel and parked at the gas pump. Corey paid cash for all his purchases with money he stole. It eliminated the need to keep receipts for the taxes he never paid. As soon as he got out, the Georgia heat slapped a sheen of sweat on his face. He headed inside.

He'd stopped here countless times before since their high school graduation, and he was pretty sure Ford Renner hadn't swept the floor or emptied a trash can since he'd bought the place. The floor was always slightly wet and slick with fish scales, and the trash cans were mostly full of empty beer cans and honey-bun wrappers. It was obvious the owner's clientele never wavered in their snack choices.

Ford Renner was a short, stocky man with a bushy red beard and long, stringy blond hair he wore pulled back in a ponytail. When he saw Corey Randall walking in, he shifted his dip of Skoal into his other cheek and spat a stream into the spit can so he'd have room enough in his mouth to talk.

"Hey, bro! Long time, no see," Ford said. "What are you doing in this part of the woods?"

"Hi, Ford. I'm just coming home to check on the old man. He's got cancer, you know. It's just a matter of time. You're looking good. How's the family?"

"Yeah, I heard about your dad. Sorry about that. As for us, we're all good," Ford said. "Me and Marcella are having another baby boy."

Corey reached across the counter and shook Ford's hand. "Congratulations, dude. What are you going to name this one?"

"We're still trying to decide, but we're gonna have to make a decision soon. The kid is already past due."

"Still gonna name him after a car?" Corey asked.

Ford nodded, then spat again. "Yep, but we done used up Lincoln, Dodge, and Chevy. I'm leaning toward Jeep, but Marcella is set on naming this one Caddie. She said she's always wanted a Cadillac and figures this is the only way she's ever gonna get one."

Corey laughed as he pulled a roll of money from his pocket.

"Here's sixty bucks. I'm gonna fill up the tank. I'll come back in for my change."

Ford looked over Corey's shoulder to the car parked at the pump.

"What the hell are you doing driving a Mazda? Stick to American cars, man!"

Corey laughed. "Find me one American car that's running on American-made parts, and I might jump on that bandwagon. Right now, I'm going for gas mileage, and this one works just fine for me." He grabbed a candy bar on his way out the door, waving it in the air. "Add this Snickers to my tab."

Ford gave him a thumbs-up and turned on the gas pump as the door swung shut behind Corey.

Corey ate the candy bar while he was waiting for the tank to fill and thought about the life Ford Renner was living. It wasn't the big leagues, but he seemed happy enough. Corey popped the last bite of candy in his mouth, licked his fingers, then wished he hadn't because he was going to taste gas now instead of chocolate.

Cars whizzed by on the highway as he waited. He recognized one driver as a citizen of Blessings and then heard a siren and saw another car speeding past going in the opposite direction with a highway patrol car in pursuit. He frowned. Good thing he'd stopped for gas. He didn't want to be meeting up with cops of any ilk.

A few moments later, the pump kicked off. Corey hung up the hose and went back inside to settle up.

"Thirty-two fifty-six plus that dollar candy bar makes it thirty-three dollars and fifty-six cents. Need anything else?" Ford asked.

Corey glanced toward the cooler where the cold pop and beer were kept. "Yeah…I need a cold pop to chase all that chocolate. Add a bottle of Mountain Dew to the total."

Ford nodded, added the pop as Corey went to get it, and then handed him his change.

"Come back when you can stay longer," Ford said.

"I'll do that," Corey said, and out the door he went.

He unscrewed the top on the bottle and took a big drink before starting the car back up, then drove away, taking care not to speed. Less than fifteen minutes later, he passed the city limit sign, then drove into Blessings. It was a quarter after two. He hadn't eaten breakfast or lunch, and since he wasn't certain of his welcome at home, he went straight to Granny's to eat.

He got out of the Mazda with his chin up and a kiss-my-ass stride and went inside the same way. He gave Lovey a thumbs-up and swaggered past her to an empty booth. She followed him with a menu and a grim smile.

"It's been awhile since I've seen you," Lovey said. "Came to check on your dad, I guess."

Corey nodded. "Yes, ma'am. We talk every day, so I know he's failing. Took off a little time from work to come see for myself."

"He'll be real proud to see you, I'm sure. Here comes your waitress. I'll let her take your order."

Lovey walked away as her new waitress, Shelly Mayberry, approached the table.

"Welcome to Granny's," Shelly said as she set a glass of ice water at his place.

Corey leaned back, eyeing her curiously.

"I don't know you. You aren't from around here, are you?"

"I don't know you, either, but my name is Shelly, and I live here with my parents…for the past eight months. Do you know what you want?" she asked.

Corey's eyes narrowed. She'd just reminded him how long it had been since he'd been back, and then blew off the thought.

"As a matter of fact, I do. Burger, fries, and a big glass of sweet tea," Corey said. "And a piece of lemon pie, if you have any."

Shelly nodded. "We do. I'll turn in your order and be back with your tea."

Corey watched the sway of her butt as she walked

away, then reminded himself he'd come home to stay low-key. He reached for his water and saw his waitress already on her way back.

"Here's your iced tea and a couple of our famous biscuits to tide you over until your food arrives. Enjoy," she said as she slid the little basket of biscuits onto the table.

Corey took a quick drink of the iced tea and pulled his bread plate toward him to reach for a biscuit. To his surprise, it was piping hot. He split it, slathered it with butter, and took a bite.

"Ohmygawdthisisonefinebiscuit," he mumbled, then chewed and swallowed and put the rest of the half into his mouth, catching the drip of butter on the edge of his lip just before it fell.

He finished off the biscuit and was buttering a second one when someone slid into the other side of his booth. He looked up and frowned.

"What the fuck do you want? No. Don't answer that. Whatever you want, I'm not your banker. Get lost, Joe."

Joe Weaver reached for a half of the biscuit Corey was buttering and got the tines of a fork into the back of his hand for his trouble.

"Ow! Shit, Corey! What's the matter with you?"

"I told you to get lost, which did not mean take my food with you when you go. I mean it."

Joe cursed as he rubbed the back of his hand.

"Watch your mouth. Lovey will throw you out, and you know it," Corey muttered.

Joe glanced over his shoulder, half-expecting her to be standing behind him, ready to escort him out.

"I remember a time when you used to hang around

me and Bo for your fun. I just wanted to say hi, so screw you," Joe said, then he got up and walked away.

Corey frowned. Even though he hadn't drawn blood, he wiped the fork on his shirt. Moments later, the new waitress was coming toward him with his food. He eyed her short red hair and the size of her boobs, then lost focus on everything but the food she set down in front of him.

"Do you need anything else?" Shelly asked.

Corey noted the ketchup already on the table and shook his head. "Just dessert when I'm done."

"I'll bring that right out," Shelly said. She came back with the piece of pie and her tea pitcher, refilled his glass, and left him to eat.

Corey was congratulating himself on coming home when he saw the police chief walk in. He froze, then inhaled slowly.

He's not here for me. He's not here for me.

The mantra seemed to work because Lon Pittman gave Lovey a wave before going into the kitchen. Corey put his head down and kept eating his burger until it was gone. Then he shook a healthy dose of ketchup on his fries and ate them. Corey didn't appreciate his food touching and ate one thing before beginning another. He was nearly done with the fries when the chief came out of the kitchen. Corey knew Chief Pittman saw him, but to his relief he kept walking. Elated to have missed that conversation, he dug into his pie and had another moment of revelation that the damn pie was as good as those biscuits, which seemed like an impossible feat.

Shelly came by to refill his iced tea again.

"Hey," Corey said. "Who made the pie and biscuits? They are really, really good."

"Oh, that would be the chief's wife, Mercy Pittman."

"She is one fine cook," Corey said.

Shelly grinned. "That's what everyone says. I'll pass along the message. Do you need anything else?" she asked.

"Just my ticket," Corey said with a wink.

Shelly's grin faded. She didn't like this guy's vibe. She went to print out the check, then slipped it on his table as she went back to turn in another order. When she returned to bus the table Corey had been using, she was a little startled by the twenty-dollar tip. She wasn't going to turn it down, but it made her a little nervous. She felt like he was one of those guys who believed he'd bought more than food with the tip. But for now he was gone. She pocketed the money and wiped down the table before resetting it for the next customers.

Outside, Corey was in a much better mood as he got back in the Mazda and left the parking lot. Like it or not, it was time to go home. He drove the backstreets purposefully, not wanting to call attention to his presence with any cops who might be looking for a stolen Mazda. Even though he'd switched license plates, if someone ran the tag on this car, it was not going to come up with the right registration. Just to be on the safe side, when he got home, he would back into the driveway, hiding the plate from easy view.

A couple minutes later, Corey arrived, backed into the driveway, and got out. The house was more run-down than he'd ever seen it, and the yard needed mowing. It looked like the house was dying with his dad.

He reached back inside the car for his bag before he went up the steps and tried the door. Like always, it was unlocked in the daytime, so he let himself in.

His dad was a shocking sight, asleep in the recliner. He was little more than a bag of bones, with a gray tinge to his skin and huge bruises on both arms that were caused by the blood draws at the hospital and all the times he caught himself to keep from falling. Corey was seriously taken aback. It was one thing to know his father was dying, but this was the first time Corey had seen what dying from cancer looked like.

He put down his bag, then stood within the silence of the house, listening to his father's labored breathing. As he did, he began remembering his childhood and how close they'd been and how happy their time together was before he hit high school. All the fishing trips. Working in their garden together. Lugging their extra produce to the park to sell, then setting it up beneath a shade tree to wait for customers. He remembered taking the money home every time and where they stashed it to save for Christmas. He'd stolen the stash when he first left home, and the next time he looked for it, it had not been replenished.

He thought of the hot summer days when they'd made homemade ice cream out under the shade trees in the backyard. He remembered his mother in the kitchen icing fresh strawberry cupcakes to go with the ice cream and the sleepovers he'd had with his friends. It was a kinder, simpler time, and for a moment, he was awash in grief.

Then angry at himself for showing weakness, he opened the door again and slammed it shut on purpose, knowing it would wake up his dad, which it did.

Moe woke with a start, blinking rapidly to clear his rheumy vision as he peered toward the front door.

"Corey? Son? Is that you?"

Corey took off his Georgia Bulldogs cap and hung it on the hall tree by the door. "Yeah, it's me. You don't look so good," he said as he walked over to where Moe was sitting. But instead of hugging, they shook hands.

Moe didn't know what to feel. He'd thought for sure he would die without seeing his son again, and now that he was here, Moe almost wished that had happened. He knew Corey too well to assume he'd come to check on his father's health. He wanted something, but only time would tell what that might be.

Moe reached for the lever on his recliner and put down the footrest.

"Have you eaten? There's food in the house. I just went to the Piggly Wiggly."

"I just left Granny's," Corey said. "I came home to check on you. I've got a few days to stay. Hope that's okay?"

"Of course it's okay. This will always be your home, too," Moe said.

Corey rubbed his hands against his pant legs, then pointed toward his bag. "I'll go put my stuff in my room then. I'll be right back."

Moe didn't comment. He was riding out a wave of pain and nausea.

Chapter 7

AIDAN WAS MOSTLY SILENT ON THE WAY BACK TO HIS grandfather's house, but the little he said was in reference to Phoebe. When they finally arrived and got out, Aidan gave Lee a big hug.

"Best day ever, Son. Take care of your mom, and come over whenever you have the time."

"Will do," Lee said and jumped in his old truck, then started it up and drove away. But his thoughts were a jumble of what-ifs as he turned the corner at the end of the block. He had seen the sad look in his dad's eyes as they parted company, and all the way home he kept trying to think of a way to eliminate the awkwardness between his parents.

He suspected his dad had feelings for his mother, and he knew she still had feelings for him despite what she'd said. He didn't know how long his dad would be in Blessings, but he intended to put them together every chance he got and pray for a miracle.

He stopped at the pharmacy to get Phoebe's prescription filled and then headed home as soon as he got it. By the time he reached the house, he had his first matchmaking idea. All he had to do was get his mom on board.

He went inside through the back door to keep from waking her up and, with his plan in mind, poked around in the deep freezer in the utility room, then in the smaller freezer in their refrigerator before taking a quick look in the pantry. Everything was on hand for a dinner guest, but he still needed to sell his mom on the idea.

Aware that one board in the hall had a tendency to creak, he stayed to the other side as he went to her room, but when he opened the door, it squeaked. He winced as she rolled over and waved.

"Did I wake you? I was trying to be quiet," Lee said.

"I wasn't asleep," Phoebe said and patted the mattress beside her. She wanted to find out what had happened between father and son today. "Come sit with me a bit."

Lee bounced into the room and eased down onto the side of her bed. The fact that Aidan's picture was still on the nightstand was encouraging.

"Is the medicine still working?" he asked and set the prescription bottle beside the lamp.

Phoebe nodded. "Yes, I'm okay. I want to know how you and Aidan got along. Do things feel weird or awkward between you?"

"No way, Mom. What's great is how easy he is to be around. I have a question for you," Lee said. "How do you feel now that the initial meeting is over? Do you hate him? Are you mad at him?"

Phoebe reached for Lee's hand. "Honey, I will never hate him, and I got over being angry a long time ago. I guess I feel hurt, but then so does he. I saw that. If I could take back the past twenty years, I think I'd make a different decision."

Lee nodded. "Yeah, that's pretty much where Dad is, too. I have to be honest. I am so happy this day finally came, but I am also very sad."

Phoebe tightened her hold. "Oh, honey…why?"

"The two people I care most about in this world once

loved each other so much they made a baby together, and now you're at odds. I feel torn between the both of you."

Phoebe hurt knowing she was the cause of his distress. "No, Lee, no! Please don't. We'll be fine."

"You didn't see him," Lee said. "There were tears in his eyes. His voice was shaking, and he kept looking at you in ER like he wanted to put his arms around you."

Breath caught in the back of Phoebe's throat. She wanted to believe she still mattered to Aidan like that, but she was honest enough with herself to guess it had more to do with Lee than her.

"Well, he lost a lot of years with you. That's probably what's happening with him."

Lee shrugged. "You didn't see him. I did, and I don't want to go to bed tonight with that memory, so I need to ask you another favor. He's so alone over there. Can I invite him to dinner tonight? I already looked in the freezer and the pantry. We have everything I need, some of which only needs to be thawed and reheated. I'm a good enough cook. I can do this…if you'll let me."

The thought of spending more time with Aidan today was painful.

"What if he doesn't want to come?" Phoebe asked.

"Then he won't be here for dinner," Lee said.

Phoebe sighed. "If only I saw the world as simply as you do."

Lee grinned. "Then I can ask him?"

Phoebe scooted herself into a sitting position. "Of course, and just for the record, you don't have to ask me this again. You live here, too, and he's your other parent. I would never refuse him entrance into our home. The door will always be open to him."

Lee gave her a thumbs-up. "Thanks, Mom, you rock! Do you care what I make for dinner?"

"No, but I can help," she said.

"No, you take it easy with your hand. I cook in my apartment at school all the time. I can do this. I'm going to call him right now."

"Be sure to tell him I'm good with the invitation, too. We don't want him showing up wondering about my reaction, okay?"

"Right! Will do, and thanks so much, Mom," Lee said and bolted out of the room.

Phoebe glanced at Aidan's photo. "You! Will I ever be free of your ability to break my heart?"

Eighteen-year-old Aidan just smiled back at her without comment.

⁓⁓⁓

But thirty-eight-year old Aidan Payne wasn't smiling. There was, at the moment, nothing humorous about his life. He'd gone to his grandfather's old office, mostly for comfort. It still smelled of Preston's aftershave and the cigars he had occasionally smoked, so when Aidan eased down into the old leather chair behind the desk and glanced up, he half-expected his granddad to walk in.

The floor-to-ceiling shelves were lined with books, some pertaining to business, others to home repair. His grandfather had a whole shelf full of ledgers, one for every rental house he owned, and detailed notations of the people who'd lived there throughout the years he'd owned them.

His heart hurt, thinking of never seeing Preston's smile or hearing that booming laugh again. Out of curiosity, he began going through the desk drawers one at a time, looking for more memories.

The big drawer in the middle had a mishmash of pens, bulldog clips, and notepads. The top drawer on the right had a stack of yellow legal pads and a bunch of sticky notes Preston had written to himself about needed repairs at rental houses. Every note had a big check mark on it, signifying completion. Then Aidan opened the bottom drawer, saw what looked like a photo album, took it out, and opened it up.

Almost instantly, the skin crawled on the back of his neck. It felt like his grandfather had just walked up behind him and put a hand on his shoulder as he read a dedication page.

For Aidan:
I made a promise to Phoebe when she needed
help most not to interfere between you two and
learned to love her like a daughter. I waited so
long for you to ask about her, but you never did.
Lee is very much like you. Please love him as
much as I did, and please forgive me.
                           Granddad

Aidan flipped to the next page and then stared at the first picture through a wall of tears. It was a picture of a teenage Phoebe with Lee in her arms, coming out of the hospital. The look on her face was one of such joy and determination that it took his breath away.

His granddad had written a caption beneath the picture.

Mother and son—going home.

"Have mercy," Aidan whispered and laid the flat of his hand on top of the photo, as if by magic he would be transported back to that day and that moment.

Anxious to see what was next, he began turning pages. There were more pictures of Phoebe and Lee, and as the months passed, he saw pictures of Lee lying on a big quilt on the floor trying to pull off his socks, another of him scooting down the hall in a walker, and another of him crawling. Then he turned the page to one moment caught in time that elicited a groan of physical pain.

First steps—just look at him smile.

And then Aidan's cell phone rang. Startled by the abruptness of the sound when he was so far away in time, he jumped, glanced at the caller ID, and quickly closed the album.

"Hello."

"Hi, Dad, it's me. Mom and I are inviting you to supper tonight at our house."

Aidan's heart skipped. "Phoebe is on board with this, too?"

"Yes, sir, she sure is, and she said to tell you that the door is always open to you here."

Aidan leaned back in the big chair and closed his eyes. "That's much appreciated, and I accept. Can I bring anything?"

"Nope. We've got this covered. Is six o'clock too early for you? As a rule, we don't like to eat late unless Mom is working the late shift at the store."

"It's perfect, and thank you," Aidan said. "I'm looking forward to it. How is her hand?"

"The pain pills are helping. Awesome that you're coming to supper!" Lee said. "See you then."

The call ended, but Aidan was still holding the phone up to his ear, his thoughts in freefall.

Please let this be a beginning to getting back what I lost.

Corey Randall had just given his dad a dose of pain meds when Moe was hit with a wave of physical pain. Corey saw his dad's body shaking so hard he thought he was having a seizure.

"Uh...hey...are you okay?" he asked.

Moe moaned. "Just pain...cold," he whispered.

Corey felt weird being the nursemaid. He felt like he'd lost the right to be there. He picked up the afghan from the back of the sofa and laid it over his dad's legs. When Moe grabbed it and pulled it up to his chin, Corey turned away.

"I'll go make some coffee. Maybe that will warm you up," he said.

Speech was beyond Moe, but he nodded with his eyes closed as he rode out the oncoming nausea.

Corey hurried into the kitchen, anxious to get away from the sight. He'd seen dead bodies before. One was a junkie; another had been shot and left to bleed out in a back alley in Savannah. But he'd never watched anyone dying from disease, and that's what was happening in the other room.

He opened a couple of cabinets before he found the coffee, then filled the carafe with water and started the coffee maker. He got down two coffee mugs and walked to the window overlooking the backyard as he waited for the coffee to brew.

His mother used to have a whole row of rosebushes against the back fence. He wondered when his dad had dug them up because there was nothing there now. He leaned forward for a closer look at the house next door, and when he did, he noticed the dust on the windowsills below him and on the ruffles of the old kitchen curtains next to his chin.

Feeling guilty was an unfamiliar emotion, and he rarely let himself go there. Ignoring the dust, he went out on the back porch, took a deep breath, and then coughed. *Damn cigarettes*. And even as he was thinking that, he sat down on the top step to smoke.

The motions were rote as he tapped the pack against his wrist, partially ejecting the cigarette, then lit it. He inhaled deeply with the first draw, letting the shot of nicotine ricochet through his system. As he sat, the neighbor to the west walked outside to put something in the garbage, saw Corey, stumbled in surprise, and then waved as he hurried back inside.

Corey gave him a nod of recognition and looked away. Screw the bastard. So what if he hadn't been home in a while. He had his own life to live, dammit.

He glanced toward the house to the east. A widow woman lived there who used to work in the public library. He took another drag on his cigarette and blew a couple smoke rings just to prove he could. When he began smelling coffee, he finished his cigarette and went back inside. His sense of smell was on point. The coffee was done.

He filled the mugs and carried them into the living

room, but his dad had fallen asleep, so he set one on the end table before sitting down to drink his. Every so often, he glanced over at his dad. Once he thought he'd stopped breathing, and it scared him. He watched in growing horror until he saw his dad's chest expand, followed by a kind of snore bubbling through his lips.

Corey shuddered. A part of him thought about leaving now while his dad was asleep, but he was in a tight spot. He needed to let the heat die down before he showed back up in Savannah, and if he left now, he'd be spending his heist money on some low-class motel. He didn't have to be a genius to figure out he wasn't going anywhere.

~~~

Lee was excited. There was a cooked ham in the freezer that he'd put in the oven to reheat and a frozen peach pie thawing on the counter. He knew his mom had made it for him to take back to his apartment after one of his visits, but tonight it was staying right here.

He had potatoes washed to bake later and two cans of green beans to heat up closer to suppertime. There was stuff for salad, and ice cream to put on the hot peach pie for dessert. It was a sampling of a lot of his favorite things.

Phoebe thought about going in to help, but she didn't want to rain on Lee's big plan and make him think he wasn't capable. However, she could make an effort to dress up a little. Aidan was a guest, after all.

She was digging through her closet when she heard Lee come thundering down the hall, talking. "Mom! Mom! Where do you keep the tablecloths?"

She backed out of the closet as he came running into her room.

"Are we setting the dining table?" she asked.

He hesitated. "Uh…I wanted to. Is that okay?"

She grinned. "This is your event. Of course it's okay. The tablecloths are all in the linen closet in the hall. The Christmas one is red. Any of the others will be fine."

"Thanks, Mom," Lee said, kissed the top of her head, and bolted out as quickly as he'd entered.

Phoebe shook her head and went back to the closet, but that didn't last long. Lee was on the move again, calling her name.

She gave up and followed him back into the dining room and directed traffic while he set the table. When he reached for the candleholders, she called a halt.

"Lee! Come on! We aren't having a candlelit dinner."

"Really? Too much?" he asked.

"Yes, way too much," she said.

"Got it," he said, giving her a thumbs-up.

"Need anything else?" she asked.

"Nope. I'm good," Lee said.

She eyed the table one last time and then went back to her bedroom to see a closet about a dress.

———

Aidan left the house at five-thirty, although it took less than ten minutes to get from his house to theirs, but like his son, he had a plan. He drove straight down Main to Franklin's Florist. He remembered George and Myra Franklin from the years when he used to buy Phoebe's corsage for the Winter Ball, or for the Peachy Keen Queen ball that happened every year after the queen was crowned. The fact that they were still the owners was slightly surprising, but Aidan did not expect them to still be working in the shop, too. Myra was behind the counter when he walked in. She looked up.

"Hello, welcome to Franklin's. How can I help you?"

"I'm on my way to a dinner at a friend's house and wanted to take the hostess some flowers. I think I'd like a mixed bouquet."

"Certainly," Myra said. "How much do you want to spend?"

"Maybe forty or fifty dollars. Don't want it to look too extravagant, but I want it to reflect my pleasure at the invitation."

Myra nodded. "Understood. You're welcome to take a seat there on that bench or just look around. This won't take me long."

"Thank you. I'm due there at six, so—"

"You won't be late on my account," Myra said and went back to the workroom, leaving Aidan on his own up front.

He was too nervous to sit, so he prowled through the store, eyeing all of the gift items and artificial displays for sale.

Within a very few minutes, Myra was back at the register with a mixed bouquet of summer flowers in a jade-green vase.

"How is this?" she asked.

"Perfect!" Aidan said, pulled out a credit card, and slid it across the counter.

When Myra saw the name on the card, she looked up in surprise. "Aidan Payne! I did not recognize you. You have grown up into a handsome man. Welcome back to Blessings."

"Thank you, ma'am," he said and then picked up the bouquet and left the store.

It was five minutes to six when he drove up to the house and parked. He grabbed the bouquet and headed to the front door. One knock and the door swung open in front of him. It was Phoebe, wearing a blue-and-white-striped halter dress that barely brushed her knees. Her bare shoulders and arms were slightly sun-kissed, and her dark hair was loose around her face. But it was the shy smile that tugged at his heart.

"Welcome. Come in," Phoebe said.

Aidan swallowed past a lump in his throat. "Thank you for the invitation. I brought you flowers, but if you'll show me where you want to put them, I'll carry the vase."

"This way," Phoebe said, taking him past their small living room to the dining room just off the kitchen. "They'll be perfect on the table, and we can look at them all through our meal."

Aidan noticed the table setting and was touched by the trouble they'd gone to.

"This is all so beautiful," he said as he set the flowers in the center of the table.

"It's all Lee's doing. He's benched me for now," she said, holding up her hand.

Lee appeared in the doorway. "Did I hear someone mention my name?"

Aidan grinned at the pink ruffled apron his son was wearing. "Nice apron. All you need is a chef's hat."

"I'm a messy cook. It serves my purpose," Lee said. "Dinner will be ready in about five minutes. Go do something, and I'll yell for you when it's done."

Aidan laughed out loud as his son disappeared.

Phoebe blushed. "That's just Lee. He is so self-assured that it is impossible to embarrass him."

"That's a great attitude to have," Aidan said, then offered her his arm. "It's your house. What can we do for five minutes?"

"We can sit and stare at each other in the living room, or we can sit and stare at each other at the dining room table."

"I'll sit with you anywhere, but I'd rather talk, if it's all the same to you."

They returned to the living room and then sat together on the sofa, but not too close. Phoebe's heart was pounding, and Aidan had so many things he wanted to say he didn't know where to begin.

"I need you to know I'm not angry. Humbled and still in a bit of shock but not angry," he said.

Phoebe sighed. "And I'm sorry for what I said to you this morning. Lord…was that only this morning? I want you to know that if I had it to do over again, I would tell you."

Then Lee appeared. "Dinner is ready!"

With too much still left unsaid, the conversation ended.

Aidan escorted Phoebe back into the dining room. In the four minutes they'd spent together and the ten feet they'd walked from dining room to living room and back again, a huge pain was lifting from his heart. She didn't hate him. And, once again, he was having dinner with family, an event he'd believed he would never experience again.

Phoebe kept resisting the urge to pinch herself. This whole day had been surreal, and she was afraid if she closed her eyes, he would disappear. But it wasn't until

Aidan seated her at the head of the table that she realized he was honoring her in the only way he knew how. As the head of this house, she'd earned the right.

Once they were seated, Lee looked at both of them with an expression of joy.

"This is wonderful! This is my dream come true!" Lee said. "I'll say the blessing, Mom." Then he bowed his head.

Phoebe had a quick glimpse of Aidan's face before she closed her eyes. He was looking at her like he used to. She realized she had completely tuned out Lee's voice until he ended the prayer with a big "amen."

"Everything looks so good," Aidan said.

"Oh, it's gonna taste good, too," Lee said. "All of this is Mom's cooking except the beans and potatoes. I just thawed and baked it for her and reheated the rest. Mom, I sliced up some slivers of ham for you so you wouldn't have to try to cut a slice."

"You think of everything," Phoebe said. "How about I just hand you my plate and you fix it for me? Then you and your dad can pass stuff back and forth to each other."

"Deal," Aidan said.

So she waited, watching the two men she loved most, thinking of how fate had twisted their lives.

They were midway through dinner when Lee got up to refill their glasses.

"I miss Granddad being here," Lee said. "Remember how he was always wanting a refill? He sure did like his sweet iced tea."

Aidan looked up. The sadness on his son's face mirrored how he felt inside. He missed Preston so much. And then something occurred to him.

"I just had a thought," Aidan said. "We're together right now *because* he's gone."

A chill ran up the back of Phoebe's neck. "You're so right. His death did for us what we couldn't do for each other."

Lee filled up the glasses and sat back down. "How about a toast to Granddad?" He lifted his glass. "To the man who taught me to think for myself."

Phoebe picked up her glass with her left hand and lifted it high. "Preston Williams, you were a white knight to me when I needed one most. We miss you, but you will never be forgotten."

Then Aidan glanced around the table as he lifted his glass. "To you, Granddad. You always told me all things happen for a reason. Thank you for bringing me home."

The clink of their glasses was echoed by the clink of ice cubes inside them. The toast was a sobering moment that could have ruined the rest of the meal but instead drew them closer.

After they'd finished the main course, Lee began carrying plates to the sink.

"Need any help?" Phoebe asked.

"No, Mom. I've got this," Lee said and carried the warm peach pie to the table. "Made with peaches from last year's Peachy Keen festival."

Aidan smiled. "I remember that! So they still hold that queen contest?"

"Oh, yes," Phoebe said. "The reigning queen is Tammy Allen, Juanita Allen's daughter. She used to be Juanita Waters."

"The same Juanita Waters who fell off the school

stage during the Christmas program our freshman year in school?"

"The same. She married Freddy Allen. He's the butcher at the Piggly Wiggly," Phoebe said.

Lee got the ice cream from the freezer and brought it and a scoop to the table before cutting the pie. The slight crunch of the caramelized sugar on top of the crust was a great intro to the brown sugar peach pie within.

"Smells so good, Mom," Lee said and cut a large piece of pie, topped it with a huge scoop of ice cream, and passed it to Aidan. "Enjoy, Dad, and don't wait for us. We're right behind you."

Aidan cut right through the ice cream, taking some of it with the bite of pie and popping it into his mouth.

"Ohmylordthisisgood," he mumbled as he chewed and swallowed. "Phoebe Ann, this is beyond delicious. It needs to go on the menu at Mimosa."

"What's Mimosa?" she asked.

Aidan stopped, then looked up at both of them in surprise.

"I guess I assumed you knew what I did for a living. I own a four-star restaurant called Mimosa in the French Quarter in New Orleans."

"Really?" Phoebe said, intrigued. "I would never have imagined you in that kind of occupation."

He shrugged. "I went to college in New Orleans and worked in the food service industry all the way through. By the time I graduated, I was hooked."

"We have to go there, Mom," Lee said as he set her dessert in front of her.

Phoebe nodded. "Sounds like a plan."

Aidan resisted the urge to cheer and took another bite.

Chapter 8

WHEN THE DINNER WAS OVER, AIDAN AND LEE CLEANED up the kitchen while Phoebe sat at the kitchen table, watching. Their expressions were almost identical—they laughed at the same things, and even the set of their shoulders was almost identical as they moved about the room. Phoebe sighed. She had been so used to living without Aidan in their world, and now he was vividly present. Part of her wanted to hope there was something left between them to build upon, but the rational part of her told her to let it go.

It was obvious he had not been pining for her for the past twenty years, and she couldn't bear to think of living that heartbreak all over again. She had to settle for Lee's happiness and forget about anything else.

Then she heard a phone ringing and realized it was hers. She hurried back into the dining room where she'd left it, glancing at the caller ID as she picked it up and smiled. It was Millie Garner, one of the women she worked with at the Piggly Wiggly.

"Hello, this is Phoebe."

"Girrlll, I just heard about you pouring Ace's beer over his head and busting his nose! I wish I'd seen that. Oh my God…what on earth did he do?"

Phoebe sighed. "Let's just say he had it coming and leave it at that. I'd rather let this die a natural death without adding to the drama."

This was not the juicy gossip Millie was expecting. "Well, that's too bad. I sure did want to know what he said an' all."

"He's already apologized to me, so I'm not going to keep the fire burning on that, okay?"

"Oh, he did? What did he say?" Millie asked.

"That he's sorry…just what I said."

"Well, then, I guess I'll see you at work on Monday," Millie said.

"See you then," Phoebe said and hung up. She glanced down at her hand and the two fingers taped together. People were bound to make the story bigger than it needed to be, but she'd control any of that. She sighed and went back into the kitchen. "Did I stay away long enough to arrive after cleanup is over?"

"You were already excused from that, and you know it," Lee said. "Who was that?"

Phoebe shrugged. "Millie…wanting to know all the dirty details about me and Ace. I'm afraid I disappointed her."

"Who's Millie?" Aidan asked.

"One of the women I work with. She's nice, but she does like to be the one with the gossip scoop, and I've been on the dirty end of that enough to know I wouldn't wish it on my worst enemy."

The moment the words came out of her mouth Phoebe knew she shouldn't have said them. The look on Aidan's face was pure horror. Before she knew what was happening, he was out of his chair and hugging her.

"There aren't enough ways for me to say how much it grieves me to know I caused you such distress. I'm sorry, Bee…so sorry."

Lee's heart skipped. Resisting the urge to cheer, he was muttering something about checking his email as he left the room.

Startled to find herself in Aidan's arms, her first reaction was to step back, but she'd spent so many years wishing the moment would happen that she hesitated.

"I'm sorry. I didn't mean to make you think—"

Aidan interrupted. "Don't say it. We have a truth between us that can't be denied or changed, don't we?"

She nodded.

"We hurt each other, didn't we?" he said.

She swallowed past the knot in her throat. "I have dreams of that phone call you made the night Daddy died. In my dream, when you ask me to believe in your father's innocence, I don't hesitate. I don't deny him or you. And then I wake up and know that I had just as much to do with the life Lee and I are living as you did."

Aidan reached for her, then stopped.

"Bee, this morning I put a Help Wanted sign in my front yard, and you knocked on my door and gave me a son instead. I had no one, and now I have family again. Am I allowed to count you as part of that family?"

Phoebe was shivering from the ache of wanting him, but the invitation was too vague for her to assume he meant anything more than including the mother of his child.

"Of course. Lee will always be the connection that keeps us linked."

It wasn't exactly what he wanted to hear, but it was something to hold on to. "Okay then, and if you can ever find it in your heart to give me another chance, all you have to do is whistle."

"Why do I feel like you just gave yourself an out? You know I can't whistle," Phoebe said.

Aidan blinked. He'd completely forgotten that about her. "You could improvise."

"We live completely separate lives," Phoebe said.

"So how's that working out for you?" Aidan said, pointing to her hand.

Phoebe's cell phone began ringing again, but she ignored it. "Let's look at it this way. You just got here. We may decide that being friends works better between us."

"Or we may decide that our first plan to spend the rest of our lives together was the best plan."

Then he leaned down, and before she knew what he intended, he was kissing her, and when he did, the distance between them disappeared.

Her phone kept ringing and then suddenly stopped as the call went to voicemail. It was the ensuing silence that ended the kiss.

Aidan's heart was racing. The magic between them was still there for him, but he was watching her face, waiting for her reaction. He didn't know that the walls behind which Phoebe had sheltered were crumbling, or he would have been overjoyed.

Phoebe's hand went to her heart, feeling the racing pulse as she struggled to find the right words.

"I'm not going to pretend that kiss didn't matter to me because it did. But I haven't lived in your heart as long as you have lived in mine. So, I guess what I'm saying is, I think we need to let go of what *was* and see if we can make something new with what *is*," she said. "Take it or leave it."

"Take it," Aidan said. "I'd shake hands on it, but you busted yours defending your own honor, so…"

She grinned. "We don't need a handshake. I trust your word."

Aidan nodded. "And on this positive note, I am going to thank you for the dinner invitation and a most wonderful meal and leave while I'm ahead. See you tomorrow?"

"We'll be in church, and then we'll be home."

"I won't be in church. It's something I'm still working on, but I have no desire to put myself on view in this town ever again and be the subject of everyone else's Sunday meals."

Phoebe heard the old hurt and anger from before and understood. "You do you, and I'll do me, and we'll see what happens, okay?"

He sighed. "Okay. I need to find Lee and tell him I'm leaving."

"He's probably in his room. It's the door on the left down the hall," Phoebe said.

Aidan ran a finger down the side of her cheek and then tapped the slight dimple in her chin before walking away.

Phoebe's phone began to ring again. "This whole Ace thing is going to piss me off. I can tell it," she muttered and let the call go to voicemail, too, as she retreated to the living room.

Down the hall, Aidan was knocking on Lee's door.

Lee answered on the second knock.

"Hi, Dad! Come in!"

"Maybe another time. I'm leaving now and wanted to thank you for such a wonderful meal…and the pleasure of your company."

Lee didn't waste time with manners. "I loved doing it. You're welcome. So, you and Mom are okay? No one is mad?"

"No, we're not mad, and we're more than okay. We're fine. This has to be one of the best days of my life, so give me a hug, okay?"

Lee's smile said it all as he threw his arms around Aidan's shoulders and thumped him soundly on the back.

"This is definitely the best day of my life," Lee said. "But the first of many, I hope."

"Absolutely," Aidan said. "And as I said before, just stay with your mother tomorrow. I'm guessing she's going to go back to work on Monday, so she's likely to need your help here. We'll work when she works."

"Yes, I will," Lee said. "I'll walk you to the door."

Phoebe was sitting in the living room when they came in. She started to get up.

"Stay where you are. Lee is seeing me out, and thank you again for allowing me into the family."

"You're welcome. Sleep well," Phoebe said and then watched the two men in her life walk out of the house together.

Aidan had just given her a new measure of hope, but she'd lived too many years on hope already. She needed substance.

Corey Randall made sandwiches and opened a can of soup for their dinner. It was more cooking than he'd done in years, but when they sat down to eat, Corey lost his appetite watching his dad's hand shaking as he lifted the soup spoon to his mouth and back to the bowl. Witnessing the progression of his father's cancer was messing with him, reminding him of his own mortality. He wished now that he'd gone somewhere else to lay low.

About halfway through the meal, Moe happened to glance up at his son and saw a look of disgust in his eyes. Struck by his son's lack of compassion, he laid down his spoon and, without saying a word, got up from the table and left the room. He loved Corey, but he didn't like him. He was a complete failure as a human being, and Moe had never been able to figure out where he and his wife, Roberta, had gone wrong.

He had been such a sweet little boy, amenable to everything they had asked of him. But then Roberta had died suddenly of a heart attack the year Corey was a sophomore in high school. It seemed to be the trigger that turned Corey into a person Moe didn't know. After that, he was in and out of trouble and ran away from home before he graduated. From that day forward, he was nothing but an intermittent visitor in Moe's life. Moe didn't know why Corey was here now but guessed he was either in hiding or wanted something.

Although it was early, Moe began getting ready for bed. He'd had enough of this day, and if God was merciful, he wouldn't wake to see another. He headed for the bathroom, pulled his little plastic stool into place beneath the showerhead, and then stripped.

The warm water felt good on his skin, and the weaker he'd become, the more ways he had adjusted his routine. Now, he shaved while in the shower so he wouldn't have to stand up at the sink. Sometimes he sat on the stool until the hot water began to run out, but not tonight. He wanted to make sure Corey had enough hot water for his bath as well.

Moe got out, dried off, and then sat down on the commode to get into his pajamas. Afterward, he carried his dirty clothes to the hamper beneath the shelf where the towels and washcloths were stored and left the bathroom.

Corey was coming down the hall as Moe crossed to his bedroom.

"Left plenty of hot water for you," he said. "Good to see you, Son, but I'll be heading to bed now."

"Yeah, uh…thanks, Dad. Get some rest. Maybe you'll feel better tomorrow."

Moe had no answer for such an inane comment. You don't ever feel better when you're in the process of dying. His son was a fool. His shoulders slumped as he went into his bedroom and shut the door, then, as an afterthought, turned the lock. He'd learned the hard way that turning his back on Corey was a quick way to lose ready cash. Corey had already stolen and pawned Roberta's silverware and the rifle Moe had inherited from his grandfather. There was nothing sacred in Corey's world when he was in need of money.

Moe turned back the covers, shook two pain pills from the bottle on the nightstand, tossed them into his mouth, and swallowed dry before crawling into bed.

The cool sheets felt good on his feverish body, but the weight of the bedspread at the foot of the bed hurt his bones. He rolled over with a sigh. Whatever Corey was doing outside this room was nothing he could stop from happening, so he closed his eyes and let the pain pills pull him under.

—∿∿—

Corey couldn't hack it. It was dark now, and he wasn't the kind who could spend time watching mindless television. He had to get out of this house, if only for a little while, but he couldn't drive that stolen car all over town. His solution was to take his dad's car, so he lifted the car keys and headed for the Blue Ivy Bar.

May Temple was in her usual spot behind the bar when Corey sauntered in. She knew who he was and was not happy to see him. The last time he'd been in here he'd torn up the place and skipped out, leaving his father to pick up the tab.

So when he slid onto the stool at the far end of the bar and yelled, "Bring me a longneck," she yelled back at him. "Last time you were in my bar, you tore up $322 worth of my property. I'm still thinking about escorting you out of here."

Corey's lips parted in shock. "My dad paid all that," he said.

"You better not be counting on him paying your debts again if you act like an ass because I won't take a dying man's money, I don't care what you do."

Corey paled and, in anger, pulled out a wad of bills and counted out five hundred dollars. "You can give me back what I don't spend when I leave."

May strode over to where he was sitting and picked up the bills. "Deal. Are you particular about your brands?"

"No. Just a longneck," Corey said.

She put the bills under a glass by the register, then opened a cold longneck beer and set it and a dish of salted pretzels in front of Corey.

"This here will start your tab. Five bucks."

His eyes narrowed as he gave her the once-over. May

looked rough. Hell, she looked old. Her hair was obviously dyed. That shade of red did not exist in nature, and her boobs were hanging low—too low for his taste. When she caught him staring, he lifted the bottle of beer in a toast to her then took a big swig. She rolled her eyes and turned away as he picked up a couple of pretzels and popped them into his mouth.

The television over the bar was on a station airing a popular fishing show. Some of the customers were laughing and telling their own fishing stories, while others were quietly watching and reading the captioning running across the screen at the bottom. Corey was too far away to see the captioning and too close to the people talking to hear what was being said on the show, so he picked up his beer and pretzels and moved to an empty table closer to the TV.

There were people in here he knew, but no one seemed inclined to speak to him, let alone join him. It pissed him off. Who did they think they were? They weren't any better than him. He quickly finished off the beer and held up the empty.

May saw his signal and took another bottle to his table. "Want to order any food to go with that?" she asked.

"No. I made dinner for my dad and me before I left."

May was surprised and made no attempt to hide it. "Didn't think you had that in you," she said and then headed back to the bar.

She'd pissed Corey off. "Say what you think, why don't you!" he yelled.

She just kept walking.

Corey settled in with his beer and attitude, and neither got better. The more he drank, the angrier he became.

He finished his fifth beer and began waving the empty bottle at May again.

She saw him and turned around. He thought she was bringing him another, but what she brought him was the change from the "deposit" he'd given her.

"I took out what you owed. The rest is yours. Go home. You do your father no good if you wind up in jail." Then she walked away without giving him time to argue.

Remembering that he had driven his dad's old car and didn't want to get so drunk that he wrecked it, Corey stuffed the change into his pants pocket, then headed out of the bar, walking with his head up and his jaw set. He passed four tables full of men, and not one even looked at him or bothered to speak. He didn't know what burr they had up their asses, but he hadn't put it there, so it was nothing to him.

He got in the old car and started it up. It was twenty minutes to one as he drove toward home, and when he turned up into the driveway, the headlights swept the front of the old house, highlighting the rundown appearance.

He unlocked the front door with his dad's house key, replaced the keys where he'd gotten them, and went to his room. He stripped down to his undershorts, then walked up the hall to the bathroom. He could hear his dad snoring as he passed the bedroom door, but when he tried the door to peek in on him and realized it was locked, he froze.

He stood there, in the silence of the house where he'd learned to walk and to speak his first words, and could almost hear his mother's voice.

Corey Allen Randall! Your father is afraid of you! For shame!

He let go of the doorknob as if he'd been burned and then slowly backed up until he reached the bathroom. He walked in and shut the door before he flipped the light switch and then stared at himself in the mirror.

He hadn't shaved in three days. His eyes were bloodshot from all the beer he'd been drinking, and he smelled like that smoke-filled room. He flashed on May's face, thinking how old she'd looked, and saw the same dissolution and age on his own. He knew his lifestyle was responsible and there wasn't a damn thing he could do to undo the damage, so he turned on the water and began to wash up. When he finally got back to his room, he fell into bed. The long day finally got to him as he closed his eyes. Within minutes, he was asleep.

———

On the other side of town, Aidan was a long way from sleep. He'd gone to bed, but the tumult of emotions he'd gone through that day was still spinning through his mind. Finally, he gave up and went downstairs. He poured a Coke into a glass of ice, rummaged through the pantry until he found the sack of cookies he'd purchased, and carried them back to the office. The pictures in the old photo album were calling his name. He'd had a glimpse tonight of what life with Phoebe and Lee was like, but he wanted to see what he'd missed.

The album was still on the desk. He set his glass onto a coaster, stacked a handful of cookies up beside it, and then popped one in his mouth as he resumed where he'd left off.

Two hours later, he was on the page with a picture of Lee in his cap and gown. High school graduation.

Someone else had taken this picture because Preston was on one side of Lee and Phoebe was on the other. There was so much to see within that image—relief on Phoebe's face of a job well done. Pride and gratitude on Preston's face that he'd been allowed into their world. And Lee was laughing, his head back and looking up as tasseled caps rained down around them.

He turned the page, wondering what would be next, but there was just a brief notation in the middle of the page where a picture might be.

> *Aidan,*
> *The next half of their lives is for you. Make it*
> *work.*
>
> *Granddad*

He shivered. It was almost as if Preston had known his time on earth was winding down.

"If I fail, it won't be for lack of trying," Aidan said, then closed the album and took his empty glass back to the kitchen.

It was nearly three in the morning when he crawled back in bed, but he felt settled, even hopeful. He rolled over onto his side and closed his eyes.

The next thing he knew, it was morning. He glanced at the time as he sat up, then headed for the shower.

Phoebe was trying to zip up the back of her dress as she was getting ready for church and finally gave up and went across the hall to Lee's room and knocked.

"Hey, Lee, I need a little help," she said.

Lee was at the door in seconds, dressed all but for his shoes. He eyed the pale-blue-and-green-floral pattern on her summer dress and the extra care she'd taken with her hair.

"You look pretty, Mom."

Phoebe smiled. "I'll look better when you zip me up. I can't get a firm grip with all this," she said, waving her taped-up fingers in the air. She turned around and pulled her hair out of the way so it wouldn't get caught in the zipper.

Lee zipped her up, then patted her shoulder. "You're good to go."

"Thanks, honey. I need to check the roast before we leave. How close are you to being ready?" she asked.

"Just need to put on shoes. I'll meet you in the kitchen in a few."

She nodded, then went back into her bedroom to get her purse before going to the kitchen. She set the purse on the table and peered into the glass lid of the slow cooker. The roast looked good. It smelled good. There was still plenty of liquid. She drained the vegetables Lee had cleaned for her, put them on top of the roast, and added salt and pepper. A couple of hours to cook while they were at church and the entree would be done. She and Lee could finish up with side dishes once they got home.

She straightened the belt of her dress as Lee entered the kitchen. She couldn't help but admire what a handsome young man he had become. The dark pants he was wearing made his legs look longer, and the light-blue short-sleeved dress shirt made his shoulders look wider. His hair was combed, after a fashion, but Phoebe knew by the time they got to church, it would be back to its usual flyaway look.

"My very handsome son, will you drive?" she asked as she took the car keys out of her purse.

"Of course," he said as she dropped them into his palm. "Do you need to take a pain pill before we go?"

"No. I took one when I got up."

Lee checked the lock on the back door before following his mother through the house and out the front door, locking it behind them, too.

The drive to church took less than five minutes. The lot was filling up as they parked. Lee saw his mother lift her chin and then watched her eyes narrow slightly and realized she was preparing herself for another round of gossip. There would be people inside who would likely frown upon a woman who'd struck a man, despite the reason. "I will stick to you like glue," he promised.

"I'm fine. They don't scare me anymore, but there are times when they do tick me off."

Lee laughed as they got out and then caught a glimpse of the car pulling into the opposite side of the parking lot and gasped. "Mom. Dad's here."

Phoebe turned in surprise. "But he said he wasn't going to come."

"And yet there he is," Lee said. "Let's wait for him."

"Of course," Phoebe said. She wouldn't have left him to walk into the church alone for anything.

Her heart fluttered longingly as she watched him coming toward them with purpose in every step, and then her vision blurred. This was how she'd always envisioned his return. Coming back to Blessings— coming for her.

"Hi, Dad!" Lee said as Aidan gave him a quick hug, but Aidan looked straight at Phoebe.

"I didn't come for church. I came for you."

Phoebe blinked away tears. "Thank you."

Lee was beaming. "So, let's go in and get our seats before we wind up in the front pew."

Aidan handed her a handkerchief as he slid his hand beneath her elbow. "You heard him. We don't want to sit in the front pew."

Phoebe dabbed at the tears on her face and then gave the cloth back to him. "Thank you again," she said.

Lee was on one side of her and Aidan was on the other as they walked into the church then down the aisle to the fifth row back from the altar and took their seats.

Chapter 9

THE PEW WHERE LOVEY COOPER WAS SITTING FELT OFF-balance. She was missing her friend, Ruby Dye. That would be Ruby Butterman now, she reminded herself, since Peanut and Ruby were on their honeymoon. She sighed. Never had two people been more suited for each other.

Then Lovey heard a slight commotion from the people behind her and turned around to see what was happening. Phoebe Ritter and Aidan Payne were coming down the aisle with their son beside them, and the sight made her smile. They might have fallen into that suited-for-each-other category, too, but for the tragedy that happened in their lives. She hoped them being together this morning was a sign of better days to come for all of them.

Rachel Goodhope tapped Lovey on the shoulder from the pew behind her, then leaned forward and whispered in Lovey's ear, "What's wrong with Phoebe's hand, and who's the hunk with her?"

"I'll tell you after church," Lovey said.

Rachel nodded and leaned back.

Vesta and Vera Conklin, who were sitting next to Lovey, worked at Ruby's hair salon, the Curl Up and Dye. They'd already heard the story about Phoebe punching Ace James and breaking his nose, but they didn't know why. In fact, no one but the people involved knew why. But they did notice some of the high school girls giving Lee Ritter the eye. He was a handsome young man with a good head on his shoulders, and lordy be, but he was nearly a dead ringer for his dad. Their attention was redirected to the pulpit when the organist struck a chord, indicating that the service was about to begin.

Lovey sat up straighter and noticed Aidan slide his arm across the back of the pew and then lightly cup Phoebe's shoulder. It made her blink back a few tears. True love never got old if you were a romantic at heart, and she was.

Phoebe's heart was hammering from sitting so close to Aidan. When he put his arm behind her and then cupped her shoulder, she swallowed back tears, then reminded herself not to make more of that gesture than what it was. He'd made it plain that he'd come as backup just so she wouldn't be inundated with questions regarding the incident with Ace.

She glanced at Aidan and caught him looking at her. He seemed at ease as he gave her a quick wink and a little pat on the shoulder. It might as well have been a pat on the head.

She sighed.

Lee was sitting on the other side of her, and she was well aware of what was going on with him, and it wasn't anything new. Girls had been enamored of him since his freshman year in high school. That was the year he passed six feet tall, and the next year he became the star running back for the high school football team, just like his dad had been. Right now he seemed to be in cruise mode. At least a half dozen high school girls were trying to catch his eye, radiating smiles so big he couldn't ignore them, or discreetly waving at him, hoping he'd wave back. To his credit, he wasn't encouraging anything, but he also was not upset about the attention. She stifled the urge to laugh.

Then the organist signaled to the congregation that the pastor was arriving. After that, everything shifted back into a sense of normalcy.

Songs.

Sermon.

Prayer.

Dismissed.

Two hours down and counting.

People rose from their seats, some stretching, while others began gathering up their things and heading for the exit. They were either going home to tend to Sunday dinner or wanting to get a jump-start on the ones headed to Granny's to eat.

Lovey had already made a break for it with Rachel Goodhope right beside her. Since Rachel and her husband were somewhat new to Blessings compared to people who'd grown up here, Lovey was filling Rachel in on what had happened to Phoebe Ritter's hand and the background of Phoebe's story as they walked to their cars.

Vera and Vesta already knew the story and were on their way to Granny's for Sunday dinner, talking about how much they missed Ruby.

But Phoebe was still stuck in the church aisle with Aidan in front of her and Lee behind her. None of

them were making much headway. When Phoebe saw
Trisha Branson waiting for her up ahead, she sighed.
She worked with Trisha, too, and expected to be grilled
by her just as Millie had tried last night. The line kept
moving slowly. Everyone up front was stopping to
shake the preacher's hand and comment on the service.

Just as they reached the aisle where Trisha was
standing, Aidan suddenly moved in front of Phoebe and
pointed to the empty pews on the other side of the aisle.

"We can get out faster that way," Aidan said and led
her out as Lee followed behind her. They backtracked
to the side door by the altar and were out of the church
in less than a minute, leaving Trisha and her curiosity
behind.

"Oh, thank goodness," Phoebe said.

"Freedom isn't going to last long, Mom," Lee muttered, then glanced toward the parking lot. "They're
loading up the church van right behind our car. We can't
leave until they get all the kids they bus to church into it
and accounted for."

"My car is free. I'll get her home," Aidan said.

"Thank you," Phoebe said. "It'll be nonstop questions tomorrow at work. I'd rather not have to deal with
them today."

"Then go," Lee said. "I'll be home as soon as I can
get out."

"Thank you, darling," Phoebe said as Aidan whisked
her away.

"Wow…hot car," Aidan said, as he started up the
engine and then rolled down a window a bit before turning on the air conditioner. "You okay?"

"I'm fine. I don't know what it took for you to go

back into that church, but don't think I didn't appreciate the effort," Phoebe said.

"I got to thinking how many times you'd had to face hardship alone. Made me ashamed that I'd even considered letting old memories keep me from doing things with you and Lee."

Then he patted her arm and drove out of the parking lot, while Phoebe sat silently beside him. When they got to the house, Phoebe dug her extra key out of her purse as Aidan circled the car to open the door.

"Oh man…what on earth are you cooking?" Aidan asked as they started toward the door. "I can smell it from here."

Phoebe smiled as she unlocked the door. "The usual Sunday fare. Roast in a slow cooker with vegetables. All I need to do is make a salad and set the table. If your social calendar is not already filled, we'd love to have you here."

Aidan reached in front of her to open the door and then followed her inside. "I'm not even going to pretend I should pass up the invitation because I was in your face all day yesterday. I accept."

Phoebe resisted the urge to add a happy little two-step to her stride as he closed the door behind them.

"I'm going to change shoes and wash up. Be right back," she said.

"I'll be in the kitchen sniffing the slow cooker," he said.

Phoebe laughed.

Aidan sighed as she turned and walked away. He had always loved the sound of her laughter. How had he lived this long without it?

The moment Phoebe got to her bedroom, she kicked off her shoes, stepped into some slip-on sandals, went to wash up, then hurried back to the kitchen.

Lee walked in as she was getting salad stuff out of the refrigerator.

"Hi, Dad. Yay, you're eating with us. Mom, I'll chop up the salad for you," he said and washed up at the sink. Moments later, he was on the job.

Aidan had already set the table, and while he wanted to be a part of all that was going on, the kitchen was small and his place was still that of a guest.

"Hey, Bee, is there anything else you want me to do?"

Phoebe turned around, eyeing the kitchen table. "I still think we should have moved everything into the dining room."

"I don't want to be company, Bee. I just want to be here. Would you and Lee have gone to the dining room table?"

Mother and son looked at each other and then grinned. "Busted," Lee said. "No, we would not."

"You're right. We would not. Okay, so you are officially no longer company. But the kitchen table is too small for all the dishes, so you're also going to get a dose of the Ritter buffet."

Aidan grinned. "What's the Ritter buffet?"

"We don't put anything onto serving dishes. We just fill our plates from the bowls on the counter and the pans on the stove," Lee said.

"After we moved away, that's how Dad and I ate all the time," Aidan said.

Lee tossed the last of the salad stuff together and then set out bowls and salad dressings.

"Tell me about your dad," Lee asked. "I don't know

much about either of my grandfathers. I know he owned and ran an auto supply store, but was he from Blessings? What was he like? Where did he meet your mother? What did he look like? I've never seen a picture."

Aidan looked startled. "Really?"

Phoebe paused what she was doing and quickly explained. "Don't blame me. Sonja, loving mother that she was, burned most of my mementos from high school that had anything to do with you or your family. And then she sold our home out from under me and she and Uncle Joe moved away as a couple."

Shock rolled through Aidan in waves. "I can't imagine her being so cold-blooded."

Phoebe shrugged. "After Daddy died, she turned into someone I didn't know."

Lee stuck a pair of salad tongs into the salad bowl. "Mom, dinner's ready. Want me to fill your plate?" he asked.

"Probably a good idea," Phoebe said.

Aidan seated her, then gently brushed his hand across her back before moving away.

As soon as they sat down to eat, Aidan began telling one story after another, dredging up every childhood memory he'd heard his dad tell about himself, along with what George's parents had been like. By the time they got to dessert, Lee was a rapt audience.

Phoebe got up to get the slices of peach pie, which she'd already plated. "Do you two want ice cream with the pie again?"

"Absolutely," Aidan said.

Lee was already pulling the carton out of the freezer. "I'll dip," he said and looked for the smallest piece of pie, which he knew would be his mom's. He put a single scoop of ice cream beside the pie. "That's yours, Mom." Then he double-dipped for Aidan and triple-dipped for himself before putting the ice cream back in the freezer.

"Lee likes pie with his ice cream," Phoebe said.

Lee grinned as he took his first bite. "I'm still a growing boy," he said.

Aidan looked up. "That's what I used to say to my mom."

"Did it work for you?" Lee asked.

"Well, she never took any food away from me, so I guess the answer is yes," Aidan said.

Phoebe ate in happy silence, listening to their banter.

Moe awakened to a quiet house, a little surprised that Corey was still asleep, and ate breakfast alone before getting ready for church. He didn't feel good, but he didn't feel any better sitting at home, and the closer he got to dying, the more he felt a need to be closer to God.

The little Methodist church he attended was where he and Roberta had been married and where Corey had been baptized. Although Methodist preachers were moved around from time to time, his friends and the location were not. He liked the pink and purple crape myrtles circling the building and the twin magnolia trees on either side of the driveway leading into the church parking lot. And he loved the way the sanctuary made him feel as he walked into the church—welcomed, comforted, and forgiven.

He was greeted with hugs and whispers from friends, reassuring him that they kept him in their prayers. By the time the preacher got to the pulpit, Moe was primed for whatever the sermon would be.

When church was over, he received an invitation from some friends to go to Granny's for dinner. He was tempted, but he thought of Corey at home alone and declined. He drove home filled with a quiet sense of peace. In fact, it was a better medicine than any of the cancer meds he'd taken.

He pulled into the driveway and got out, thinking of what he had in the refrigerator that they could make for their meal. His steps were slow, and because they were, they were also quiet. He got all the way into the house and down the hall before he realized the door to his bedroom was open. As he got closer, he heard someone moving around inside and frowned. Corey's door was still closed. Surely he didn't have a prowler. But the thought made him move even more quietly. When he peered around the doorway and saw Corey digging through drawers and shuffling through his things, a slow rage went through him. It was happening again.

"What the hell are you doing?" Moe shouted.

Corey dropped the handgun he'd just pulled out of the back of his dad's drawer and then jumped when it went off and into the wall only inches from Moe's shoulder.

"I'm sorry, I didn't mean to—"

"Shut up!" Moe said as he stormed into the room and snatched the gun off the floor. "Shut up and get out! Get out of my house and don't come back."

Corey was stunned. Through all these years and all the arguments they'd had, he'd never heard those words come out of his father's mouth.

"But who's gonna take care of you?" Corey asked.

"Like you care? We both know that's a lie. Now get your stuff because whatever you leave behind, I'll burn, and if there are any keepsakes that mean anything to you in your room, you better get them, too."

Corey's shock was slowly being replaced with anger.

"This is what you've wanted to say for years, isn't it?" he shouted. "You haven't been able to look me in the eyes for years."

Instead of backing up, Moe moved into Corey's personal space. "Can you blame me?" he shouted. "Look me in the eyes, and tell me that I'm wrong."

Corey blinked then looked away. "Fine, I don't care what happens to you either."

"Time's running out. You have fifteen minutes," Moe said.

"Or what?" Corey shouted.

"Do you really want to watch me set fire to your stuff out in the yard in front of God and everybody?"

Corey reeled as if he'd been slapped, then stormed out of the room.

Moe heard him throwing things around in his room, but he didn't care. His eye was on the clock. Twelve minutes later, Corey stormed out of the house and drove away without looking back.

Moe stood in the living room, listening to the thunder of his heartbeat, then locked the door and went into the kitchen. He puttered around for a couple of minutes, then got a can of soup from the pantry, dumped the contents into a pan, added some water, and put it on the stove to heat.

As he moved from counter to table and back again, adding crackers and a cup of reheated coffee at his place setting, the solitude of his little space wrapped around him like a familiar blanket, calming his rage and racing heart.

When the soup was ready, he poured it into the bowl at the table and then sat down to eat. He crumbled a couple of crackers into the soup, blew on the first spoonful to make sure it wasn't too hot, and then put it in his mouth. The warmth of the soup rolled down his throat and into his belly. He ate until the bowl was almost empty, then carried it to the sink to rinse.

This mindless routine was what was left of his life, and he didn't intend to squander it on anger or share it with someone he no longer knew.

Corey continued his journey by heading south, putting as much distance between himself and Blessings as he could manage and getting farther and farther away from Savannah, the scene of his last crime.

He was still reeling from being kicked out. The knowledge that he now had nowhere else to go when the going got rough was frightening. He belonged nowhere and to no one.

Emotion gathered in his midsection, swelling in size as the pain of rejection bloomed. He kept seeing the shock on his father's face when he dropped that damn gun and nearly shot him. He tried to tell him he didn't take anything and didn't mean for that gun to go off, but it appeared that no longer mattered. Probably because he'd taken so many things before.

How the hell had he gotten to this place in his life? Where did it all start to go so wrong? And then the minute he thought the questions, he sucked up the feel-sorry-for-myself mood. He knew. He'd always known. The past twenty years of his life, he'd been running from the truth.

———∽∽∽———

Monday rolled around without incident. Lee got ready and headed to meet his dad to start painting at one of the rental houses, and Phoebe went back to work as if nothing had happened.

She walked into the Piggly Wiggly at 7:00 a.m. and clocked in before heading up front to get her cash drawer.

Wilson Turner was up front in the office and saw her coming. He'd already heard about the incident between her and Ace James but didn't know why it had happened. However, he also knew Phoebe Ritter well enough not to ask. He saw that the two last fingers on her right hand were taped together and then looked up at the expression on her face. *Alright then. Don't even ask how she feels. Got it.*

"Morning, Wilson. Which register do you want me on today?"

"Millie is on three. I want you on one." He handed over her cash drawer. "Have a nice day, and holler if you need something."

"Thank you," Phoebe said. "It is a good day already." Then she flashed a rare smile and left.

He watched her pause to say hello to Millie then move on to where she'd be working today. Despite her taped fingers, she quickly counted out the money, opened the rolls of quarters, nickels, dimes, and pennies, and then slid the drawer into her register and turned on the light switch at her station. She was open for business.

Wilson sighed. She looked different, but he couldn't quite put his finger on why. Most likely had to do with the fact that Aidan Payne was in Blessings. And then Arlene, another Piggly Wiggly cashier, showed up for her cash drawer.

"Morning, Arlene. Take register four today. I'm keeping two open today unless we get busy. It's right in front of the entrance doors and likely to be hotter than the others."

"Thanks, Wilson." Then she leaned a little closer. "How's Phoebe doin'?"

Wilson shrugged. "Judge for yourself. Appears to be just fine to me."

Arlene glanced over her shoulder and saw Phoebe laughing and talking as she scanned a customer's groceries.

"Yes, well, we'll talk on break. I'm sure she'll let us know what happened."

"Don't count on it, and don't piss her off," Wilson said. "She's about had her fill of crap from the good people of Blessings, don't you think?"

That silenced Arlene, at least for the moment, as she stomped off to her assigned location, while Phoebe was oblivious to the undercurrents going on behind her back.

Police Chief Lon Pittman was in his office, finishing up transfer paperwork for a prisoner they were holding for a U.S. Marshal, when he got a phone call.

"This is Chief Pittman."

"Chief, this is Detective Gerber from the Savannah Police Department, Robbery Division."

"Morning, Detective. How can I help you?"

"We're searching for a man named Corey Randall. Last info we have on him is he has a father still living in Blessings."

"Yes, Moe Randall. Really nice guy, but he's dying of cancer."

"Umph…my sympathies. That's tough. Lost my dad to cancer. So, back to my perp. Has anyone had eyes on Corey Randall in the past few days?"

"I can't say I have personally, but I heard he was here visiting his father. What's he wanted for this time?"

"We have a tentative ID on him for a car heist and a possible on a robbery at a liquor store. By any chance was he driving a blue 2012 Mazda?"

"I don't know, but I can find out soon enough. Give me a contact number, and I'll do a go-see for you."

Detective Gerber gave the chief his cell number. "And many thanks, Chief. Just let me know what you find out."

"Absolutely," Lon said. He tore off the phone number from the pad, grabbed his hat, and hit the intercom. "Avery, I'll be out of the office for a bit. Radio if you need me."

"Will do, Chief," the dispatcher said.

Lon settled his hat on his head and went out the back door. A few minutes later, he was pulling in the driveway of Moe Randall's house. He frowned as he got out. Moe Randall's car was the only one here. He jogged up the steps and knocked.

Moe had dozed off in his recliner but woke up when he heard the sharp rap on the front door. He lowered the footrest, eased himself up, and peeked out a window before opening the door. His heart sank when he saw the chief of police. His footsteps were dragging even more as he opened the door.

The chief smiled at him and took off his hat.

"Morning, Moe. I wonder if I might come in for a few minutes. I need to ask you a couple questions."

"Sure, Chief. Take a seat," Moe said and eased back down in his recliner. "Excuse my manners, but I don't have much energy these days."

"I'm sorry to bother you," Lon said and hung his hat on the back of his chair.

Moe sighed. "Just get to the point. What did he do now?"

Lon felt bad for the old man. As long as he'd known Moe, he'd been dealing with his good-for-nothing son's escapades.

"Is Corey here?" Lon asked.

"No. He left this morning for parts unknown. Why?"

"I'm doing a follow-up for the Savannah police department. I guess they're looking at him for a car theft and robbery. By any chance, did you notice what he was driving when he got here?"

"A late-model blue Mazda," Moe said. "Did he steal it?"

"It looks like that might be the case," Lon said.

Moe leaned back in the recliner and closed his eyes.

Lon thought he was drifting off to sleep until he saw tears rolling down his cheeks.

Lon jumped up and went to Moe, gently patting his shoulder. "Moe. Can I get you anything? Do you need your meds? Maybe a drink of water?"

"No, sir," Moe said and then wiped his cheeks as he

opened his eyes. "Do you have some time to talk? I have been living with a horrible secret. I reckon living with it has just about killed me, but I find I cannot go to my grave with it on my conscience."

Lon frowned. "Of course I have time."

Moe waved toward Lon's phone. "Does that thing video people?"

Lon's frown deepened. "Yes. Do you want me to video your statement?"

Moe nodded. "I'm likely to die any day now, so if I can't show up in court to testify, you can play it."

Lon set the camera in his phone on video and aimed it straight at Moe's face. "You're on, Moe. Say what you have to say."

Moe licked his lips, then stared straight at the phone. "My name is Moe Randall. I'm seventy-one years old, and even though I'm dying of cancer, I am very much of sound mind. I've lived with this secret for twenty years, and I don't want to take it to my grave."

Then Moe started talking, and Lon's eyes widened as the storytelling ensued. He heard the words coming out of Moe's mouth and stifled a gasp. Sweet lord in heaven! This was going to tear Blessings apart.

Chapter 10

SONJA AND JOE RITTER LIVED IN AN AFFLUENT NEIGHBOR-hood on a hill in St. Louis. From her front windows, she could see all the way to the Mississippi River flowing past the Arch.

After they left Blessings, Joe flew planes for commercial airlines for years and had only recently retired. These days they puttered about in their garden and spent weekends together antiquing or fixing up something on their Victorian-era home. They entertained occasionally, but their friends weren't close. They kept to themselves when it came to hanging out.

Sonja rarely thought about Blessings or her first husband, Marty, and most days forgot she'd left a daughter behind. But on the days when she got emails or phone calls from her cousin, Myra Franklin, who ran the florist shop in Blessings, Sonja got snippets of what was happening in Phoebe's life, whether she liked it or not.

Once she'd learned that Preston Williams had stepped in and taken on the role of elder in Phoebe's life, Sonja had washed her hands of any lingering guilt and let the years go by.

Then last week, a friend of theirs from across the street had dropped dead walking from her front flower bed to the steps, and Sonja had witnessed it happen. She had run across the street thinking her friend had just fainted only to find the woman already gone. The shock of that was upsetting enough, but then she had to be the one who stayed with the body until the police and ambulance arrived. Witnessing a passing like that bothered her greatly and made her think of Marty's death, which then made her think of Phoebe.

So when she went to bed that night, Sonja dreamed, reliving seeing her friend fall. Only when she ran across the street to go to her aid, the dream changed. Sonja turned the body over like before, and the dead woman had her face. In essence, Sonja had watched herself die.

She woke up shaking, thinking it was a premonition, and spent the next day praying for forgiveness for all her sins. That night when she went to bed, her dream picked up where the first one had left off, and now she was standing before God and he wouldn't let her pass into the light for what she'd done to her daughter.

Sonja woke up in hysterics. It took Joe hours to calm her down, and she couldn't be consoled until he promised to take her back to Blessings to right her wrongs.

They packed the next morning and within hours were on their way to Georgia. Now Sonja had another worry. Facing the residents of Blessings would be only slightly less daunting than facing her daughter. She'd broken all kinds of rules people lived by, like being seen with another man before her deceased husband was even buried and then shunning her pregnant daughter for the child she carried. But the worst was moving away without telling anyone where they were going—basically abandoning a teenage girl, leaving her homeless and helpless. But with the lack of foresight that had gotten her to this point in life, she had convinced herself she could make this work.

They took I-64 out of St. Louis to Mount Vernon and then I-57 until they could connect to I-24 and drove all the way to Nashville, Tennessee, to spend the night.

They were tired and Sonja was short-tempered as they entered their motel room.

———

Sonja walked into the bathroom and threw up her hands. "This place is disgusting. They have a plastic shower curtain. The towels are rough… Oh my God, Joe! Feel this!"

Joe pushed past her and went to get his toiletry kit from his bag.

"Don't push me!" Sonja screamed and threw the towel at his back.

Joe turned around and pointed a finger in her face. "I didn't push you. I pushed past you, which means I'm not listening to this bullshit. You whine about everything. We are not on vacation. This was all your idea. So either shut up and deal with it, or spend the night in the car. I couldn't care less which one you choose as long as I get some peace and quiet."

Sonja blinked. It had been years since she'd seen this side of Joe, which meant she wasn't on the solid ground with him she'd thought she was. Her face crumpled as she turned away in tears.

Joe sighed then put his arms around her. "Don't cry, baby. I'm sorry I yelled, but I'm also sorry you yelled at me. Savvy?"

She nodded. "I'm sorry, too. I'm just scared."

He shrugged. "It's not too late to turn around and go home. As far as I'm concerned, we should not be doing this."

Sonja panicked. "No, no, we have to. You didn't have my dream. I don't want to be turned away from heaven when I die."

Joe rolled his eyes. They didn't go to church, so this sudden interest in getting right with God seemed strange.

"So go clean up and we'll find a good steak house to have dinner."

Sonja dabbed at her tears with a wad of toilet paper and kissed the side of his cheek. "Thank you for understanding."

And so the night passed.

The next morning after breakfast they were back on I-24 southbound, and when they reached the connection to I-75 that took them into Georgia, Sonja began to fidget.

———

Sonja glanced at her reflection in the visor mirror, checking to make sure there was no lipstick on her teeth, then sighed. Her hair was blond and cut short like a cap on her head. She had Botox in her lips and a ten-year-old boob job that was steadily going south. She was thirty pounds thinner than she'd been when she left Blessings and had a tendency to dress far too young for a woman in her late fifties, and she was bored.

After giving herself the once-over, she glanced at Joe. He was twenty pounds heavier than he'd been when they first left Blessings, and he was now completely bald. Sonja thought it made him look tough and sexy. She liked his rough ways and hard-line talking. Even after all these years, Joe Ritter still made her hot. Marrying him had been easy. She'd wanted him for years and prayed in church every Sunday for the want to be taken away. Instead, fate had handed him to her with such

ease that she still considered being widowed a blessing
in disguise. She shivered, then made herself focus on
something besides their sex life.

Her gaze shifted to the scenery of the passing countryside. "How much farther?" she asked.

"We are hours from Atlanta, where we will spend the
night. I don't like the frantic pace you have set for us and
so as the driver, you'll have to indulge me."

"That's okay," Sonja said. "I was just asking."

"Are you worried about how people will feel toward
us?" Joe asked.

Sonja waved her hand as if people's opinions were
of no consequence. "I don't care what anyone thinks."

He grinned. First of all, he knew better. Sonja cared
deeply about what other people thought of her. She just
didn't care for other people. That trait alone should have
put him off, but Sonja intrigued him. She was a woman
with hidden depths, all of which bordered on sexually
submissive. They'd had themselves some kinky romps
over the years, and she showed no signs of slowing down.

"So tell me again why this is a good idea," Joe said.

"So I don't go to hell," Sonja said.

Joe burst out laughing.

Sonja tried to look hurt, but his laughter was infec-
tious, and before long she was laughing, too.

Much later, they stopped for the night, this time in
Atlanta as Joe had promised. They had another opulent
meal, went back to the motel, and broke out the sex toys.
Sleep came later, and morning came next. One more
breakfast on the road, and they were on their last leg of
the journey. Good idea or bad idea, they would spend
the night in Blessings.

Sonja spent most of the trip either fighting with Joe or praying. It never occurred to her that she was defeating her own purpose going from anger to feeling sorry for herself.

———ⵗ———

"You don't understand anything," Sonja said. "You were never a parent."

"You didn't spend all that much time out of your fifty-nine years being a parent either."

Sonja glared. "I raised my daughter. She was out of high school and legal age when we parted company. Besides, Myra says she's doing great."

Joe shrugged as he took a curve in the road. "I wouldn't count on anything Myra said as fact. She was always full of gossip. So you have rationalized the way you parted from Phoebe, but what about from her standpoint? You dumped her, sold the house out from under her, and left her pregnant and homeless. What in hell makes you think she'll want to see you again?"

Sonja shrugged, then turned away to stare out the window again. There was a small part of her selfish heart that regretted that part of her past, but there was no way to take it back, and she was counting on the mother-daughter thing to kick in.

"So, you don't have an answer for me?" Joe asked.

"Maybe I just want to see my daughter again," Sonja snapped.

Joe grinned. "And maybe you're just the selfish, conniving little bitch I fell for who's trying to buy her way into heaven?"

Sonja's eyes widened, and then she smirked.

"Maybe so…maybe not. I guess we'll both just have to wait and see."

Joe shook his head slowly. "I don't wait for any woman, and you know it."

Sonja shivered. Trying to beat him to a climax was a turn-on all its own.

A short while later, they passed the Blessings city limit. "I made a reservation at a motel," Sonja said. "Take a left at the next street. I think it'll get us there."

"Will do," Joe said and turned their car off Main with no idea they were driving straight into a hornets' nest.

Chief Lon Pittman walked in the back door of the station past the empty holding cell, guessing the U.S. Marshal had finally come and gone.

Lon was still reeling from the statement Moe Randall had given him and needed to find Corey Randall ASAP. Corey was the key to closing a very old cold case, and now both he and Detective Gerber knew Randall was in the wind.

Phoebe was in the break room eating her lunch when Arlene popped in.

"Hey girl, how's it going?" she asked.

Since her mouth was full, Phoebe waved the half-eaten sandwich at her and gave her a thumbs-up.

"So how's your hand?" Arlene asked.

Phoebe gave her another thumbs-up and kept chewing.

"So, I heard you punched Ace James in the nose. What happened?"

Phoebe swallowed her bite. "I broke it," she said and took a drink before taking another bite.

Arlene frowned. "Well, I know that. I meant…why?"

"I'm not talking about it. Ask him if you want details."

Arlene's lips parted, but she couldn't think of any other way to ask what she wanted to know.

"Okay…so, I gotta get back to work."

Phoebe's eyes narrowed as the door closed behind the other checker, then she tossed the rest of her sandwich and finished her drink. Her lunch break was over.

—⁓—

Corey Randall was driving south on I-75 and had just crossed into Florida. He'd driven all night and had already drifted off onto the shoulder of the road once. He needed sleep. Wrecking a stolen car was a sure way to wind up in jail.

He kept watching the roadside for signs and saw one stating that Jennings, Florida, was only a few minutes away, so he took the Jennings exit to Highway 143 and drove straight into town.

He stopped at the first motel he came to and got a room. He locked himself inside, adjusted the air conditioner, crawled onto the bed, and passed out from exhaustion, unaware the police departments in both Savannah and Blessings had warrants out for his arrest.

—⁓—

Lee and Aidan spent the day together painting one of the empty rentals as Aidan's opinion of Lee continued to rise.

When three o'clock rolled around, Aidan called a halt.

"It's almost time for your mom to get off work.

We've been at this all day and can finish up tomorrow. I'm thinking she's going to be ready to get home."

"I think she will be exhausted, too, Dad. I've been thinking about her off and on all day, hoping she hasn't been hassled too much. I'll meet you here same time tomorrow?"

"Yes, and many thanks for today. You are really good at this stuff."

Lee grinned. "I've been doing it for years. Have a good night, Dad. You're the best."

Aidan was still smiling when Lee drove away.

———

Phoebe's steps were dragging by the time she clocked out and headed to her car. She was almost there when she heard someone calling her name. She turned. Her heart sank. *Crap. My high school nemesis—Tiffany "the Tiff" Snowden. Ex-cheerleader and once a Peachy Keen Queen.* She noticed Tiff's hair first. Last month it had been brown with red highlights, and now it was blond—a little brassy, but to each his own. Tiff was wearing shorts, a pink blouse tied so that her midriff was showing, and silver sandals with a serious amount of bling.

Then Tiff caught up and gave Phoebe one of those half-hearted hugs people give as a means of insinuating themselves into other people's personal space.

"Hi, girl! I'm glad I caught you. Heard all about your fight with Ace. What on earth?"

"Hello, Tiff. Calling it a fight is misleading. That would mean we'd traded blows, which didn't happen."

Tiff's smile slid a bit sideways, and then she took a fresh breath and attacked from another angle. "Oh. Well, that's not what I heard. I see you broke something. Are you in pain?"

"Nope, nothing is broken. I just dislocated a couple fingers. They're sore, that's all."

Tiff frowned. "But I heard down at the Curl Up and Dye that something was broken."

Phoebe laughed. "So you're getting your info from the beauty shop now? You used to have better contacts. The only thing broken is Ace's nose. How are your kids? Still living with your ex?"

Although it was a subconscious move, Tiff took a step back because she'd never known a woman who'd broken someone's nose before—on purpose.

"They're fine, and yes, they're still with Dudley. It's hard to compete with a beach house in Florida. Where's your Lee now?"

"Oh, he's here. Just finished his first year of college with a four-point GPA. He came home for the summer and is helping his dad paint some of Preston's rental properties."

Tiff's mouth opened, closed, then opened again. "His dad? As in Aidan?"

Phoebe laughed again. "You must be the only one in Blessings who doesn't know. I'm the talk of the town again. Gotta go. Need to make supper for Lee."

Then she wiggled her taped fingers at Tiff and got in her car, well aware Tiff was still staring as Phoebe drove off.

Her tension eased as she drove out of the parking lot, and the closer she got to home, the better she felt. Her hand hurt, but not unbearably, and the first thing on her mind was to jump in the shower and wash off the scent of deli-fried food that permeated the whole store.

To her delight, Lee was already home, and when she walked in the door, she called out, "I'm home!"

"So am I!" Lee yelled.

She sighed. Just hearing the sound of his voice, and the last bits of crap from her day were gone. She headed to the kitchen. He was making a fresh pitcher of sweet tea.

"Hi, Mom! How was your day? Do you hurt?"

"It was fine, and yes, it hurts some, but I can fix that. I have to go shower before I do anything. I smell like the deli."

Lee laughed, and then his phone signaled a text. He glanced at it and grinned. "It's Lola."

Phoebe gave him a left-handed thumbs-up and left the kitchen, leaving Lee with privacy to talk to his girl.

She showered and then dressed in shorts and a T-shirt, re-taped her fingers together, and went barefoot through the house to the kitchen, but Lee was nowhere in sight. She looked out the kitchen window and saw him standing beneath the shade trees at the back of the yard. She could tell by the look on his face there was trouble. She turned away. He was pretty much a grown man, however young. He would take care of his business his way. Still, she hoped he wasn't going to be hurt by what was happening. She opened the refrigerator. They had leftover roast and vegetables, and she decided to cut up the vegetables into smaller pieces and cube up some of the roast to make stew. It was cooler-weather food, but she and Lee ate what they had regardless of seasons. She stirred up some corn bread batter and put it in the oven to bake, then began the prep work for the stew. She was about to start slicing up some roast when Lee came back inside. He saw what she was doing and went to help.

"What are we making here?" he asked.

"Corn bread is in the oven, and I thought I'd make some stew out of the leftover roast and veggies."

"Let me do the meat," he said as he began washing his hands at the sink. "Are we dicing it like usual?"

"Yes," she said and gladly handed him the butcher knife.

He went right to work without mentioning a thing about Lola, which told Phoebe he didn't intend to talk about the call.

"How was work, Mom? Did people bug you much?"

"Nothing I couldn't handle," she said. "Do you want bay leaf in the stew, or should we go the spicy route and add some hot sauce and a jalapeno?"

"I vote spicy, unless you'd rather have the other. I like both," he said.

She grinned. "I vote spicy, too," she said and got a jalapeno from the refrigerator and began cleaning and dicing it. Then she added it to the vegetables she'd already prepared.

"Did you and your dad get a lot done today?" she asked.

"Yes. We spray-painted the outside of one of the empty rentals and then repainted all the rooms inside except for the kitchen. I think Dad's toying with the idea of painting the cabinets, too. They're pretty dated as is and would look great painted white with some new hardware. He mentioned the possibility of putting the empty rental up for sale, which I think would be great. There aren't a lot of houses that go up for sale in Blessings, and it would give people the chance to own instead of rent."

"That's a really good idea," Phoebe said.

Lee nodded. "Dad is smart...a good manager, I think. And he's kind...reminds me of Granddad. You know how he was always thinking of ways to ease his renters' financial burdens."

Phoebe had a moment of déjà vu, listening to Lee talking about his day. It was like he always had after spending the day with Preston. She missed Preston so much, but if he was still here, Aidan would not be. It was a hard thought to balance in her mind.

The stew was finished. Corn bread came out of the oven, and they sat down to eat. Somewhere between buttering his third piece of corn bread and asking about dessert, Lee looked up at Phoebe and announced, "Lola and I broke up. Don't feel bad about it because I don't. Whatever we felt had run its course the week before finals. We both knew it, I think. I told her I was going home for the summer and letting my apartment go, and the next day she told me she and her parents were going to Europe for the summer. We didn't say anything more except goodbye, but she finally let go."

Phoebe watched Lee bite into the hot, buttered corn bread. His eyes were a little watery, but she knew her son. He was telling her the truth.

"Okay. Glad it was a mutual decision. Do you want molasses to pour on your corn bread?"

Lee licked the butter off a thumb. "Yes! That would be good."

Phoebe went to the pantry and came back with the jar.

"Knock yourself out. I'm going to put apple butter on mine."

"I might want some of that, too," Lee said.

She laughed. "There's plenty of everything."

Sonja Ritter was sitting cross-legged on their motel bed eating pizza and watching Joe drying off from his shower. He was such a hunk, and naked, he was a hot hunk.

"Save me some pizza, dammit," Joe yelled.

"Calm down," she said, waving the pizza in the air. "This is only my second piece."

Joe wrapped a towel around his waist and strode into the bedroom, lifted a piece of pizza from the box, and took a big bite.

"Good stuff," he said. "I didn't think there was a pizza place in Blessings."

"There's not. It's from the deli in the Piggly Wiggly."

Joe swallowed and took another bite, talking as he chewed.

"They deliver?"

"No. I ordered it and picked it up while you were in the shower."

He frowned. "Did anyone recognize you?"

"I don't know. Does it matter? We're not in hiding, and we hardly came incognito. Chill out and eat your pizza. And don't look at me like that."

"Fine," Joe said, stuffed the last bite of pizza in his mouth, and went back into the bathroom, slamming the door behind him.

Sonja shivered. She wasn't afraid of Joe, but she also didn't like it when he was angry. She glanced down at her pizza, laid it back in the box and drank the rest of her Coke.

She just needed to chill out. They were both on edge coming back here. She was afraid of facing her daughter. Phoebe had shut down the day Aidan and his father left Blessings, and when she'd found out she was pregnant, she hadn't cried, hadn't begged for help, hadn't asked for anything. But the part Sonja still felt a bit guilty about was the fact that she hadn't offered to help her own daughter, she'd just given her an ultimatum: Get rid of the kid or you're on your own. It was the shame of her life. She and Joe basically left her on the streets. She didn't know until months later that Preston Williams had taken her under his wing. She was relieved to know Phoebe was safe but guilt-ridden that she'd had nothing to do with it.

She was rethinking the wisdom of trying to get back in Phoebe's good graces. Phoebe was a real hard-ass when she wanted to be. Maybe Sonja and Joe should just get back in the car and go home.

Then Joe came out of the bathroom wearing a pair of undershorts. He eyed Sonja, sat down on the bed beside her, and took another piece of pizza from the box.

"You didn't finish your pizza?"

Sonja shrugged.

"I'm sorry if I upset you," Joe said and ran his finger down the side of her face. "You're my baby, and I don't mean to make you sad."

Sonja started crying. "I think this visit is a mistake. We left Phoebe behind like an unwanted dog. I am a horrible mother. I don't want to see that in her eyes and know she's right."

Joe sighed. "Look, we can't undo the past, but maybe there's a way to build a future."

Sonja shook her head. "No. She won't want anything to do with me, and I don't blame her."

"Well, we're here, so if it's a bust, we can't say we didn't try," Joe said. "Your turn in the bathroom. You'll feel better once you've showered."

Sonja sighed. "You're right. As always. I won't be long," she said and rubbed her hand on his bald head as she passed by him. "For good luck," she added and heard him chuckle as she closed the door behind her.

Chapter 11

AIDAN SAT OUT ON THE BACK VERANDA UNTIL THE MOON came up, then sat a little longer, listening to the night sounds. A breeze rustled the leaves on the trees, and lights were on all over the neighborhood. He remembered sitting outside at Phoebe's house and listening to the television through the open windows. Marty, her dad, watched football religiously, so if there was a game on anywhere, he was watching. They'd hear the roar of the crowd and then Marty yelling at some player, "Run, you son of a gun, run!"

They always laughed. The laughter died with Marty.

Aidan slapped at a mosquito and then got up as another buzzed around his neck. "Time to go inside," he said, letting the screen door bang shut behind him as he did.

Phoebe left the house at six thirty in the morning dressed in the uniform of the day, which was long pants of any color and a clean Piggly Wiggly T-shirt. Her hair was loose because putting it up was too difficult with taped fingers, and the only makeup she had on was lipstick. Her lunch was in the back seat beside her umbrella because there was a chance of rain before she would get off work. When she backed out of the driveway, she went in the opposite direction to give Millie a lift to work.

Phoebe was a creature of habit and hardly ever deviated from her normal routes, so it had been a while since she'd driven in this part of town. She knew Millie lived near the Blessings Motel and was driving slowly, looking for her house number, when she saw it on a gray brick house up ahead. As she pulled up into the drive, she saw Millie watching for her at the window and waved. Millie came out a few moments later, already talking as she opened the door.

"I sure appreciate you picking me up, girl! My car won't be ready until later today."

Phoebe nodded, waiting for Millie to buckle up. "It's no trouble."

She backed out of the drive and accelerated slowly, cruising past the motel with her mind on the day ahead.

Millie pointed as they passed the motel. "Oh, look at that calico cat sitting on the roof! How funny. Probably waiting for some bird to land nearby."

Phoebe was smiling as she glanced toward the motel. She saw the cat, and then she saw the door opening to the room below it, and for a moment in time, she thought she was hallucinating. She glanced at the street and the traffic and then in disbelief back to the person still standing in the doorway.

What fresh hell is this? You're twenty years too late to rescue me, Mommy Dearest.

Phoebe looked away again, devoting her attention to driving, but there was a roar in her ears so loud she couldn't hear Millie's chatter. They arrived at the store fifteen minutes ahead of schedule, and when Millie got out, Phoebe stayed behind the wheel. "I have a call to make. See you inside," she said.

Millie nodded and waved as she walked away.

Phoebe's first thought was to call Aidan. Lee didn't know the woman, but Aidan did. The phone rang twice and then Aidan answered, slightly breathless and sounding a bit concerned, and no wonder. It wasn't even seven o'clock.

"Hello? Phoebe? Is everything alright?"

"No!" Phoebe said and then unloaded. "I just saw Sonja standing in the doorway of one of the rooms at the motel. I don't know what she's doing here, but it can't be good. Please watch out for Lee today. He won't know her from Adam, but you will. Her hair is blond now and short, but it's still her."

"You're sure it wasn't a look-alike?" Aidan said.

"Positive."

"Then don't worry about Lee, and if she happens to show up looking for you, what do you want me to tell her?"

"That I don't want to see her ever, and if she persists, I will make her sorry."

Aidan felt the rage in her voice and was suddenly so very grateful that his arrival here had not elicited the same emotions.

"I got your back, Bee."

The promise was as comforting as the sexy rasp of his voice. She shuddered as the shock and rage began to dissipate.

"I have to clock in."

"Call if you need us. Lee and I can be there in minutes."

"Yes, alright," Phoebe said. "And thanks."

Then she disconnected and made one more call, this time to Lee, who answered with a mouthful of something.

"Hi, Mom! Miss me already?"

"Swallow. I have something to tell you."

The joking was immediately over. "What's wrong?"

"Sonja is in Blessings. I just saw her at the motel. She didn't see me, but it's only a matter of time before we're all blessed with her presence. I have no idea why she's here, but I am not pleased. I have already alerted Aidan to be on the lookout for her and to protect you from whatever shit she has planned."

"Sonja, the grandmother we don't like? And why did you call Dad? I can take care of myself," he said.

"Yes, that Sonja, and do you know what she looks like?" Phoebe asked.

Silence, and then Lee answered with a less challenging attitude, "No."

"Well, he does, so now you know why I called him, okay? I love you. I have to go clock in. She can't hurt any of us. Just remember that."

"But she can hurt you, Mom, and that's not okay. Whatever is going on with her, you do not have to deal with it alone. Not anymore."

Phoebe blinked back tears. "Thank you. I don't deserve you but I am grateful to God that you're mine."

She got out, grabbed her lunch and umbrella from the back seat, and hurried inside. She clocked in a couple minutes shy of seven a.m., put her lunch in the break room fridge, and went up front.

Wilson started to chat as he gave her the cash drawer then saw the look in her eyes and changed his mind.

"Take number one today, okay?"

"Yes, thank you," Phoebe muttered and walked away.

The frown on Wilson's face deepened. He didn't know what was wrong, but something told him it might be wise to keep an eye on her today. She was spoiling for a showdown with someone, which was so unlike her. Then he was sidetracked by a customer wanting to buy a money order, and the day began.

———ᴡᴡ———

Lee was shaken by his mother's call. He'd always hoped one day to meet his father, but he had nothing but disregard for the woman who'd abandoned her pregnant daughter without so much as a goodbye. By the time he got to Preston's house, he was glad for his dad's backup.

Aidan met him in the front yard and gave him a quick hug.

"Your mother called you, right?"

Lee nodded. "I can't believe this is all happening. Why do you think she came back now?"

Aidan shrugged. "Who knows? Preston's death brought me back. Maybe it had something to do with her return, too."

Then Aidan looked past Lee's shoulder to see the neighbor from across the street coming toward them at a fast pace.

"I wonder what Elliot wants," Aidan said.

Lee turned around and then smiled. "Hi, Mr. Graham! Good to see you," Lee said.

Elliot nodded but seemed a little distracted. "Good to see you, too, Lee. Give your mother my regards."

"Yes, I will," Lee said.

Then Elliot reached for Aidan, his fingers curling around his wrist.

"You need to know it's all about to come undone. Prepare yourself. Guard your words so that what happened to your father is not repeated in Blessings. This matters. Do you understand?"

Lee gasped. "What do you know, Mr. Graham?"

When Elliot turned to walk away, Aidan stopped him.

"Does this have to do with finding out who started that fire?"

"Yes," Elliot said. "And that's all I can say. Just be prepared for revelations."

"Are they happening now?" Lee asked.

Elliot was silent a moment, and then he frowned. "No, not tomorrow. I have to go," and hurried back to his house.

"What's going on with that old man?" Aidan asked.

"Granddad said Elliot knew things, like, before they happened. And he said Elliot was never wrong."

Aidan's eyebrows rose. "Like he's psychic?"

"I don't know, Dad. But I've known him all my life, and he's a good man. He only became a kind of hermit after his wife died. I guess we'll have to wait to see if he's right."

Aidan shook his head in disbelief. "It will take some doing to make me believe anything like that."

Lee grinned and let the subject drop. "So, what are we doing today? Going back to finish that last room?"

Aidan nodded.

"Yes, but we were running out of paint. I have some more ordered. It's due to be delivered here within the hour. We'll store all but what we need for today in the storage shed. I have a phone call to make to my manager back in New Orleans, so I need you to wait here on the porch for the truck from the lumberyard. Have them put two gallons in the back of my truck and the rest in the storage shed in the backyard, okay?"

"Absolutely, Dad. No problem."

Aidan grinned. "Thanks, and hopefully, my call won't take long."

Then he loped back toward the house, clearing the front steps in two long strides, and went inside.

Lee followed him at a much slower pace, then sat down on the porch in one of the white wicker chairs.

———

Sonja was antsy to get the day started. She and Joe were on their way to Granny's Country Kitchen for breakfast. She hadn't had good grits since she'd left Georgia and wanted them as part of her meal. Joe was in a good mood, thanks to the way she had woken him this morning, so when they walked into Granny's, they were both smiling.

Lovey was manning the register as usual, and when she saw Sonja and Joe walk in, she thought she was hallucinating. *What the heck? First Aidan returns, then these two?* Everyone was glad to see Aidan come back, but this couple was another story. Lovey picked up two menus and smiled.

"Two for breakfast? This way, please," she said and led them to a table right in the middle of the room. "Your waitress will be right with you. Enjoy," she said and walked off before they could ask for another seating.

Sonja frowned as she slid into her seat. "She did that on purpose."

Joe sat in the chair to her right. "Did what?" he asked as he picked up a menu.

"Seated us in the middle of the room. Prepare yourself to be stared at all through our meal."

Joe glanced up, looked around, and then shrugged. "Screw all of them. I don't care."

Sonja sighed. "I guess I don't either. What are you having?"

"I want sausage, three eggs, and a side of pancakes. How about you?" Joe asked.

"Eggs, bacon, biscuits, and a side of grits."

A waitress swung by their table with a pot of coffee. "Hi, I'm Shelly. Y'all want coffee?" she asked.

Joe nodded. "Yes, please, and we're ready to order."

She filled their cups and then set the hot coffeepot on an empty table behind them to take their order.

Sonja ordered first and then Joe.

"And don't forget to bring us some hot sauce," Joe added.

"Will do," Shelly said and left them sitting, filling cups at other tables along the way to turn in the order.

They were waiting for their food to arrive when from outside there was a large boom and the sound of crashing metal, and then a car horn began to honk.

"What the hell?" Joe asked and got up to look out the front windows along with everyone else. "Looks like a pretty bad wreck. Someone call 911."

"Oh my God, that's Betty Purejoy's car!" someone yelled.

"That truck is from the lumberyard!" another man said.

Lovey ran outside with her cell phone, already on the line with 911. The truck driver was climbing out of the cab. He sat down on the sidewalk, his forehead bleeding.

"I called 911. Don't move!" Lovey said and headed for the car. She knew it was Peanut Butterman's secretary, Betty, and she was unconscious.

Smoke was coming from under the hood of Betty's car, and Lovey was scared to death it would catch on fire or explode before help arrived. Then Betty started moaning and moving, and Lovey yanked and pulled on the door until it opened and she could lean in.

"Betty, honey, this is Lovey. Don't move. You had a wreck, but help is on the way."

Betty moaned again and reached toward her face. Blood was coming out of her nose and mouth. It looked to Lovey as if she'd hit the steering wheel.

"Oh God, oh God, please let them both be okay," Lovey whispered and took Betty's hand. "Hold my hand, Betty. Hang onto me. I'm right here with you."

Within moments, Lovey heard and then saw an ambulance coming up the street and two cop cars coming from opposite directions.

"Help is here, Betty. Hang on! Help is here."

Betty moaned again, but she was holding onto Lovey's hand with all the strength she could muster. It was reassuring to Lovey that Betty heard her, even if she couldn't speak.

And then all of a sudden the parking lot was swarming with rescue units. Another ambulance arrived, and then Chief Pittman was on the scene, directing traffic and sending sightseers on their way.

Paramedics loaded up the truck driver and took off to ER with him, while the second ambulance crew began working on Betty. As soon as they had her stabilized, they removed her from the wrecked car and also sped away to the ER with sirens screaming.

Lovey stood back, watching. The whole sight was surreal and a horrible reminder of how swiftly a life could change. A wrecker was already on site, getting ready to tow Betty's car to the police impound, while a couple of employees from the lumberyard had shown up with another vehicle and begun transferring the deliveries. All she could do was say a prayer for both of the drivers and go back inside.

People were beginning to return to their tables and booths, and the waitresses were bringing out the food. Lovey noted that Sonja and Joe were back at their table, their heads were together, and they were talking with some urgency. She wondered what they were up to and then got busy again and forgot. Before she knew it, they were at the register to pay.

"Was everything satisfactory?" Lovey asked as she took their ticket and the credit card Joe handed to her.

"It was delicious," Sonja said. "I haven't had good grits since I left here, and my mind was set on having some. They were just as good as I remembered, but it was those biscuits that hit the spot. You sure do have a good baker."

"Thank you," Lovey said.

Sonja kept expecting her to say something and finally asked her outright. "Lovey, do you know who I am?"

Lovey met her gaze, looked her up and down, and glanced at Joe and then back at Sonja.

"Yes, I know who you are. You're the woman who left her pregnant daughter broke and homeless when you skipped town with him." She pointed at Joe. "If it hadn't been for that girl's determination not to fail and Preston Williams's charity, God only knows what would have happened. Have a nice day."

Sonja's lips parted, but she didn't have a comeback.

Then Joe grabbed her by the forearm and escorted her out of the cafe.

"Oh my God," Sonja moaned. "That was awful, just awful what she said to me."

Joe frowned at her. Sometimes the woman was oblivious. "What the hell did you expect, Sonja? You can't deny one thing she said. Now get in the car."

Sonja let herself be led away, but as soon as they got in the car, she was already in recovery mode.

"I want to go see Phoebe. Myra said Preston gave her the family house. I want to go there now."

Joe sighed, put the car in gear, and drove away.

Aidan walked out of the house just as the sound of sirens erupted. "What's going on?"

"I don't know, but I just heard what sounded like an explosion or a really bad wreck somewhere toward Main," Lee said. "Everything okay back in New Orleans?"

Aidan sat down in the other chair to wait with him. "Yes, just a few little snags to iron out."

Lee was silent for a moment, then glanced up. "How much longer are you going to stay here? Is there pressure to get back to your business?"

Aidan leaned forward. "I'm not in any hurry to go anywhere, and there's no pressure."

Lee exhaled slowly, relieved.

A couple moments later, Aidan's cell phone rang. He glanced down and then frowned. It was the lumberyard.

"Hello? Aidan Payne speaking."

"Mr. Payne, this is Newton. I wanted you to know that our truck was just in an accident, so your delivery will be just a bit delayed. We're in the process of transferring the orders to another vehicle and will be there soon."

"Oh no! I hope no one was injured!" Aidan said.

"There were injuries, but we don't think they're serious. Thank you for asking."

"Yes, yes, no problem," Aidan said and disconnected. "That explosion you heard was an accident. Our delivery truck was in a wreck. We'll have to wait a bit longer. Want to go inside?"

"I'm good sitting out here if it's okay with you," Lee said.

Aidan grinned. "Anything you do is okay with me. If you want something cold to drink, help yourself."

"I know it's a bit early to be hitting the pop, but I think I will have a cold Pepsi."

"Help yourself," Aidan said.

"Want one?" Lee asked.

"Not now," Aidan said.

Lee headed inside at a lope.

Aidan leaned back, thinking about him and Phoebe finding their way back to each other and all of them together in New Orleans, and then closed his eyes.

They were still closed when a car began slowing down in front of the house. But when he heard it coming up the drive, he opened his eyes, saw the maroon Lincoln and the man driving it, and then stood and walked to the top of the steps, unaware his hands were already curling into fists.

The man driver got out first, then circled the car to open the door for the woman with him. The moment she stepped out, the hair crawled on the back of Aidan's neck.

Then Lee came out of the house to stand beside him, staring. "Who's that, Dad?"

"That's Sonja. And the man is Joe Ritter. Don't talk to either of them. I've got this."

Lee didn't have to be told twice. The man looked scary as hell, and the woman was nothing like his mom. Her hair was bleached and shorn, and her clothes were too tight on her skinny, sagging body.

Aidan watched them approaching until they reached the bottom step. "Stop! Don't come any closer. Say what you came to say, and get the hell off my property!"

Sonja gasped. "Your property! I thought it belonged to my daughter!"

"You don't have a daughter, and you're wrong!" Aidan said.

A dark flush swarmed up from Sonja's neck onto her face as her eyes narrowed in anger. "You don't speak for my daughter."

"I do today!" Aidan said.

Sonja's gaze slid to the young man beside Aidan Payne. He looked so much like Aidan had at that age that she knew this must be Phoebe's son.

"You must be my grandson, Len," she said.

Lee shook his head. "You are nothing to me, lady, and my name is Lee."

Aidan took a step closer to his son. "We're done here. Get off the property!" Aidan said.

"Not until I see my daughter!" Sonja shouted and then started screaming. "Phoebe! Phoebe! Come out! I just want to talk to you!"

"She's not in this house. She doesn't live in this house. No one does."

"You're lying to me," Sonja said. "I know because my cousin lives in this town, and she told me Phoebe inherited this house."

Aidan glared. "Your cousin? Hmm, if memory serves, that would be Myra Franklin, who is notorious for spreading gossip without verifying facts. Preston deeded a house to Phoebe alright, but it's the one he gave her to live in when you left her homeless. It's barely a thousand square feet and there's no room for you...not in their house...and not in their lives."

Sonja was in shock. Joe grabbed her arm, trying to pull her back to the car, and she yanked out of his grasp and went after Aidan.

"You went off and left her pregnant! You don't deserve to speak for her!" she shouted.

"Oh, hell no," Aidan said and came down the steps so fast that Joe Ritter doubled up his fists, thinking he was going to have to fight.

Sonja screamed, thinking she was going to be attacked, and then Aidan stopped just short of arm's reach.

"You don't get to play that card! You two are the reason all the trouble happened between us. I didn't run off. You did that...with him." Aidan pointed at Joe, who looked like he wanted to take a swing at him. "I moved away, with my father, who did not abandon me. You're the one who went off without your child. I found out exactly two days ago that Lee existed. You knew he was on the way when you left her here. You are an unnatural bitch of a mother. Everyone in Blessings knew she was pregnant. You knew. Granddad knew. But no one told me. You and Joe Ritter told lie after lie about my father, even after the law proved he was innocent. Why? Why did you do that? Was it to keep everyone in Blessings so stirred up about my dad that they wouldn't see what you two were doing right under their noses? And you a widow less than a month! You get off my property. If you come back, I'll call the cops."

Sonja was furious. She kept looking from father to son and back again, and though the hate emanating from them was palpable, she couldn't let go of the need to justify herself.

"You don't speak for her! You aren't her husband."

And that was when Lee had had enough. He stepped in front of his dad and poked a finger hard against Sonja's shoulder.

"I speak for Phoebe Ritter! I am her son. You think you know her? You think she's still the scared teenager you abandoned? Lady, you mess with my mother, and she will take you apart."

Sonja audibly gasped and then backed all the way up against Joe's chest.

"Joe..."

"I'm here," he said. "But you're the one who wanted to come. I warned you, but you wouldn't listen. Are you ready to go home now?"

Sonja turned on him in rage. "I'm not leaving this town until I talk to my daughter. I have to make this right!"

Lee glanced at his dad. "What do you think?"

Aidan shrugged. "She isn't going to shut up."

Lee frowned. "Mom might wind up hurting herself again."

Sonja turned on them and screamed, unaware that people on both sides of the street were now out on their front porches, watching. "I want to know where she is!"

"Dang, lady, stop screaming. She's right where she's been every workday for the past twenty years…checking groceries at the Piggly Wiggly," Lee said.

The expression on Sonja's face sort of froze and then melted, leaving her with her mouth half-open and all the loose skin under her neck mottled and quivering.

"I'm going to see her right now," she said in a challenging tone, as if daring one of them to argue again.

"Don't say we didn't warn you," Aidan said.

"Are you going to call and tell her I'm coming?" Sonja asked.

Aidan nodded. "Hell yes. I'm not the kind to blindside someone I love. Now get off this property and don't come back. You do, and I'll have you arrested for trespassing."

Joe dragged Sonja back into the car and drove away, leaving rubber behind as he accelerated.

"Call your mother," Aidan said.

Lee knew from experience she wouldn't answer calls at work, but she left her phone beside her register so she could watch for his texts. He wasted no time sending one.

Chapter 12

PHOEBE HAD JUST FINISHED A TRANSACTION WITH A CUSTOMER and was watching another lady with a full shopping cart coming toward her register when she got Lee's text.

> Sonja is headed your way. Be prepared. Dad and I have pissed her off royally. XXOO

The heat that shot through her was pure rage. She reached up, flipped off the Open light at her station, and turned around to face the entrance.

Wilson saw her light go off and then zeroed in on the look on her face. Whatever had been bothering her this morning appeared to be coming to a head. He didn't want a disturbance in the store and was walking toward her, but he wasn't fast enough. He saw a man and woman come rushing into the store, and then all hell broke loose.

Phoebe started toward them, pointing a finger as she walked, her voice so tight with anger that everything she said came with a visceral blow.

"I saw you this morning. Couldn't believe my eyes. Twenty years ago you gave me an ultimatum: kill my baby or find a new place to live. You and your lover left me behind, homeless and broke, and I have waited a really long time to say this to you, but I do so now with a great sense of relief. You, Sonja Ritter, are not only a coward, but you are also a pathetic excuse for a parent."

Sonja held out her hand like she would have to a feral dog, praying it didn't bite.

"I need to explain," Sonja said. "I'm—"

"I just told you what you are!" Phoebe shouted. "Get away from me! I don't need you. I don't need either one of you. You mean nothing to me."

Sonja was painfully aware of the expressions on the shoppers' faces. They were looking at the both of them like they were garbage. Then she noticed Phoebe's hand and pointed to the obvious injury.

"What happened to your hand?"

"Oh, you mean this?" Phoebe asked, waving it in the air. "I dislocated a couple knuckles when I punched a man in the face for saying something I found offensive."

Sonja's eyes widened. Now she was beginning to understand what Lee meant about his mother. So, her daughter was no longer a pushover. She shrugged.

"I'm sorry you were hurt."

"I wasn't hurt. I was offended!" Phoebe said. "Do you know how many times I was offended as a pregnant, unwed teen? At one time, most of this town felt it their business and their right to criticize me. You two made the Payne family's life a living hell with your lies, and it turned Aidan against all of us. He never came back for me, and you left me behind. I couldn't be worth much. Why would the fine citizens of Blessings treat me better than the two people I needed most?"

Sonja was losing ground fast. "No, Phoebe, you have it all wrong! You don't have any idea what was going on after your father's death! I was—"

Phoebe walked closer, her voice rising with every word she uttered. "I know everything that was going on." She pointed at Joe. "He was at our house from morning until night, interfering in our family, trying to act like he was my boss. And I know you called Social Security to see about receiving money from Dad's death before he was even buried."

Sonja's face paled. "I was within my right to—"

"You! Shut up!" she shouted. "I'm not through talking. I also know that you tried to get more money for yourself by claiming me as a dependent child. I know because I called them myself hoping they could help me after you two disappeared, only to find out you'd already inquired on my behalf and found out that since I'd turned eighteen, that offer was no longer available to me as Dad's child. So how did that work, Sonja? Since I wasn't worth anything to you financially, you just forgot I existed?"

Sonja's legs went out from under her. If Joe hadn't been beside her, she would have gone to her knees.

"Good. Now you know how I felt. Get out of my life," Phoebe said.

Sonja let herself cry, knowing she looked awful when she did, but it was her last-gasp effort to sway public opinion.

"I can't do that," Sonja said. "What I did was wrong, and I'm trying to make it right."

Phoebe turned around and caught Wilson's attention. "Have you called the police yet?"

He shook his head.

"Then would you please do that for me? Tell them there are people causing a disturbance in the Piggly Wiggly and they need to be removed."

Now Joe stepped in, glaring at Phoebe and muttering

beneath his breath. "Oh, hell no. We don't need the cops. We're leaving, we're leaving."

Phoebe leaned forward and lowered her voice to the point that no one but Joe and Sonja could hear.

"Stay away from us—from Lee, from me, from Aidan—or I will make you sorry."

Sonja shuddered.

Joe started to comment, but when Phoebe just shook her head, he thought better of it. He took Sonja by the arm and then tried to leave by the same door they'd come in, but it wouldn't open.

Phoebe rolled her eyes. "You're standing on the sensor."

He flushed a dark, angry red as he circled the handrail separating the doors and went out the other one.

When Phoebe turned around and realized a good half dozen people were still videoing with their phones, she threw her hands up in the air.

"If I'd known you were doing all this, I would have turned my better side to the camera."

They had the grace to be embarrassed, put their phones away, and suddenly got very busy.

Phoebe glanced at her boss and then spoke to all the customers waiting to check out, who seemed stunned by what they'd witnessed.

"I am sorry my dirty laundry was dragged up in front of you. That wasn't fair. You came to shop for your family and instead got a dose of the Hateful Housewives of Blessings, Georgia. I apologize, and rest assured, I will not speak of this again." Then she looked at Wilson again. "Do I still have my job?"

Before he could answer, every customer in the store

shouted, "Yes," and then glared at the manager, as if daring him to say otherwise.

"Of course you still have your job," Wilson said. "However, if you wish to leave early today, I would certainly understand."

"No, thank you, Wilson. I can't afford to leave early. However, if you will allow me a bathroom break, I do feel a need to calm down before I throw up."

Millie walked to her, whispering in her ear as she hugged her tight. "You are my new hero. Now go pee."

But when Phoebe started to the break room, every witness in the store met her with either an apology for how she'd been treated or praise for how she'd taken care of herself and Lee. By the time Phoebe got away, she was in tears, but after that, the morning seemed to fly by.

——〰——

It was almost noon when Phoebe heard someone behind her say her name. She turned around and saw Myra Franklin from the florist with a beautiful bouquet of roses.

Phoebe blushed. "For me?" she said.

Myra smiled and nodded. "Yes, for you, and this card goes with it," she said, handing Phoebe a sealed envelope along with the bouquet.

Phoebe's customer was beaming. "What fun, Phoebe! Who sent them?"

There was only one person in Blessings who would feel the need to do this. She slipped the card into her hip pocket, sniffed the roses, and then took them as Myra left the store.

Phoebe turned to the woman waiting to be checked out. "Excuse me just a moment. I need to take these to the office."

"No problem, honey," the woman said. "I'm in no hurry."

But Phoebe was. "Hey, Wilson. I just received a flower delivery. Can you find a safe place for them in the office with you, or do you want me to take them to the break room?"

"Yes, you can leave them with me," he said as she handed him the flower-filled vase. "Really pretty," he added.

"Yes, they are," Phoebe said and hurried back to her register with a smile on her face.

As soon as there was a lull in customers, she opened the card and recognized Aidan's handwriting.

I told Sonja today that I love you, then realized I should have told you first. So, we're on a new path here, but I want you to know that I'm falling for the woman you are just like I fell for the girl you were.

Aidan

She shivered, then slipped the card into her hip pocket and sent Aidan a quick text.

Just don't break my heart. I wouldn't survive it again.

She saw another customer approaching and put down the phone. It was Vera from the Curl Up and Dye with a shopping cart full of paper towels and toilet paper. Vera began unloading the merchandise onto the conveyor belt as Phoebe scanned the items.

"Heard from Peanut and Ruby since they went on their honeymoon?" Phoebe asked.

Vera grinned. "Not a word! Isn't that exciting? They must be having a ball."

Phoebe laughed. "That's one way of looking at it," she said and then hit Total.

Vera slid her credit card into the chip reader, talking to Phoebe while she followed the prompts, and then pushed the cart full of bags to her car.

Wilson came up behind Phoebe and switched off her light. "Take your lunch break now while there's a lull. Darla is coming in anytime now, so we won't be shorthanded."

"Thank you. For everything," Phoebe said.

Wilson nodded. "I wish you nothing but the best, Phoebe. It's all I've ever wanted for you, and I'm happy for you that things are changing for the better in your life."

Phoebe smiled. "Thank you, Boss. That means a lot to me."

She got a cold bottle of pop to have with her lunch and then stopped by Millie's register to pay for it before heading to the break room.

Her lunch was a roast beef sandwich, a sandwich bag full of potato chips, and another sandwich bag with a handful of dill gherkins. She opened her Pepsi and took a drink, grateful to be off her feet. A few minutes later, she was reading the local paper between bites and hoping that Aidan would text back.

But when he showed up in the break room with two pieces of Mercy Pittman's best coconut cream pie from Granny's, it took everything she had not to fall into his arms.

"Surprise," Aidan said. "Your boss gave me permission to eat dessert with you. Hope it's okay with you, too."

Phoebe's smile was so wide it felt fake on her face. "It's very okay. Sit with me," she said.

He grinned, unpacked the slices of pie from the sack he was carrying, and set one at her place. She was wiping the pickle juice off her fingers when he reached across the table and laid his hand on her arm.

"I won't hurt you, Bee, ever again. I'll wait as long as you need, and if you can't get past what happened, I won't like it, but I won't let it change a thing about my relationship with our son. Okay?"

She nodded, suddenly too emotional to speak.

He saw the tears in her eyes and pointed at the pie. "Lovey said it was good for what ailed me, so I'm assuming the same goes for you. Dig in."

Phoebe managed a slight smile and then removed the plastic cover from the pie, took the fork he handed her, and took a big bite. She rolled her eyes as the sweet taste of rich vanilla pudding mixed with shredded coconut settled on her taste buds.

"Yummm, this is good stuff," she said.

He took a bite, nodding in agreement. "Yes, this is good stuff. Indeed, very good stuff. But this stuff is not as good as your stuff…if you know what I mean."

Phoebe was so startled by his foolishness that she burst out laughing. "It's good to know you still have the same slightly dirty sense of humor."

He grinned. "Just making sure you're paying attention."

Phoebe sighed. "I haven't missed a word you've said since you walked back into my life."

His smile disappeared. "Did I say the right things? Did I say enough? I'm not joking about this, Bee."

"Just know I'm still listening and waiting," Phoebe said.

"What are you waiting for? What can I do to make you forgive me?" Aidan asked.

Phoebe hesitated, then reached across the table and clasped his hand. "I forgave you when I realized I was also at fault."

Aidan groaned. "Then what are you waiting for?"

She was silent for a few moments, then looked up and met his gaze. "I think maybe now I'm waiting to forgive myself."

He started to argue the point, but something in her expression stopped him. "Okay, understood. Not to be changing the subject on you or anything, but if you don't finish your pie, I'll do it for you."

And just like that, the seriousness of the moment had passed and he had her laughing again.

―――∽∽∽―――

Joe and Sonja drove back to their motel room and walked in without speaking. Joe locked the door as Sonja kicked off her shoes and curled up on the bed.

The silence within the room was acute. There was nothing to drown out the reality of what had just taken place.

Joe sat down on the other side of the bed and then reached for her hand. "It's not all your fault," he said. "I never once argued with you about your decisions. I never told you it was okay if she went with us. I never told her I was sorry for treating her as I did. It's not all your fault."

Sonja shook her head. "Yes, it is. She was my daughter. Mine and Marty's. I didn't just let her down, but I let him down, too. We'd been fighting for months before he died, so I took my anger at him out on her. I am a horrible mother."

Joe leaned back against the headboard. "I knew you guys were fighting."

Sonja froze. "You did? But you never told me."

He shrugged. "He talked about it to me once. Asked me what I thought he should do. I told him that wasn't for me to say."

Sonja gasped and then sat up, wiping her eyes. "Why am I just now finding out about this?"

"Because it makes me look like an even bigger jerk for coming on to you when what was left of Marty was lying in a drawer in the morgue. I knew you were vulnerable, and I took advantage. Phoebe became collateral damage to lust."

Sonja put her hands over her mouth to keep from screaming.

"I want to go home," Sonja said.

Joe nodded. They stared at each other for a long time without speaking, and then Sonja finally lay back down and closed her eyes. But she reached for him as she was falling asleep, and he saw it. He lay down beside her, pulled the covers up over both of them, and held her hand as she slept.

—◦◦◦—

Betty Purejoy was lying in the hospital bed feeling sorry for herself, thinking about how fast life could go wrong.

She'd left home having a good hair day. Her soft blond curls were behaving. She'd looked good enough for a woman in her late forties to feel pretty and for once was not bemoaning her baby-face features.

She'd worked all morning at Peanut Butterman's law office, even though her boss and his new wife were still on their honeymoon. She'd left just before noon to have lunch at Granny's, and the last thing she remembered before waking up in an ambulance was pulling out of Granny's parking lot to go back to the office.

Now she was in the hospital with a broken nose and a concussion. Her lips were swollen, and she had a couple of loose teeth, an assortment of butterfly bandages for small cuts, and six tiny staples along her jawline. She still didn't know what had happened, but it was the honesty in the truck driver's statement that ultimately told the tale.

He told the officer he had looked down to check the address of his next delivery stop, and when he looked up, he realized he'd run a stop sign and then hit Betty's car. He had bruised his ribs, jammed the fingers on his right hand, and suffered a small cut on his forehead, but he was otherwise fine. It was Betty who'd suffered the more serious injuries.

"I'm just so sorry," he kept saying as the officer wrote him up for causing the accident.

Betty was sorry, too, but blame didn't change her situation. She was in charge of the law office until her boss returned from his honeymoon. There was paperwork to be filed and work to be done. She couldn't let him down, but she didn't know how soon she could get back to work. Right now she was seeing double, which wasn't good, and her car was a mess.

She wanted to weep, but her nose was packed with gauze, so she couldn't cry and breathe at the same time. She knew they'd already called her husband, Jack, but he worked out of town and she had no idea how far away he was when he'd gotten the call.

She was at the point of feeling very sorry for herself when Jack burst into her room, his short, graying hair standing up on end like he'd run his hands through it a thousand times. He was still wearing his uniform from the trucking company he worked for, and for a big, stocky man, he could sure move fast.

"Oh, Betty! Oh, honey! I'm so sorry," he said as he rushed to her side and took her in his arms.

It was the sympathy that did Betty in. Tears rolled, and then she had to make herself stop. Between the gauze up her nose and the pain from her concussion, sobbing was not an option.

Jack ran to the sink with a clean washcloth, wet it, then wrung it out, and brought it to her. The cool cloth felt good against her flushed cheeks.

"You have a broken nose and a concussion," Jack said. "And your poor little mouth. Did you hit the steering wheel?"

"I don't remember," Betty said. "I must have. Most of my injuries are to my head and face."

Jack patted her cheek, kissed her jaw near the staples, and then sat beside her, patting her hand over and over as he spoke.

"From the moment they told me about the wreck until right now, all I could think about was that I forgot to tell you I love you before I left for work. I'm sorry, darlin'. I love you with all my heart, and I won't ever forget to tell you again."

Tears rolled down Betty's face again. "It's okay, sweetheart. You show me your love every day in the smallest of ways. I don't always have to hear it."

But Jack wasn't satisfied. "I need to hear myself say it, just as a reminder of how lucky I am to have you. What can I do? What do you need?"

Betty wiped at her eyes. "I should notify Peanut. I'm not behind on paperwork, but there are things that need to be filed this week, and I'm not sure I'll be well enough to do it. Right now I'm seeing two of you."

"Lord have mercy," he said and hugged her again. "Want me to call him for you?"

Betty nodded. "His number is in my phone, which should be in my purse, wherever that is."

Jack began to look around, then found it in the bottom drawer of the nightstand.

"Here it is," he said.

"Just pull up my contact list. He's under *P* for *Peanut*."

Jack nodded, found the name, clicked on it, and made the call.

Chapter 13

PEANUT AND RUBY WERE STANDING ON THE RIM OF THE Grand Canyon using her phone to take pictures of themselves with the canyon in the background. Peanut had just told her it was the scariest piece of land erosion he'd ever seen, which had her laughing in every shot. And then his phone began to ring.

"Hang on a sec, sweetheart." When he saw the call was from Betty, he answered with a laugh. "I thought I told you not to call unless you were bleeding."

"Hi, Peanut, this is Jack, Betty's husband. Actually, she has been bleeding, but I think they have most all of that either stapled up or bandaged."

Peanut gasped and quickly put the phone on speaker so Ruby could hear, too. "No! Oh my God, I am so sorry. What happened?"

"She was in a wreck. She's going to be okay. She has a concussion, some staples on her chin, a few smaller cuts, and a broken nose. She's worried about papers she needs to file for you this week because right now she's seeing double and doesn't know when that will clear up."

"Oh good lord!" Peanut said. "You tell her I'm sorry she's hurt and to quit worrying about paperwork. I can call a temp agency and have them send someone down from Savannah, and Betty can direct traffic from home. Just tell her she's not to go to the office, and she can talk the temp through anything she needs to know over the phone, okay?"

"Yes, okay."

"I have Betty's number, so tell her I will give that number to the temp agency. Then when the temp gets to town, she'll call Betty for further instructions."

Ruby leaned in toward the phone. "It's me, Jack. Tell Betty I send her love and get-well-soon wishes."

"Thanks, Ruby, I sure will, and thank you, Peanut. Really sorry to break in on your honeymoon like this."

"You didn't mess up anything," Peanut said. "Just tell Betty we're thinking of her and I'll check in on her when we're back."

"Will do," Jack said, disconnected, then put the phone on the nightstand. "He's going to call a temp from Savannah. The temp will call you at home for instructions, and you're not to go to the office at all."

Betty sighed with relief. "I was just so worried."

"And now there's nothing to worry about, right?" Jack said.

Betty nodded.

"Just rest. I'm not going anywhere," Jack said.

―∾∾―

Ruby was still fretting about Betty after the phone call was over until Peanut took her in his arms and kissed her senseless. When he finally stopped, Ruby was reeling. "Not that I'm complaining, but what was that all about?" she asked.

Peanut tapped the end of her nose. "You are not allowed to start planning rescues for anyone but me until we finish with this honeymoon."

Ruby laughed. "So, when are you going to need saving?"

"Oh, you already saved me," Peanut said. "However, you never know when I may need more mouth-to-mouth resuscitation."

"I'm on it," Ruby said and planted a sweet, long kiss squarely on his mouth. When she stopped, she looked up at him and smiled. "Feeling better now?"

"Hell no," Peanut said. "I've lost my senses, I'm losing control, and I'm hyperventilating like crazy. You better do that again."

Ruby's laughter rang out across the canyon, echoing over and over and over until Peanut stopped it with yet another kiss.

"I've seen enough holes in the ground for today," Peanut said. "Wanna go back to the motel and make love?"

"You know it," Ruby said.

It was the perfect first course to a much later lunch.

———

Everyone at the Piggly Wiggly had heard about the wreck and who was driving. The employees spent their down time talking about wrecks they'd been in, wrecks they'd witnessed, or wrecks they'd caused.

As for Phoebe, every time she had a break between customers, she looked toward the front office to where the very top of her bouquet of roses could be seen. Both Aidan and the flowers had been a surprise at lunch, and she was coming to the realization that, after waiting twenty years and regardless of how it had happened, he'd returned still holding feelings for her. Maybe his return wasn't the romantic scene she'd envisioned, but she wasn't willing to turn down a second chance with the love of her life based on a fantasy reunion.

"Hey, Phoebe, look how dark the sky is getting!" Millie said. "It's going to pour."

Phoebe glanced toward the front entrance and frowned. The sky was so dark it looked like nightfall. She was trying to remember if she'd closed that little window in the utility room at home when the sound of thunder rumbled overhead. She shuddered. Storms made her anxious. So much uncontrolled energy. Then another customer came hurrying up and began unloading groceries to be checked out. It was Melissa Dean, who had recently inherited the dry cleaner in town.

"Hi, Phoebe. I knew I should have done all this earlier but kept putting it off. Now I'm not going to get home before this storm hits, and I left a kitchen window open," she said.

Phoebe nodded. "I hear you. I was just wondering if I'd closed the window in my utility room. I'll hurry. Maybe you'll get home before too much mess has been made."

"Thank you," Melissa said and started sacking her own purchases to hurry the process along.

Within a couple of minutes, she'd scanned her card and was on her way out with the bags in her hands. It was already raining.

An hour later when it was time for Phoebe to go home, the rain had amped up to a downpour. She retrieved her roses, and while still under the shelter of the store overhang, she opened her umbrella, used the remote to unlock her car, and then took off running.

By the time she got to the car, her shoes were full of water and her clothes were soaked. But the flowers were safe. She used the umbrella and her purse as props to keep the vase from spilling over in the seat, then settled in behind the steering wheel and headed home.

It was raining so hard that visibility was limited, but traffic had thinned out. She was almost home and turning a corner when the car suddenly hydroplaned and went into a skid. Phoebe screamed, grabbed the steering wheel hard as she could, and steered into the skid, quickly righting the car. But she'd gripped the steering wheel so tightly she'd hurt her hand. When she finally pulled up beneath the carport and killed the engine, she was shaking and her hand was throbbing, but she was home.

Grateful for the carport and shelter getting into the house, she gathered up her things, including the bouquet of roses, and went inside. She was dripping water as she walked, but that was easy to mop up.

She set the flowers on the counter, wincing from the ache in her fingers. The very idea of cooking supper tonight was almost more than she could handle, so she dried her hands and made a quick call to Lee.

―⁂―

Aidan and Lee were finished with the paint job on the first empty rental, leaving a clean and freshly painted house ready to put on the market. They got home and unloaded their painting equipment into the storage shed and were in the house before the sky unloaded.

"It's really coming down. How is the roof on your house?" Aidan asked as he stood at the kitchen window watching the water pooling in a low spot in the backyard.

"It's good, Dad. Granddad reroofed it for us about

four years ago. I'm gonna call Mom and see if she got home okay."

But when Lee went to make the call, he couldn't find his cell phone. "Maybe you left it in the truck," Aidan said.

"I'll go check," Lee said and went out through a side door to get to the portico.

The door had barely shut behind Lee when Aidan began hearing a phone ringing, and it wasn't his. He followed the sound to the top of the refrigerator. He found the phone, and when he noticed the caller was Phoebe, he answered the call for Lee.

"Hey, Phoebe, it's me. Lee is outside at his truck. Want me to have him call you, or do you want to hang on? He'll be right back." Then she sighed, and he heard the weariness in her voice. "Are you alright?"

"I'm hurting and so tired. I thought I'd take a pain pill and go rest a bit. Would you tell Lee to pick up some burgers on his way home?"

Before Aidan could answer, thunder rumbled overhead so loudly it rattled the windows. Phoebe turned toward the sound as well and then turned around to grab a tissue from the counter just as a bolt of lightning hit the roof. The flash was blinding, and then the ceiling above her exploded. She was screaming when everything went black.

Aidan heard the crack of lightning over the phone, then a loud boom followed by Phoebe's screams. The sounds nearly stopped his heart.

"Phoebe! Phoebe! Are you okay? Answer me, dammit! Are you okay?"

But the phone had gone dead. He ran toward the back door and out onto the portico, yelling Lee's name.

"Lee…get in my truck!"

"What's wrong?" Lee asked, even as he was running.

Aidan tossed Lee's phone onto his lap as he started up the truck.

"I found your phone when your mom called. Something blew up as we were talking. Call 911 and get fire and ambulance there ASAP."

"No, no, no," Lee moaned and dialed the number with shaking hands. He gave them the information and address and then put the phone in his pocket.

Aidan was flying through streets, taking corners in a skid, and the silence inside the cab was telling. They were both too afraid to speculate and bracing themselves for the sight.

As Aidan turned the corner onto their street, he saw a fire truck coming up from the other direction. Even in the downpour, smoke was coming up through the roof.

"Oh my God…Mama," Lee moaned.

Aidan gripped his son's wrist. "Don't. We don't know. We don't know. Don't make it worse."

Lee's fear turned to tears, but Aidan was already in rescue mode as he came to a sliding halt behind rescue vehicles.

"Wait for me," he yelled and leaped from the car into the storm before Lee could take a breath.

But Lee wasn't about to wait. He was right behind his dad and running.

For Aidan, the whole moment was surreal. A fire had been the reason he'd lost Phoebe once. He couldn't believe it was happening all over again. He kept running toward the house. He wouldn't lose Phoebe twice.

Firemen were pulling a hose toward a fireplug, and a cop was already blocking off the street when Aidan ran past the fire truck. No one saw him until he had run up the steps and kicked in the door. Someone was yelling at him to stop as smoke billowed out, but he didn't heed them as he disappeared inside.

Lee was close behind when he stumbled. A cop caught him, then held him back to keep him from following.

"Let me go! My mother is inside!" he cried.

"No, son. You'll only make it worse."

Lee swayed, then dropped to his knees as the rain came down.

The smoke was disorienting, but Aidan remembered the kitchen was a straight shot from the front door and the house was small. Only a few steps and he should be right there.

"Phoebe! Phoebe! Where are you?" he shouted as he ran and then choked on his own words as the acrid smell of smoke burned his throat.

A heartbeat later, he was in the kitchen. There was a hole in the roof that had taken on the aspect of a chimney funneling out the smoke. He glanced up. The flames were up in the ceiling, and the moment he took a step forward, he tripped on something and fell facedown near the bottom cabinets with the rain falling on his legs. And then he realized he was lying across Phoebe's body.

"Oh God, oh no, please no," Aidan mumbled as he scrambled to his feet and scooped her up into his arms.

Following the draft flowing from the open door in the living room, he began backtracking through the smoke with Phoebe held fast against his chest. He was on the way out the front door when he had to dodge two fire-men entering the house with hoses spraying.

"Get out, get out," they shouted.

But that was already his intention as he leaped through the open door. He stumbled going down the steps as the rain hit him in the face. When he realized it was pounding Phoebe, too, he pulled her closer, shielding her from the downpour with his body. He heard shouts but saw nothing but shapes and movement coming toward them. All of a sudden Lee's voice was in his ear and he was guiding him forward.

"This way, Dad, this way. An ambulance is waiting."

Aidan reluctantly gave Phoebe over to the EMTs and then staggered. His eyes had been aggravated by the smoke to the point that they were raw and burning.

Lee was trying not to lose it, but he'd never been so scared. His mother was unconscious, and his dad was stumbling around like a blind man.

An EMT pulled Aidan up into the ambulance and sat him on a bench against one side of the interior wall.

"I'm Roger. I'm going to put this oxygen mask over your face to help you breathe. Bud and Art are taking care of the woman."

"Her name is Phoebe," Aidan said, then tilted his head back as Roger began flushing his eyes until most of the burning had stopped.

Two other EMTs already had Phoebe on a backboard with a cervical collar stabilizing her for transport as they lifted her into the ambulance, too.

Lee was in a panic and kept looking from one parent to the other in disbelief. How had everything gone so wrong so fast?

"What's wrong? Is she breathing?" he asked.

"She's breathing," Art said as Roger worked on starting an IV on Phoebe. "Hey, Lee, we're leaving now. You can follow us to the ER."

"Dad! I'll see you there," Lee said and took off toward the truck.

Aidan's chest was tight with emotion as he watched Lee leave.

"You can sure tell he's yours," Roger said as Bud took the driver's seat and Art slid into the passenger seat, riding shotgun beside him. "You pretty much cloned yourself there. I remember him sacking groceries at the Piggly Wiggly. Real nice kid. Okay, Art, I've got a line in, let's move!"

Aidan shifted the mask enough to answer. "His mother gets all the credit for how he was raised."

At that same moment, Phoebe stirred. Her arms were strapped down, and it was obvious the oxygen mask was bothering her.

Roger touched her shoulder to let her know he was there. "Phoebe…you're in an ambulance, and that's an oxygen mask. You need to leave it alone, okay?"

She moaned but quit trying to get to it.

The lights were flashing, the siren a continuing scream as the ambulance picked up speed, leaving the burning house behind.

—◆◆◆—

It was the sound of Aidan's voice that Phoebe heard first, but when she tried to talk, it felt like someone had put a hand over her mouth. Then she heard an unfamiliar voice tell her it was an oxygen mask and that she was in an ambulance. She didn't know what had happened, but she was beginning to hurt—all over. She was scared and in pain, and this felt like a bad dream.

"Lee? Where's my son?" she mumbled.

The EMT patted her arm. "Your son is fine, Phoebe."

"Aidan?"

"I'm here, sweetheart," Aidan said.

Phoebe blinked several times to clear her vision and then saw him. "What happened?" she said.

"Lightning struck your house," the EMT said. "Firemen were putting out the fire as we left. Your house will still be there."

Phoebe started to cry.

The silent tears hurt Aidan far worse than outright sobs. He knew how she was feeling and reached across the space between them until his hand was on her leg.

Her gaze locked on his face.

"It's okay, Bee. I promise."

Chapter 14

WORD SPREAD THROUGH TOWN ABOUT THE INCIDENT, AND the story was still being told even after the fire had been put out. The kitchen had the most damage; the smoke and water from the fire hoses had done a number throughout the rest of the house, but the house was still standing.

As soon as the fire was no longer an issue, men from the neighborhood climbed up on Phoebe's roof and nailed a tarp over the hole, then went inside and began shoveling out the debris, while outside the rain continued to fall.

Aidan's injuries were minor. Phoebe ended up with a slight concussion and a couple of butterfly bandages on her head. Her throat was raw from inhaling the smoke, but because she'd been lying unconscious on the floor, the thin layer of air between the floor and the smoke had served her well. The deluge of rain that had almost caused her to wreck going home in the end had been what saved her house. She still didn't know how she missed being struck, but she considered it a miracle.

The ER doctor had recommended Phoebe be admitted for observation, but she refused, and Aidan didn't argue with her. Except for scratches and bruising, she seemed to have escaped serious injury.

They were both in Phoebe's exam room waiting to

sign release papers, and Lee had gone to the parking lot to bring the truck to the entrance to take them home.

Phoebe wouldn't let herself think of what had happened to her house. Not when the most important thing was that she was alive. She'd already heard how Aidan had run into the fire to get her and was being touted as a hero. She couldn't help but wonder how this all would have turned out if she had not been on the phone with him when it happened.

However, she was sitting up beside him now, her legs dangling off the side of the bed, as wet and as dirty as she'd ever been, and all she wanted was to hug him.

Aidan was just as wet and almost as dirty as she was, sitting so close to her that their shoulders were touching. When he'd carried her out of the house, he had not known if she was alive. Now, just knowing she was still in the world was a gift.

Phoebe leaned her head against his shoulder. "Do you have any idea of the extent of damage to my house?"

He patted her leg, knowing she deserved the truth but hating to be the one to deliver it.

"I know there's a hole in the roof because I felt rain on my face when I found you. And the house was full of smoke, which probably means furniture, carpeting, and curtains will have to be replaced. The only flames I saw were in the ceiling, so if the firemen got it out in time, the damage might not be as bad as I first thought."

Her eyes welled. "I have insurance to cover everything, but it makes me sad that the little house that has sheltered us for so many years has been hurt. I won't feel right until it's been fixed."

When he slid his hand beneath her palm, she threaded

her fingers through his, holding on tight for the strength to say what she needed to say.

"There's something else I want to tell you," Phoebe said. "Remember what I said the day I told you about Lee? About wanting you to come back to Blessings for me? Well, you did that today when it mattered most. No matter how everything else plays out between us, thank you for saving my life."

There was a joy spreading through Aidan that he hadn't felt in years. A weight lifting from his heart. A release of guilt and of regret. "Sweetheart, this may not seem like the time or place, but extenuating circumstances often force big decisions, and today I thought I'd lost you. I have no words for how that made me feel. All I know is that I want a life with you and Lee so bad I ache. Do you still want a life with me?"

Tears rolled down Phoebe's face. "Yes, I want that. It's all I've ever wanted. I just thought you didn't want me."

"Thank you, God," he said and kissed her, and this time she kissed him back. He cupped her face, rubbing a thumb beneath the curve of her bottom lip. "I have a beautiful two-story home in the Garden District of New Orleans just waiting for a family to fill it. Will you marry me? Will you and Lee come live there with me?"

Every sad day of the past twenty years was fading from Phoebe's memory as she thought ahead to the years of waiting joy. "Yes, yes, yes…twenty years' worth of yes."

Weak with relief, he smiled. "The ring will come later. Right now I'll settle for another kiss."

Phoebe wrapped her arms around his neck. All of a sudden she was seventeen again, kissing the boy who loved her.

Lee walked in on that scene and could have wept for joy.

"Want me to go back out and come in again, or can I say how happy that just made me?"

Lee's arrival ended their moment and they pulled away, but they were smiling.

Aidan saw the joy on Lee's face. "It's making me pretty happy, too. I have you, but I need your mom back in my life, too. I asked her to marry me, and she said yes. Do I have your blessing?"

Lee let out a little whoop and began hugging them.

"This is my dream come true...right here...today. Yes, you have my blessing! Now let's get those papers signed and get out of here."

Chapter 15

AFTER THEY LEFT THE HOSPITAL, LEE DROPPED HIS PARENTS off at his granddad's house and went back to their house for clothes. Rain was still coming down but not in the deluge it had been, and the big blue tarp on the roof was a reminder of what had happened. He dreaded going into the house, and it was a fear worth having.

It was as shocking as he expected it to be. The power was off, so he needed a flashlight and knew there was one in his mom's nightstand. He made his way down the hall, splashing in puddles as he went into her bedroom. The flashlight was still there.

He switched it on, shining it over his dad's high school photo, then rounded up a duffel bag and a small suitcase and began to fill them with clothes and toiletries.

He glanced into the kitchen on his way out, swinging the beam of light from one side of the room to the other. It was a sickening sight. He kept thinking of all the meals they'd made in here and all the homework he'd done at the little table while his mom was cooking their supper. His whole life had been lived in this house. He looked up to the big hole in the ceiling and then down to the blackened hole in the floor where the lightning had gone through. It was nothing short of a miracle that his mom had survived this.

He saw her phone lying on the dining room table and tossed it into the bag with her clothes, then gave the little house one last look. They would never live here again. They would have mementos, but this house belonged to their past, and Dad was their future. Lee walked out of the house with a measure of regret but glad he'd had this chance to say goodbye.

As soon as he returned to his granddad's house, he plugged in his mom's phone to see if it worked and saw it taking the charge. She would be relieved. Then he began putting their clothes in the washer in hopes of washing away the smell of smoke. The phone was still charging when he transferred the wash load into the dryer.

Aidan came through the kitchen once to get a bottle of water from the refrigerator and saw Lee kicked back with a bottle of Coke and some cookies, playing a game on his phone.

"Hey, Son, do you need anything?" Aidan asked.

"I'm good. Having myself a snack while I'm waiting for the clothes to dry. They smelled so smoky I knew we wouldn't want to put them on."

Aidan stood there a minute, thinking about what a self-starter Lee was. He saw things that needed to be done and did them without being asked. He was competent and reliable, and he was also smart.

"Your mother raised a good man," Aidan said.

Lee looked up, started to grin, and then realized his dad was serious.

"Thanks, Dad. I know she worked hard to do it. I had rules, and every time I broke one—and yes, I did do that now and again—I got punishment to fit the crime. Not once did I ever get away with it. After a while, I realized I didn't like disappointing her…and then I got old enough— maybe mature enough would be a better phrase—that I didn't like disappointing myself. So, here I am."

"Good job," Aidan said. "Your mom just got out of

the shower and is lying down, resting a bit. I'm going to shower now. We'll deal with supper later, okay?"

"Sure thing, but you need to rest, too. Your eyes still look red, and your voice is raspy. Keep in mind I'm a pretty good cook. When you get hungry, let me know. I'll whip something up for us."

"You rock," Aidan said. "Maybe I will rest after I shower. When those clothes are dry, just bring them up. I'll put them away for her."

Lee gave him a thumbs-up and stuffed another cookie in his mouth.

A half hour later, the buzzer went off on the dryer. Lee folded the clothes and started upstairs, paused at the door to his dad's room, and knocked once.

Aidan came to the door with his finger to his lips and pointed toward the bed. Phoebe was asleep.

"Clean clothes," Lee whispered. "Yell if you need me. Otherwise I'm going to shower and change. Is the third bedroom down the hall okay for me? It's the one I always slept in when I stayed over."

Aidan gave him a thumbs-up and went to hang Phoebe's clothes in the closet as Lee walked away.

It was just after six p.m. when people began to come to the house. Some wanted to donate money to Phoebe to help repair what she'd lost, while others brought food or flowers. Some came not just to check on Phoebe but also to praise Aidan for saving her life, and some just came to shake his hand and welcome him back. For Aidan, it was a kind of redemption, but he wished his dad could be here on the receiving end, too.

It was after eight when people finally stopped coming.

Lee announced he was hungry, and so they went to the kitchen to check out the food they'd been given.

"Oh man, fried chicken," Lee said and then he took the cover off a bowl. "Potato salad," he announced and went to get a spoon.

As they began eating, the conversation shifted to the food they'd get to eat living in New Orleans. When it came time for dessert, Lee wanted a little bit of everything, which consisted of three pies, cupcakes, and brown-sugar bread pudding with caramel sauce.

Phoebe rolled her eyes at the size of his plate while Aidan just grinned.

"Oh…you are now witnessing the symptoms of your son's one affliction," Phoebe drawled. "He has hollow-leg syndrome. It's sad, really. He'll eat the scraps of anything sweet from nearly anyone's plate."

Lee pointed his fork at her. "No fair. I have my own rules about that. I have to know them. They can't be gross, and I have to like them."

Aidan burst out laughing.

Phoebe rolled her eyes. "Don't encourage him. He's pathetic…makes people think I never feed him enough."

Aidan laughed again. "Oh my God…this is what's been missing from my life! Family! Family quirks…family jokes…family ties." Then he leaned forward and scooped a spoonful of the bread pudding off Lee's plate. "Good stuff," he said. "I'm going to have some of that."

"If it's that good, I want some, too," Phoebe said.

"I'll get it for you," Aidan said. "Typical Phoebe-size serving?"

She nodded, pleased that he remembered she loved

sweets but in minimal quantities, and thanked Aidan when he brought her the plate.

"Yummm, good," she said when she took her first bite. "It's the brown sugar instead of granulated that makes such a good difference…and the caramel sauce instead of regular hard caramel doesn't hurt."

"Agreed," Lee said. "Do we know how to make this?"

Phoebe grinned again. "Translated to 'does Mom know how to make this,' and the answer is yes, I do. Does this need to go in the keep-for-Christmas file?"

Lee nodded. "This might be my new favorite dessert, and I'm not kidding."

Aidan reached across the table and patted her hand. "Bee, you are going to be a stellar addition to the menu team at my restaurant!"

She beamed. The idea of working with him in any capacity was exciting. She finished off her dessert, right down to licking the spoon when it was gone.

"Oh my gosh, that was good," Phoebe said.

"I'll clean up," Lee offered.

"I'll help," Aidan said. "Four hands work faster than two. We can freeze part of this and make it last longer, too."

"Don't freeze the bread pudding," Lee said.

Aidan nodded and began clearing the table. When Phoebe stood up to help, he took the dirty plate from her hands and shooed her into the living room.

"Sit here in Granddad's chair, and put your feet up, honey. The remote is on the table beside it." Then he draped an afghan over her legs. "The air-conditioning might make you shiver a bit," he said.

Phoebe grasped his hand. "You make me shiver."

He leaned down, kissed the side of her face beside her lips, then cradled her face. "I love you, Phoebe Ann," he said softly.

"I love you," she said.

"Give me half an hour to help Lee get stuff cleaned up and in the freezer, and then I'll join you."

"I gave you forever to come find me again, and it only took you twenty years. Take your time. I'm not going anywhere."

Aidan was at a loss for words as he leaned down and kissed her. Then he nodded once and hurried back into the kitchen.

After their supper, the evening passed slowly.

Lee was upstairs checking email. A part of him wanted to hear from Lola, but at the same time, he hoped she had not reached out. Goodbye had been hard enough the first time.

Phoebe went upstairs while Aidan was locking up and setting the alarm. She went into the bathroom to brush her teeth and wash her face, then stripped without looking in the mirror and pulled a clean nightgown over her head. She'd washed her hair and lightly combed it when it was wet, but now that it was dry, she wanted to brush it. Only she couldn't see where all the cuts were and didn't want to make anything bleed.

This nightly ritual was something she'd done all her life, but tonight she felt different. She wasn't anxious. This was Aidan. He'd seen her bare body a hundred times, and while it was thinner now, it was the woman she'd become while she'd been waiting, and if he wanted her, this is what he would get.

She walked back into the bedroom and pulled down

the covers. But then she didn't know whether to get in bed or wait, so she sat on the edge of the bed with her legs dangling down, her feet barely touching the floor.

When she heard his footsteps coming up the stairs, her pulse went up a notch. And then she heard him pause, and when the doorknob began to turn, she suddenly stood. Sitting down she felt too vulnerable. Tonight they met halfway.

He walked in without speaking, locking the door behind him and turning out the lights, leaving only the glow from the bathroom night-light by which to see as he began taking off clothes. He walked out of his shoes at the door, stripped off his shirt by the settee, dropped his pants on the floor, peeled out of his briefs in front of her, then reached out and pulled her nightgown up over her head and hung it over the bedpost.

Phoebe shivered. He was so big...bigger than she remembered, and she was smaller, thinner.

He cupped her face and kissed her forehead, then the tip of her nose. When he laid a hand over her heart and felt the wild, frantic rhythm, he sighed. "We know what we're doing here, don't we, Bee?"

She nodded and slid her arms around his waist as she pulled herself closer. Despite the slight changes in their physical bodies, together they felt the same. "We still fit," she said.

He leaned down and picked her up off her feet. "I carried you out of your house today not knowing if you were even alive. Are you okay to do this now? We have the rest of our lives to make love."

Phoebe slid a hand across his chest to where she could feel his heartbeat.

"Yes, I am okay, and I need to do this now. I've been living a half-life ever since you left me. I may need a jump-start, but there's never been anyone for me but you. Make love to me, Aidan. Remind me that I am more than the life I have been living."

The brutal honesty of her words was gutting. Another reminder of what she'd given up to raise their child.

"I'll spend the rest of my life proving you aren't just more, you are my everything," Aidan said.

He laid her down, then eased in beside her and began stirring memories. First with his mouth and then his hands, he lit her up like a firecracker with a short-burning fuse, waited until she started to beg, and slid between her legs.

Three strokes and Phoebe went off in a burst of light so bright she closed her eyes against the glare. There was a roar in her ears, and she was trembling like a virgin, trying to catch her breath when he took her up again. It was just like when they were young, learning together the difference between sex and love.

Hours later, they fell asleep in each other's arms, and soon afterward, it stopped raining.

When they woke, it was to the alarm going off on Aidan's phone.

Aidan rolled over to shut it off and then raised up on one elbow to watch Phoebe waking up. They'd had sex many times in their past, but they'd never slept in a bed the whole night through and never had the pleasure of waking up together. He squinted his eyes, looking past the cuts and bruises to the woman she had become. They'd just taken the first step into a new life.

Phoebe tried to stretch, moaned, then felt the heat

of Aidan's body beside her and remembered. She was smiling when she opened her eyes. She reached out to touch him and sighed. "This is real, isn't it? You're not a dream."

"It's as real as it gets," Aidan said. "This is the best wake-up call I've ever had in my life."

In the bright light of day and after that night of lovemaking, all of Phoebe's normal defense systems were down…maybe off for good.

When Sonja and Joe finally left Blessings, it was in the rainstorm. They knew nothing of what had happened to Phoebe and set their minds to driving straight through to St. Louis without stopping, taking turns driving all through the night while the other slept.

Sonja was driving the last leg home, letting Joe sleep, but she was depressed. Her single reason for going to Blessings was to reconnect with Phoebe and hopefully put herself back in God's good graces, but she had failed. She needed to refocus—do something that would take her mind off her dwindling mortality. And then it occurred to her that she and Joe did not have a will. That was it! Oh my God, that would fix everything!

She glanced at the GPS. Only a half hour longer, and they'd be home. She reached across the console and punched Joe on the arm.

"Joe! Wake up! Wake up!"

Joe shot up in the seat so fast he hit his head on the roof of the car, thinking they were about to crash.

"What's wrong?" he yelled, frantically looking all around them, and saw nothing but the shoulder of the interstate they were on and the lights of passing motorists. "Dammit, Sonja! You scared the shit out of me."

But as usual, Sonja was focused on her agenda, not his thundering heart and lack of sleep.

"We don't have a will. We need to make one and make Phoebe our heir."

Joe rubbed his eyes as he settled back into his seat. "Okay, but where the hell did this come from?"

"If we give everything to Phoebe, God will see our generosity and we'll be forgiven," she said.

He frowned. "You're the one trying to make bargains with God. Me and Him are good."

"Oh, just shut up," Sonja said. "We're doing it anyway. We're making a will and leaving everything to my daughter, who, I remind you, is also your niece."

"Fine," Joe said and then leaned back in the seat again and closed his eyes.

It aggravated Sonja no end that in less than five minutes he was already snoring. She could feel the heat emanating from his body and it pissed her off, so she turned all the air-conditioning vents straight at his face and turned the knob to High.

Within seconds, Joe was awake and fumbling for the air-conditioning settings.

"Leave it alone!" Sonja muttered. "I'm having a hot flash."

"You are over hot flashes, like, nearly ten years ago, remember?" Joe said.

"That is so not the truth," Sonja said and accelerated as if to punctuate her statement.

"Okay then," Joe said, turning all the vents so they were blowing into her face. "Enjoy, and don't pull any more shit. I'm not in the mood to put up with you. Understand?"

"Don't tell me what to do," she said.

"Then stop pretending, Sonja. I like you better when you're the bitch, not the reformed saint."

She started to argue, then stopped. Maybe he was right. She wasn't good at being a saint. Not even a reformed one. But she was still going to have that will drawn up—as insurance—just in case Joe was wrong and she was right.

Moe Randall was awake by daybreak, going through his desk, pulling out papers that would be needed after he died. He found his will, the instructions for his burial, and confirmation that he had named Peanut Butterman executor of his estate, such as it was. He was looking for his address book for family to notify. He had distant cousins in Florida and West Virginia, not that he thought any of them would come. But they did communicate now and then with a card or a call, and he wanted them to know what had happened to him.

He reached all the way to the back of the drawer before he finally felt the raw leather cover beneath his fingers and pulled it out. It had been a while since he'd had occasion to use the book and didn't remember what all he'd kept in there, but when he opened it, a piece of paper fell out. He turned it over, his eyes widening. It was the number to Corey's cell phone. He'd forgotten Corey had ever given it to him. He sat staring at the number with thoughts running through his head. He didn't have any way of knowing if the number was still good, but he had an idea.

He went to get the car keys and headed straight for

the police station. It was a little before nine a.m. when he walked into the lobby and told the dispatcher he needed to speak with the chief.

Avery took him back to Lon's office. When Lon saw Moe, he got up smiling, shook his hand, and escorted him to a chair.

"Good morning, Moe. You're up early this morning."

"I don't sleep so good anymore," Moe said and handed him the piece of paper with the phone number on it. "I found this a few minutes ago, and I had an idea that it might help you corral my boy. Corey gave this to me probably two or three years ago. Forgot I had it. It was the number to his cell phone. I don't even know if the number is good anymore."

"This is very helpful, and I know it wasn't easy for you to bring this in."

Moe shifted nervously in his seat. His voice was shaking, but he was determined to see this through. "If you want him back here and you want him to come in on his own without knowing what's going on, tell him I died."

Lon was startled. He hadn't seen this coming. "You want me to tell him you died?"

"Yes, and don't feel bad about lying to him when you do it. He has done nothing but lie, cheat, and steal his entire adult life. And then there's what I confessed to you to go along with it. Hell yes, lie…I'll look him in the eyes when you lock him up and tell him I'm the one who turned him in, too."

"Yes, that's a good idea, and thank you. This is going to mean a lot to those two families," Lon said.

"You haven't told anyone else about me keeping that secret, have you? I'm asking because I figure at the least

I'll be shunned when everyone finds out, and I accept I'll likely be charged with aiding. Doesn't matter if I die here or in prison, I just want to be prepared."

"No, I haven't talked about it, Moe. I wanted to get Corey into custody first."

Moe nodded. "Alright then. And once he's locked up, I have to confess this to the whole town as well."

Lon didn't argue. He didn't even disagree. It was a hell of a thing to have done.

"We'll keep this between us for now, but if he answers this number and takes the bait, I'll let you know."

Moe's shoulders slumped. "I just want this over with," he said.

Lon felt sorry for the man. He was old. He was sick, and he was dying with a horrible amount of guilt. "Why don't you wait in the lobby? If he answers, I can let you know right now."

Moe shuffled out of the office and back up the hall to the reception area while the chief sat down at the desk and dialed the number.

Corey was just getting out of the shower when his cell phone began to ring, which surprised him. Very few people knew his number, but for the ones who did, he wouldn't ignore the call. He ran into the bedroom and grabbed it from the nightstand and then froze when he saw the caller ID was Blessings PD. How the hell had they gotten this number?

"Hello?"

"This is Chief Pittman from the Blessings Police Department. I need to speak to Corey Randall."

Corey sat down on the side of the bed, buck naked and shaking. "This is Corey."

"Corey, I have some bad news. I'm sorry to inform you that we found your father's body on the front porch of his home this morning. He had been dead for several hours."

The news hit Corey like a fist to the gut. He wasn't surprised, and yet it was the end of one entire aspect of his life.

"Oh man, I can't say I'm surprised. I was just there, and his health was in obvious decline, but I never thought it would be so soon."

"Yes, well, he left his final papers on his desk—the will, deeds to the property, stuff like that. That's where we found your number, too, so it appeared as though he had a premonition of his own passing. There are things that need to be dealt with. Setting up the funeral services, that kind of thing. When can we tell the funeral director to expect you?"

Corey glanced at the clock. "I'm in Florida. It will likely take all day at least…maybe longer. Regardless, I'll be there in the morning."

"Okay…see you then," the chief said. "I'll pass along the information, and when you get to town, stop by the station first. I have some papers for you to sign, and then I'll turn over the personal belongings that were on your father's person…his wallet, house keys, stuff like that, and again, I am so sorry for your loss."

"Thank you," Corey said and then disconnected.

He felt something running down the front of his leg and looked, expecting some kind of bug, but it was just water from the shower. He swiped at it with the towel he was holding and then got up and went back inside the bathroom to finish drying.

There was a weird feeling in his chest, not unlike the first time he'd been sent to prison. That had been a fifteen-month sentence that ended at six months, with the rest spent on probation. He'd been scared to death of what would happen to him in there, but as it turned out, it wasn't much different than what he had to deal with on the streets.

Only this knot had no release date and no parole. The last words he and his father had said to each other were loud and ugly. There was no way to apologize. Another regret he would have to live with.

Corey got dressed, tossed his things back into his bag, left his room key on the nightstand, and drove out of the parking lot. Before he left town, he stopped for breakfast. The eggs and bacon were good enough, but he didn't taste them. He was remembering instead the cereal he and his dad had shared the other morning in total silence.

But there was a bright side to this news as he headed back to Georgia. The house would be his, and he was wondering if his dad had left him any money. Maybe he could get a job there in Blessings. It was something to consider, but he wouldn't know where he stood until he got back.

—◦◦◦—

Lon disconnected from the phone call and then walked up front.

Moe was sitting in a chair listening to Avery dispatching an officer to a call when he saw Lon approaching. His gaze shifted to the look on the chief's face. Then Lon gave him a thumbs-up. "Corey will be here in the morning. I told him to come to the office first to pick up your personal belongings and the keys to the house."

Moe stood and shook Lon's hand. "Thank you for helping me do the right thing. Let me know when he shows up. I need to be face-to-face with him when he finds out what I've done."

Lon nodded. "I will."

Moe moved slowly to the door and left the station.

Avery glanced up. "One of our park joggers just called in to report a drunk asleep beneath the flagpole and when Deputy Ralph went to arrest him, he started a fight."

Lon shifted focus. "I'll be on the scene," he said and went back to his office to get his hat before going out the back way to his cruiser.

Aidan was in the kitchen making coffee when the phone rang. He pressed Start on the coffee maker and then picked up the receiver.

"Hello?"

"Aidan, this is Chief Pittman. Hope I'm not calling too early. I wanted to check in and see how you both are."

"We're doing well. Definitely counting our blessings," Aidan said.

"That's good to hear," Lon said. "Look, I know this may seem like an odd request, but I would like to know if you and Phoebe would be available to come by the station tomorrow morning."

"Yes, we can, but why?"

But Lon didn't want to give anything away or get hopes up in case Corey Randall blew them off and didn't show. "It has to do with tying up some loose ends from the past, and that's all I can say about it at this time."

All of a sudden Aidan was remembering Elliot

Graham's strange warning about the truth of Marty Ritter's death coming to light. "Yes, we can do that. Just tell us what time."

"Um, that's a little iffy right now, but could you be ready around eight in the morning just to be on the safe side? I ask because when I do call, I will need you to get here as fast as possible," Lon said.

"Yes. We'll be ready and waiting for your call," Aidan said.

"Thank you. You won't be sorry you came, I can promise you that."

"Is it okay for Lee to come, too?" Aidan asked.

"Yes, of course. This indirectly concerns him, too. Just wait for my call."

"Will do," Aidan said and hung up.

"What's going on?" Phoebe asked as she and Lee walked into the kitchen.

"I'm not sure. That was Chief Pittman on the phone. His call was kind of vague, but the bottom line is sometime early tomorrow, like around eight a.m., the chief is going to give us a call, and when he does, we have to get to the station as fast as possible."

"But why?" Lee asked.

"He wouldn't say, but I'm thinking back to that weird warning Elliot Graham gave me. If he knows what he's talking about, it might have something to do with your dad's death."

Phoebe gasped. "Are you serious? Does the chief finally have a lead on who set that fire?"

"I don't know," Aidan said. "We'll find out tomorrow."

Corey Randall was on his way home to Georgia, and for the first time in years, he had hopes for a new start. Too bad it had come at the cost of his father's life. He had no job skills to speak of and couldn't imagine what kind of work he'd find in Blessings, but he'd figure it out as he went along. He'd wasted a lot of years he couldn't take back, but shit happened. The way he looked at it, his ship had finally come in.

Moe Randall felt every day of his seventy-one years and then some as he walked back into his house. There were things he'd planned to do today, but now that the trap had been set for Corey, he didn't feel like doing any of them. Instead, he settled into his recliner to watch some television. He dreaded tomorrow. The people of Blessings would shun him, of that he was sure. He could handle that, but he was scared of facing God. He had never considered George Payne as just a boss. He'd thought of him as family, and then he had betrayed George in the most horrible of ways.

He kicked back, lifted the footrest, and then used the remote to flip to one of the channels that aired TV classics and closed his eyes. The canned laughter from an old *I Love Lucy* episode wrapped around him like a hug. Roberta loved this show, reruns and all.

"Is it loud enough for you, honey?" he murmured and then upped the volume. "There you go…your favorite show."

Chapter 16

AFTER BREAKFAST, LEE WENT TO THE LIBRARY, HEADING FOR the bookshelves to get one of his granddad's favorite books. He'd read it many times before, but he was missing him so much, and this was one way he could visit him again.

He found the book, then went to the big leather recliner near the window and settled in. It smelled a bit of the cigars Preston liked to smoke. Lee rubbed his hand over the old book jacket like he was saying hello, then glanced at the title.

On the Road.

He opened the book to the first page and began to read. "I first met Dean…"

He sighed and settled back a little farther, ready to take the trip once again with Jack Kerouac's prose. He could almost hear his granddad's voice reading the words aloud, just like he had the first time he took Lee on the journey.

The day passed with Aidan winding up even more of Preston's affairs and talking to the bank president, Carl Buckley, about the possibility of finding someone interested in purchasing Preston's business as well as getting recommendations for someone capable of managing the rental properties.

"I'll send out some feelers, and if I get any hits, I'll tell the interested parties to contact you. How's that?" Carl asked.

"Thank you," Aidan said and shook his hand before leaving.

A few doors down from the bank, Myra Franklin was on the phone, waiting for Sonja to answer her call. Just when she thought it was going to voicemail, Sonja finally answered, and she sounded impatient.

"Hello."

"Hi, Sonja, it's me, Myra."

"I know who it is. What do you want? I'm rather busy."

Myra frowned. "Too busy to hear about your daughter's house being struck by lightning and catching on fire with her in it?"

Myra was satisfied by the gasp she heard but disappointed by Sonja's response. "Is she alive?"

"Yes, she is," Myra said.

"Was she burned?"

"No, because Aidan Payne ran into the burning house and saved her life."

"Of course he did," Sonja muttered. "Thank you for calling," she said and disconnected in Myra's ear.

"Well, I never! She always was a hateful child," Myra muttered and dropped her cell phone back into the pocket of her smock.

Conversation at the evening meal consisted of Lee asking Aidan what Mardi Gras was like, whether he ever attended blues performances, and whether he had a housekeeper.

Phoebe's questions leaned more toward his circle of friends. Aidan could tell she was nervous about fitting in. Finally, he laughed and told her this was just like Christmas. She was simply going to have to wait and see.

"That is not an answer," Phoebe said as she got up to go refill her glass.

But when Aidan took the glass out of her hands and pulled her down onto his lap, Lee chuckled.

"And…that's my cue to retire for the night," he said and took his bowl of ice cream with him as left the room.

"Aw man, I didn't mean to embarrass him," Aidan said.

"Trust me. He wasn't embarrassed," Phoebe said. "He just got himself out of doing dishes with that move."

"Good lord, he *is* a character, isn't he?"

"Yes, and about that question you refuse to answer," she said.

"Honey…it's not a refusal. I just can't answer for you. Everything will be new, yes, but it will be your experiences and judgments, just like the ones I had to make when Dad and I first moved there. You're going to be fine. They're all going to love you and Lee. You'll see."

Phoebe sighed. "Okay…I get it."

Aidan hugged her, then whispered in her ear, "What's it worth to you if I do the dishes?"

Her eyebrows arched. "Are you coming on to me, mister?"

"I'm sure as hell trying to," he said.

She whispered against his ear, "You get whatever you want."

He grinned. "You know that big old claw-foot tub in the master bathroom?"

Her eyes widened. "I know I would fit, but are you sure the two of us could get in there together?"

He ran a finger down the valley between her breasts. "If you sit on my lap, I'm absolutely positive you will."

She shivered just thinking about it. "We'll likely make a horrible mess."

"I'll bring a mop up with me," he said.

Phoebe laughed and then leaned into his hug and kissed him. "Then I say you have a deal."

"Hot damn," Aidan said, dumped her out of his lap, and started gathering up the dirty dishes.

He could still hear her laughter as she was walking up the stairs, and when he got to their room later, he could hear the water running in the tub. He heard the water go off as he locked the bedroom door and stripped, hoping to make a good impression as he walked into the bathroom carrying the mop.

The tub was full of bubbles, and all he could see of Phoebe was her head and neck.

He grinned. "Bubbles?"

"You better park that mop and join me. But be careful when you step in. Everything, including me, is so very, very slick, slick, slick."

He grunted as she rose up from the bubbles like an underwater goddess coming up from the sea.

"HavemercythankyouLordHolyMaryMotherofGod."

"You're not Catholic," Phoebe said.

"Just covering all the bases," Aidan said.

She eyed his magnificent body, thinking of them

together, and shivered. "Oh, I'm counting on a home run before we get rained out."

They mopped twice before the water got cold, at which point Aidan took her to bed and made love to her again, proving he was just as good dry as she was wet.

———◦◦◦———

When the alarm went off at six a.m., Phoebe started to roll over and turn it off only to find herself pinned beneath one very strong arm and one exceedingly long leg.

"I'll get that," Aidan mumbled but didn't move.

Phoebe laughed. "I'm thinking we have to hurry this morning, don't we?"

Aidan rolled over, shut off the alarm, and sat up. "I almost forgot. Yes, we do. I don't know what's going on, but I have a really good feeling about it, and while I'm thinking about it, I need you to know how much I love you. You are an amazing woman. Therefore you get first dibs on the bathroom."

"I was in the water so long last night I could skip baths for a week. However, I won't."

He laughed, and kissed the hollow of her neck, then groaned. "Go before you make me lose my mind again."

Phoebe smiled. "It won't take me long, but I'm going to need a little help brushing my hair. I can't see where the butterfly bandages are, and I don't want to make anything bleed," she said and eased herself gently out of bed.

He frowned. "I'll brush it for you, Bee, but are you okay? You're moving like you're in pain."

She looked over her shoulder. "I'm fine, but I do feel like a roof fell on me. I can't imagine what's wrong."

Then she went into the bathroom, shutting the door behind her. She could still hear him chuckling as she looked at herself in the mirror. Bruises were shining. Little cuts were beginning to scab. Then she shook her head at her reflection.

"Good morning, Phoebe Ann. You look like you've been rode hard and put up wet. Might have to put on more than a little lipstick today."

And then she began to hustle. She didn't want to make them late.

Moe was up, showered, shaved, and dressed in his Sunday clothes, eating a bowl of Cheerios while waiting for Chief Pittman to call, unaware his son was just driving into Blessings.

Aidan, Phoebe, and Lee were ready and on edge as they finished their breakfast, anxious to find out what was going on at the police station that would require their presence.

Unaware of the waiting hell he was driving into, Corey Randall drove straight down Main to the police station and parked.

Avery was already on dispatch duty and per the chief's instructions had been watching for Corey's arrival. When he saw him drive up, he buzzed the chief.

Lon picked up. "Chief Pittman."

"He's here, Chief. Pulling up front right now. Want me to send him back?"

"Tell him I'm taking a long-distance call and have him sit. I'll be up shortly."

"Yes, sir," Avery said.

Lon made a call to Moe, who answered on the first ring. "Hello."

Moe's voice was shaky. Lon didn't know if it was from his illness or from what was about to happen.

"Moe, this is Chief Pittman. He's here. Are you okay to come down?"

"Yes. On my way," Moe said and hung up.

The chief had one more call to make, this time to Aidan Payne.

Aidan answered. "Hello?"

"Good morning, Aidan. Chief Pittman here. I need you here now."

"We're on the way," Aidan said and hung up. "That's our call. Head for the door."

The air was already hot and steamy as they filed out of the house to the truck—a promise of the day to come. Lee helped Phoebe into the passenger seat then jumped in the back as Aidan slid behind the wheel. They sped through the neighborhood, heading for the police station as fast as they dared drive.

Chief Pittman sat for a couple of minutes, trying to give Moe enough time to arrive, and then went up the hall.

Corey stood as soon as he saw the chief. "Thank you for calling me about this," Corey said.

"Part of the job, but one I'd rather do without," Lon said, then glanced at his dispatcher. "Avery, make sure one of my officers stops by here shortly. I'm going to be needing him later."

Avery knew what that meant and nodded. "Will do, Chief."

Then Lon smiled at Corey. "Follow me. I have the paperwork ready."

Corey straightened his shoulders from the usual slump he favored and followed the chief to his office.

"Have a seat," Lon said and motioned to a chair close to his desk.

Corey sat, eyeing the file on the chief's desk. He saw a ring of keys and a manila envelope with objects inside, likely his dad's wallet and pocket change.

"Bear with me," Lon said. "There are priorities to this, so I'll begin with his personal belongings. I have an itemized list that I want you to look over, and then we'll go through what was on his person, making sure it's all there."

He handed Corey a sheet of paper with a list, hoping Moe would get there soon.

And Moe arrived less than two minutes later. "The chief is expecting me," he said to Avery.

"Yes, sir, but we're waiting on two more people. As soon as they get here we can—"

Aidan walked in holding Phoebe's hand, with Lee only steps behind. He frowned, puzzled by Moe Randall's presence.

Avery stood. "Follow me, all of you. Don't talk, just walk, and when you get to the chief's office, again, do only what he says. You'll understand what's happening soon enough."

Then Avery took off down the hall with them following him in silence.

When Lon saw them coming, he stood up.

Corey saw the chief stand and turned around to see what was going on. When he saw his father coming into the room, he almost fell out of the chair in an effort to get up. But it wasn't until he saw all the people coming in behind him that he felt the ground going out from under him.

"What the hell? What the fuckin' hell?" Corey screamed, then turned on the chief. "If this is your idea of a joke, I'm not laughing!"

"Sit down and shut up," Moe said. "It wasn't his idea, it was mine."

Corey dropped back into the chair. His head was spinning with possibilities but still had not grasped the full meaning of the situation.

Lon heard the back door to the precinct open and then footsteps running up the hall. Seconds later, Deputy Ralph was in the room, shutting the door behind him.

Aidan put his arm around Phoebe and pulled her close. Lee was standing behind both of them, at a loss as to what was going on. Then Lon suddenly grabbed Corey's arm, and before Corey knew what was happening, he'd been shoved face-first against a wall, handcuffed, and dropped back into the chair he'd just vacated.

Corey groaned. This had to be about the Mazda or the robbery…maybe both. Shit. He'd been tricked into coming back and walked straight into a trap, but what the hell did all these other people have to do with anything?

Lon pointed to the onlookers.

"Everyone…take a seat. Deputy, please stand guard at the door. No one else comes in or goes out until I say so."

"Yes, sir," Ralph said.

Corey was just resigning himself to another stint in jail when his dad started talking.

Moe sat down, afraid he would pass out if he did

not, then grabbed onto the armrests and leaned forward, looking straight at Corey.

"Every one of us here is connected because of something you did."

And that's when Corey got it. Phoebe Ritter. Aidan Payne. Paynes and Ritters, all connected to the Ritter who'd died.

Corey looked at his father in disbelief. "No. No. You can't do this. You swore you wouldn't! I'm your son!"

Moe just shook his head. "I've already done it. I'm not dying with your sins on my conscience. I gave a statement to Chief Pittman. I told the chief everything about what you did. He has it all on video in case I die before you go to trial."

Corey's mouth opened. He began shaking his head as reality surfaced. "You didn't! You couldn't! Why, Daddy, why?"

"Yes, I did," Moe said. "Twenty years ago, I lied for you because a man died and I didn't want you to go to jail. And then the lie grew into a big ugly thing I didn't know how to stop. I lied because you were just a boy. I lied because you were my son. It didn't seem to bother you, because you didn't show remorse. You just kept walking in that dark life, taking things that didn't belong to you, stealing other people's money without a hitch to your conscience, while that secret festered in me and turned into cancer. I will die for keeping quiet about your sins, and it is no more than I deserve."

Corey threw his head back, screaming in rage.

When Aidan heard Moe's confession, he lost all color in his face, and when he turned loose of Phoebe, she grabbed him to keep him from charging forward. They

looked at Corey, and then at each other, wanting to wail
at the price they'd all paid for Moe Randall's secret.

Lon had the arrest warrant in front of him. "Corey
Randall, you are under arrest for one count of attempted
robbery of Payne's Auto Supply and for one count of
arson. That's when you set the place on fire as you tried
to blow up the safe. And for one count of second-degree
murder in the death of Marty A. Ritter."

Then he began to read Corey his rights. The chief's
words had turned into a roar inside Corey's head. He
looked at his father and the cold look of contempt on
his face and then at Aidan and Phoebe. They'd all been
in school together and once had been friends before life
took them in different directions. The horror on Phoebe's
face and the rage on Aidan's were something he'd never
forget. He closed his eyes and dropped his head. His life
had just come to an end. Who would have guessed that
when he came back to bury his father, his father would
bury him instead? For all intents and purposes, his life
was over.

The chief pulled him up from the chair and handed
him over to the deputy.

"Lock him up. I'll be back there shortly to help you
book him into jail," the chief said.

"Yes, sir," Ralph said, and he took Corey by the arm
and led him out of the office.

Phoebe couldn't wrap her head around what was
going on.

"I don't understand, Moe. You kept quiet all these
years. Did you know he was going to do it?"

"Of course not," Moe said. "George Payne was my
friend. I did not know my son was planning a robbery. I

didn't even know he'd done it until late the next morning when I went into his room and saw the burns on his arms and his charred clothing."

Now Phoebe was shaking with frustration and anger. "But you still stayed quiet about how my daddy died. You were his friend and you stayed silent about what your son did, and let the people in Blessings persecute Aidan's dad."

His shoulders slumped even more. "I know, but I thought after it was proven George was innocent it would stop, and it did not. I accept my guilt." Then Moe turned to face Aidan. He saw anger and could not blame him. "I accept your condemnation. I deserve whatever it is you need to say to me. Your father was my friend, and I let an entire town persecute him just to save my son."

Aidan was so angry he was shaking, and then he felt Phoebe thread her fingers through his and caught a glimpse of his son at his side. Was revenge the answer, and if it was, was it something he wanted his son to see?

He took a slow, steady breath, and as he did, he remembered Elliot's warning. It was Aidan's task to make sure the town of Blessings did not persecute another man as it had once done his dad. Now he understood what that meant. If he raised hell now, everyone would know, and Moe Randall's last days on earth would be torture. He didn't want that on his conscience.

He patted Phoebe's hand, then wiped a shaky hand across his face and reached out to Moe. They were standing face-to-face now. Aidan could smell the death waiting for Moe, the same way it had been with his mother. He saw abject terror in the old man's eyes. It didn't feel good to know this old man was afraid—of him. But instead of striking him, he put his arms around him.

The old man was trembling so hard he could barely stand. "I'm sorry, Aidan. I'm so damn sorry," Moe whispered.

"It's okay, Moe. What you did you did out of love, not revenge. Every one of us in here made horrible mistakes during that time, and they were things we couldn't take back either. But one thing remained when everything was over. One thing I didn't even know I had. A piece of Marty still lives on in Phoebe's son. My son. I don't want him to be a part of hate, even as a bystander. Hate changes who you're meant to be, and I don't want Lee Ritter to be changed in any way because he's perfect as he stands."

Aidan glanced at the chief. "I'm going to ask if you could just release the news of the arrest by stating that the mystery of what happened to Marty Ritter has been solved. Tell the people of Blessings that Moe Randall found out about his son's guilt and came forward with the truth, and I will support that release."

"I will too," Phoebe said.

Lee couldn't see for tears, but his father's words and the heroic gesture it had taken to forgive a dying man wrapped around him like a warm hug on a cold night.

"Can this happen, Chief, or do you intend to arrest Moe, too?" Aidan asked.

Lon sighed. "I can't lie to the district attorney, but there are certainly extenuating circumstances, and I will relate everyone's wishes as well while reminding him that it was Moe's testimony that brought an end to a cold case."

Moe kept patting Aidan's arm and shaking his head. "I never expected this. I did not see this coming. I am humbled by your gentle heart, Aidan Payne. And you, Phoebe...it breaks my heart to know my son was responsible for taking your father's life. I know what it cost you, and I am so sorry."

Phoebe took a deep breath. Regardless of the circumstances, Moe did not have a part in the theft, or the accident that started the fire. His only mistake was staying silent about what he knew.

"Apology accepted," Phoebe said.

Then Moe turned to the chief. "Well, sir, you know where to find me."

Aidan thought of his father, wishing to God he had lived to witness this, and then let the thought go. The past belonged in the past. He turned around and walked into his family's arms.

"I'm glad it has all worked out," Lon told them. "Go home and get some rest now. You deserve it."

He escorted them to the lobby and then hurried back to help his deputy book Corey Randall into jail. After he sent Deputy Ralph back out on patrol, he put in a call to the DA, informing him that the warrants had been served and explaining what had been requested regarding Moe Randall. Then he closed the door to his office and called his wife. After knowing of the ugliness that had gone on in their lives, he had a sudden need to hear the sound of her sweet voice.

Chapter 17

DAN AMOS WORE SLACKS AND SHIRTS WITH BUTTON-DOWN collars at the office, but his off-duty clothes usually consisted of rodeo gear. Well-worn Justin boots, comfortable Levi's, his daddy's old gray Stetson, and a belt with his granddaddy's World Champion Bull Rider buckle. The big shiny buckle made a statement riding just below Dan's navel, as did the long scar across his right cheek. He glanced in the mirror, finger-combed the black hair away from his face, and then carried the packed toiletry bag into his bedroom and added it to his suitcase.

He had a phone number and directions to his next job, which would be in a town called Blessings, about an hour from Savannah. He'd worked for Business Temp Enterprises for almost two years now and knew they should have already notified the employer he was coming, but on the off chance someone dropped the ball at BT—and it wouldn't be the first time—he was making his own call, too. He picked up the info BT had given him, sat down on the corner of the bed, and called the number.

Betty Purejoy had just finished the worst breakfast of her life—lukewarm coffee, unsalted oatmeal with no sugar packets, and skim milk to pour on the cereal. She'd already fussed at the nurse for the menu.

"Who cooks this stuff?" Betty asked when the nurse came back to pick up the tray.

"Why, didn't you like it?" the nurse asked.

"No, I didn't like it. Just because I busted my mouth and loosened a couple teeth doesn't mean they had to send me water and gruel."

The nurse laughed.

Betty didn't. She felt awful, and she missed Jack. Last night was the first time in thirty-six years that she'd slept alone. Even when they were mad at each other, they still crawled into bed and cuddled up.

She took a deep breath and then slowly exhaled. There was no sense in having a fit about the food when the real reason she was so upset was that she hurt and was thinking about the temp who would be coming, hoping it was someone capable enough to do the job. She didn't want anything going out of the Butterman Law Office that wasn't perfect.

She closed her eyes and was about half asleep when her cell phone began to ring. She reached over the bedrail to pick it up.

"Hello, this is Betty."

"Hello, Betty. This is Dan Amos from Business Temp out of Savannah."

Betty raised the head of her bed. "Oh, hello, Dan. Glad to hear from you. I guess Mr. Butterman called, explaining what our needs are right now."

"Yes, ma'am. You were in a wreck and need help keeping up with paperwork until you're well enough to return to the law office, is that correct?"

"Yes. The temp will need to be up to speed on typing and filing legal documents. Do you have someone with those skills?"

Dan suddenly realized that BT had not called her after they'd assigned him to the job. "Oh, I am the someone who's coming to help," Dan said. "Sorry. I assumed BT had already called you."

"Oh…well…and I just assumed it wouldn't be a man, and that sounds very sexist. I'm sorry, too."

Dan chuckled.

Betty liked the sound of his laugh. "Maybe we can start over now," she said. "Are you coming today?"

"Yes, ma'am."

"Are you driving back and forth every day, or do you need a place to stay? Because I can recommend the bed-and-breakfast here."

"Thank you, but I have the address of a place to stay. I'm told it belongs to Mrs. Butterman. I'm to get the key from a woman named Lovey Cooper at a café called Granny's Country Kitchen, so I'll give you another call after I get settled."

So Ruby was letting the temp stay in her little house! Betty was filing all that information in her news-to-be-passed-on as opposed to her news-she-kept-to-herself.

"I'll have my husband meet you at Granny's with the office key and a list of things that need to be done. The most pressing ones are at the top of the list. Call as soon as you get into the office, and I'll give you passwords and tell you where everything is."

"Will do," Dan said, "and I'm sorry about the accident. Feel better soon."

He dropped the phone in his shirt pocket, grabbed his keys, and headed out the door.

—◠◠—

Phoebe was sitting in the front seat beside Aidan, trying to absorb everything that had happened in the chief's office, when she thought about the Piggly Wiggly.

"Before we go home, take me by the store. I need to make sure they were able to get a sub for me today."

Aidan reached across the seat and gave her hand a soft squeeze.

"Phoebe, honey…you don't need to do that."

Phoebe frowned. "But why not? If she didn't show, then I don't want the bosses to blame me for the short-age. I need that job. It's all that I know how to do and—"

"No, you're not hearing me," Aidan said. "If you want to go by the store, I'll gladly take you, but you have the option to tell him you're quitting. You don't have to do that job again as long as you live. Not here and not in New Orleans either. Mimosa is one of the best restaurants in the city. We have reservations booked weeks in advance. You can forget about clip-ping coupons and getting up to alarm clocks. You've been taking care of yourself and Lee for so long, please give me the honor of stepping into your shoes. Let me baby you now."

Phoebe's eyes widened, and then she looked in the back seat at Lee. He was grinning.

"Wow, Lee! Can you believe it? No more days when chickens go on sale and me coming home smelling like that pink runny juice seeping out of the packaging. No more smelling like the deli!" She started laughing, and then she cried, and then it turned into laughter again. "Yes, take me by the store. I need to tell Wilson that all the Piggly Wiggly T-shirts smell like smoke, but as soon as I get them washed, I'll be turning them in."

Lee let out a little whoop, but it was Aidan who suddenly felt like a king.

"Thank you, Aidan, thank you!" Phoebe cried.

He grinned. "You ain't seen nothin' yet. I have way more to offer than just this hunky body."

Lee burst out laughing, while Phoebe turned red. "Oh man, Dad! That's perfect. I need to remember that…for future reference, of course. Right now, a hunky body *is* all I have to offer."

They were all still laughing when Aidan pulled up to the store to let her out. "Want me to go in with you?" he asked.

"Thank you, but no. I got this job by myself. I'm gonna end it by myself."

"You go, Mom," Lee said.

Aidan leaned across the console and kissed her. "Yeah…you go, Mom."

Phoebe got out, lifted her chin, and walked into the store—cuts, scrapes, bruises, and all.

Lee leaned forward between the bucket seats, watching her go.

"She's something else, isn't she, Dad? For as long as I've been alive, I have never seen her back down from anything. She told me once that she lost you because she let her family bully her, and that she'd never let that happen again. I was never supposed to be angry you weren't with us because it was her fault you were gone."

Aidan's heart hurt just hearing that. "And now you know that's not entirely true. The best part is that this time when I leave, I'm taking my family with me."

—―∾∾―—

Everyone in the front of the store, customers and employees alike, saw Phoebe come in. There was instant pandemonium at seeing her upright and walking after surviving the lightning strike and the fire.

Everyone started talking at once, and she spent a good ten minutes trying to get to the office. Finally, she called a halt.

"Guys…thank you. I'm really happy I'm still alive, too, and, yes, Aidan Payne is one hundred percent my hero. I need to talk to the boss right now."

"Tell him you need a whole week off," Millie said as everyone began to scatter.

Phoebe winked. "I'm taking more than that."

Millie gasped. "Are you quitting?"

"I need to talk to Wilson," she said.

Millie stepped in front of her. "Did Aidan ask you to marry him?"

Phoebe laughed. "Move, Millie. I have stuff to do here."

Millie lowered her voice. "Oh, my sweet lord! You're moving away. Take me with you."

Phoebe threw her arms around the woman. "You couldn't leave your grandkids if you tried. Now hush and let me go quit my job in private."

Millie squealed.

"Hush now," Phoebe said.

Millie did a little dance step on her way back to her register.

"What's going on?" Trish asked.

"Tell you later," Millie said and then pulled herself together as a shopper started unloading groceries at her register.

Wilson was waiting on a customer when Phoebe

walked up, so she just got in line behind him and waited. She knew Wilson had seen her come in. He would have had to be blind to miss her entrance. And she knew in her heart that quitting would make him sad. He'd tried for a really long time to take her out, and this would be her final no.

Finally the man in front of her left.

Wilson leaned across the counter. "You are the Unsinkable Molly Brown of Blessings, aren't you, girl?"

Phoebe smiled. "I can see why you might think that. I need to talk to you…about work."

Wilson sighed. "First I want to say how very glad I am that you survived all that. And then I want to add how much I appreciate your gentle heart in not breaking mine. You managed to stay my friend even though I bugged the heck out of you to date me far past the time of being polite."

Phoebe's eyes filled with tears. He already knew, but she let him continue.

"And last…I wasn't here when you were hired, but it would be my honor to hear you say what you came to say…and with a grin, please."

She wiped her eyes. "Boss, I can't say it's been fun, but it was certainly appreciated. However, I came to tell you that I quit."

Wilson sighed, then extended his hand across the counter. Phoebe offered her left hand, and he shook it.

"Thank you for your service, and it has been a pleasure to know you. Where should I mail your last check?"

"I'll still be in town for a bit. I'll come pick it up like always and bring back the clean Piggly Wiggly shirts with it. Right now they smell like smoke."

He nodded. "Alright then. See you in the cookie aisle."

Phoebe turned on one heel and walked out.

"Finally," Lee said when he saw her coming out the door.

But Aidan laughed. "Look at her! That smile on her face is a mile wide."

"She's free, Dad. That's what it is. She's finally free."

———

Dan Amos arrived in Blessings before noon, found Granny's café on Main Street, put his Stetson on as he got out, and went to find Lovey Cooper. There was no one manning the cash register and only a few customers, so he flagged down a passing waitress.

"Miss, I need to speak to Lovey Cooper. Is she here?"

Della had lived in Blessings all her life, and she couldn't remember seeing a real cowboy come into Granny's even once. This one was a heartbreaker.

"Yes, she's here. I'll go get her," Della said and flashed him a quick smile.

"I thank you," Dan said and touched a finger to the brim of his hat.

Della scurried into the kitchen, fanning herself with a napkin as she went.

"Lovey! Lovey!" she hissed. "There's a cowboy in the dining room who wants to talk to you, and oh my lord...hold onto your britches 'cause he looks like the kind of man who could talk you out of 'em real quick."

Lovey's eyes widened. "What does he want?"

"You!" Della whispered.

"Oh, for the love of Pete, Della. Get yourself back to work," Lovey said and then rolled her eyes at Mercy, who was standing there with a big grin on her face. "So, we're cutting the meeting short, but I say yes to trying out a cold dessert on the menu since it's so dang hot outside."

Mercy nodded. "So, since Blessings holds the Peachy Keen Queen contest every year, how about the peach cheesecake I was telling you about?"

Lovey slapped her hands together in delight. "I love it. You do your thing, girl. I guess I better hitch up my drawers and go see what this cowboy wants."

Lovey exited the kitchen and saw the stranger standing in the middle of the room like he owned the place. Then he smiled at her, and her heart skipped at least a couple of beats. Dear lord, even with that scar on his face, he was a knockout. He reminded her of her second husband—or was it her third? He was a piece of work, for sure.

"You wanted to see me?" Lovey asked.

Dan took off his hat. "Yes, ma'am. I'm Dan Amos, the temp who's gonna work for Betty Purejoy until she's well. I'm supposed to get a key to Mrs. Butterman's empty house from you."

Lovey's mouth fell open, but her thoughts were still trying to connect.

"Yes, Ruby called me. I've got the key. You're the temp?"

"Yes, ma'am," Dan said.

"You type and file?" Lovey asked.

Dan grinned. "Among other things."

It was the glint in his eyes that ended Lovey's questions. She wasn't sure what other things he did that she ought to know. She pulled the key from her pocket and handed it over.

"Do you know where to go?" she asked.

"I have the address, and Gertie Pearl Sala will get me there."

Lovey blinked. "You brought a woman with you?"

Dan threw back his head and laughed, and Lovey's hand instinctively went to her waist to hold onto her drawers. It was her third husband, for sure.

"No, ma'am, Gertie Pearl Sala is my GPS. I just named her…like some people name their cars."

"That's real clever," Lovey said. "I detect an accent… but not exactly Southern. Where are you from, if I may ask?"

"I'm from Texas by way of Savannah. Raised in Texas. Been living in Savannah for a while now. I'm going to get settled in the house and then come back here for lunch before I go to the office. Really nice meeting you, and I'm guessing from the wonderful aromas coming out of your kitchen that we'll be meeting again."

He tipped his hat and left Lovey standing, her mouth still a bit slack as she watched him walk out.

"You're drooling," Della whispered as she passed Lovey with an order.

Lovey sighed. "Not really, but I thought about it."

———

Aidan loaded Lee up with paint and equipment and sent him to the next empty rental house to begin painting. Lee was happy to have something productive to do, and Aidan was grateful he was so reliable. As soon as Lee was gone, he went back into the house in search of Phoebe. He found her in the kitchen making a list and stroked the back of her hair as he sat down beside her.

"What are you doing, honey?"

"Making a list of things that have to be done at the house. I need to call the insurance agent first and let him see the extent of the damage. The power is off, so I need to get the frozen food out of the freezer today. The food in the refrigerator will have to be thrown out, and then I need to get our clothes and launder everything."

"Well, you can call the insurance agent, and I'll go with you to move the frozen food and empty the refrigerator for you. That won't take long."

She sighed as she leaned her head against his shoulder. "You are going to spoil me, aren't you?"

He tilted her chin so they were looking eye to eye. "I am going to do my damnedest. I so love the woman you have become."

Phoebe leaned into the kiss. God how she loved him.

Aidan reluctantly pulled away from the sweetness and got down to business.

"I have garbage bags here. Do we need to take them with us?"

"No, I have pl—" She stopped. "I *had* plenty. They might have burned. Yes, to be safe, we should take some of yours."

"I'll get the box," he said.

Phoebe looked back at the list, then Googled the number of her insurance office and made the call. By the time Aidan was back, she'd finished her call. The agent had already heard about the fire and contacted an adjustor. He commiserated with her about what had happened and what a fortunate woman she was for surviving it. He told her the adjustor would call her and set up a time for inspection, and they'd go from there.

"Well, the insurance call is off the list," she said.

"Now I wait for the adjustor to call so we can make an appointment for him to see the damage."

"You want to go empty the refrigerator now?" he asked.

"Yes. The longer I wait, the bigger of a mess it will be in this heat."

"Right," Aidan said, then eyed her shoes. "When we get there, if you have older shoes, you might want to change."

"Good idea. I will." She got her purse off the side-board and followed Aidan out of the house.

Elliot Graham waved at them from his front yard as they exited the house.

They waved back, and Aidan added a thumbs-up.

The old man nodded and smiled like he already knew what had gone down.

Aidan suspected Elliot was the real deal. If that was true and he lived in New Orleans, he'd have people lined up at his door for readings. But he was in Blessings, living a calm, quiet life, obviously the way he liked it.

Aidan and Phoebe drove in comfortable silence, with Aidan occasionally commenting on who used to live in a certain house and asking where they were now. He didn't think about the fact that Phoebe hadn't seen the damage to her home until they turned the corner and drove down the block.

All of a sudden she gasped and then moaned. "Oh my God! Oh my God! The roof. Someone put a tarp on the roof. Is the hole that large? And the kitchen windows are black."

"Ah, Bee, I didn't think. I'm sorry. I can't imagine what a shock this is to you."

She shook her head. "It's okay. I don't know what I was expecting, but it sure wasn't this."

"There's water and smoke damage, but the fire was contained in the kitchen."

She nodded, her eyes wide in disbelief as they parked and got out. Aidan grabbed the box of plastic bags and a couple large cardboard boxes for the frozen food.

Phoebe unlocked the door, took a deep breath like she was going into battle, and led the way. She saw a flashlight on the table by the door and picked it up, guessing it was what Lee had used when he came to get them some clothes, and then took it with her as they headed for the kitchen.

The stench in the house was awful, as was the temperature. Aidan left the front door open as they entered to get some fresh air circulating.

The rooms were a disaster from the smoke and water damage. Phoebe could already smell the beginning of mold. In this hot climate, with wet curtains and furniture…it wouldn't take long.

She eyed the warped top on the dining room table and the ruined cushions on the matching chairs with despair, remembering how long it had taken her to save up to buy the set. She'd been proud of its presence in their home, but the dull ache in her chest was for the house. It had sheltered them so snugly for all these years, only to come to this fate.

"It can be repaired to look like new," Aidan said.

She stepped into the kitchen and looked up at the six-foot hole in the ceiling, down at the hole directly beneath it where the lightning strike had gone, at the water still pooled on the floor, and in the black, grimy sink and groaned.

The curtains had melted off the rods, and the walls were black and scorched. The cabinets had burned off the walls. Their contents had fallen to the floor. What hadn't gone up in flames had shattered into fragments.

The little kitchen table where she and Lee had shared all their meals was blackened, partially from the fire and partially from smoke. The varnish had bubbled and then burst, leaving the surface looking more like the hide of a crocodile rather than the polished wood it had been.

"I lived through this because of you," Phoebe said.

Aidan set the boxes down on the table and took her in his arms. "I'm so sorry this happened."

Phoebe turned around. "Where was I when you found me?"

Aidan kept staring at the floor. "I never saw the hole, but I think you were closer to the cabinets because I literally tripped over you. Rain was pouring in through the hole, and smoke was going out. I just picked you up and ran."

She kept shaking her head. "I don't remember that. I don't remember anything but being on the phone with you." She buried her face against his chest. "Thank you. Just thank you."

"It's over. You're safe, and you're healing. Now let's get this job over with and get out," he said.

Phoebe nodded. "Yes. I'll start dumping food from the refrigerator into garbage bags if you'll get the frozen stuff from the freezer."

"Just don't try to carry anything. Just fill the bags and set them aside. I'll take them out for you," Aidan said.

But before they could begin, they heard footsteps on the porch and then voices coming inside. "Phoebe? Are you here?" someone called.

It was her neighbors from up and down the street, all coming in to help.

"In the kitchen!" she yelled as they piled inside the little house.

"What can we do? What can we do?" they began to ask.

Her neighbor from across the street opened the refrigerator door. "You want that all cleaned out?"

"Yes, ma'am," Phoebe said.

The woman took the garbage bag from her. "I can do that," she said. "Want to save any of the dishes the food is in?"

Phoebe looked in, then looked in the freezer above the refrigerator and shook her head.

"No. Just toss it all."

"We've got this," she said and waved at a couple more women who took Phoebe's place and shooed her aside.

As for Aidan, there hadn't been a lot of frozen food in the bigger deep freezer, so there wasn't much to recover, but as soon as he got one box filled, a couple of men came and carried it to his truck, then came back for the next box. The freezer was emptied in less than fifteen minutes and the refrigerator in less.

When Phoebe started down the hall with the flashlight, a string of neighbors went with her. They began emptying the closets and carrying the clothes out to the back of Aidan's truck. Then they put all the shoes and the contents of the dressers into garbage bags and carried them out as well.

Phoebe went into her bedroom, and while everyone was lifting and carrying things out, she took down all the framed pictures of Lee that she had on her wall and stacked them on her bed, adding the photo of Aidan from her nightstand to the pile.

"Want these carried out, Phoebe?"

She turned to see who was talking and saw Vera and Vesta Conklin from the Curl Up and Dye.

"I didn't know you were here," Phoebe said.

"We were on our way to lunch and saw the crowd. Figured we could afford to skip a meal to help."

"Thank you so much. And yes, please carry those out and put them in the back of Aidan's truck."

"Will do," they said, divided up the load, and left the room.

Phoebe was across the hall in Lee's room, rolling his sports trophies and keepsakes into bath towels to keep them from breaking and putting them into plastic bags when the twins returned.

"You want these in the back seat?" they asked.

"Yes, put them somewhere inside the cab. Just save me a place to sit."

"You got it," they said, and each grabbed a bag and left her again.

The next person who came looking for her was Aidan.

"We're finished up front. What else do you want to take out of here?" he asked.

Phoebe turned around. Tears welled, and then she fell into his arms.

"This is breaking my heart. When Preston moved me into this house to live for free, I felt like I'd won the lottery. Every time something went wrong here, he was on the job fixing or replacing it. And it's so broken now... and Preston is gone, too. It makes me feel like I'm losing him all over again."

Aidan held her while she cried, unaware that all of the people who'd come to help had quietly slipped away, giving them the time alone that they needed.

She cried until her head was hurting almost as much as her heart and then finally pulled herself together. "I've cried enough for a week, and we need to get that food into a freezer."

"Then let's go home."

Phoebe sighed. Home wasn't a house anymore. It was Aidan.

"Yes, I'm ready," she said.

He left the flashlight on the table where they'd found it and pulled the door shut behind them when they left.

Dan Amos easily found the address that would be his temporary home in Blessings and was pleasantly surprised when he entered. It was definitely feminine in decor but with a feeling of comfort. The floor was shining, the curtains were crisp, and the sunshine coming through the windows lit up the rooms.

He walked over to the thermostat and turned on the central air and then carried his bag down the hall and dropped it off in the master bedroom before checking out the bathroom. It had soap, shampoo, and linens, and when he opened the medicine cabinet, he found a small assortment of first aid items. *A very thoughtful hostess*. He went from there to the kitchen, which he also found fully furnished.

"Weird. Like she just walked out and didn't come back," Dan said.

The pantry and refrigerator were empty, but the refrigerator was cold and at the proper temperature.

After he closed the office this evening, he would find a grocery store and stock up on food. He found a washer and dryer and even a box of detergent and fabric softener sheets. After a quick walk through checking entrances and exits and making sure all the windows were locked, he went to unpack.

There were a few hangers in the master closet, enough for his needs, and after he changed into tan slacks and a cream-colored short-sleeved shirt for work, he traded his cowboy boots for loafers and drove back to town, leaving the belt and the Stetson behind.

He was just pulling into the parking lot at Granny's again when his cell phone rang. He saw Betty Purejoy's name come up. "Hello, this is Dan."

"It's me, Betty. Where are you right now?" she asked.

"About to go in and eat lunch at Granny's Country Kitchen."

"Good. My husband, Jack, will meet you there with a few more office details and the office key. Have a nice lunch, and when you get to the office, remember to call me to navigate it with you."

"Yes, ma'am. I will do that. Oh…what does your husband look like, so I can recognize him?"

"Don't worry," Betty said. "He'll know you right off because you'll likely be the only stranger there."

Dan smiled to himself as she hung up. He was so used to Savannah he'd forgotten what it was like to live where you knew pretty much everybody. This small-town living was going to make him homesick for Texas. He'd grown up on a ranch outside of a town with a population of about five thousand people, which might make it larger than Blessings.

He parked and hurried inside out of the heat. The dining area was far busier than it had been the first time he'd been in here, and Lovey, who was up front now, saw him come in.

"Whoa! That's quite a costume change," she said as she picked up a menu.

"Can't mix business with leisure," he said.

"Booth or table?" she asked.

"Table at the back of the room," Dan said, and when she looked a little startled, he blew it off with a joke. "It's my Wild Bill Hickok syndrome. Don't turn my back to a door."

Thinking he was making a joke, she laughed as she led the way to a table that was at the back of the room.

Dan was well aware of the eyes upon him as he followed Lovey. They'd all know soon enough who he was. There would inevitably be one jackass who would challenge him in some way, thinking if he knew how to type, he must be some kind of wimp. After that mistaken presumption was dealt with, the status quo would level out.

Shelly Mayberry, the new waitress, caught his table, took his order of fried catfish with fries and coleslaw, and brought him a sweet tea brimming with ice and no lemon. When she set the basket of biscuits down with it, he looked up in surprise.

"A little something to tide you over until your food arrives," she said. "I suggest loads of butter and the peach preserves, although I could eat a dozen of these plain and never regret a bite."

He grinned. "They're that good, huh?"

"You'll see," she said. "Knock yourself out."

He picked one up and, without anything added, took

a bite all the way to the middle and began to chew. The hot, flaky bread literally dissolved in his mouth.

"I stand corrected," he muttered. He buttered the second half, stuck it in his mouth, rolled his eyes, and put butter and preserves on the next one, half at a time, taking the time to savor it.

Shelly came by with an order for another table and grinned at him.

"Was I right?"

"Yes, ma'am, you sure were," Dan said and finished the last half of the second biscuit with as much finesse as he made love — slowly, savoring every lingering bit of pure lust.

⁓

Aidan took Phoebe home so they could clean up, and while she was in the shower, he called to check on Lee.

"Hi, Dad. Everything is going great," he said.

"When you get to a stopping point, why don't you take a break, pick up some burgers and fries, and come home for lunch?"

"My pleasure," Lee said. "And I have some news about that rental we just painted. You have a potential buyer if the price is right."

Aidan grinned. "That's great! Tell me all about it when you get here."

"Okay…one other thing. Do you want one burger or two?"

"One and a side of fries is more than enough," he said. "Do you have enough cash on you, or do you want me to go get the food?"

"No, I have enough," he said. "See you soon."

Aidan was still smiling when he went up to check on Phoebe.

She was dressed in shorts and a blouse and trying to comb out her wet hair, and for a brief moment, he flashed on the girl she'd been, running barefoot on the football field at midnight and laughing when he finally caught her beneath the bleachers.

They'd made love there.

Then she saw him and smiled, and the memory faded.

"Lee's bringing burgers and fries," he said.

Phoebe paused. "That's what I was going to have him do when lightning struck." Then she poked a finger in his chest. "We're still on the same wavelength, aren't we?"

He wanted to take her to bed, but he considered their son and the burgers.

"Yes, we are, Bee. I'm going to clean up, too. Sweet tea and cold pop are in the refrigerator. Make yourself comfortable. I won't be long...and if Lee gets here before I get downstairs, don't let him eat my fries."

"If you'll comb those last tangles out of the back of my hair, I'll safeguard your fries."

"Deal," he said and proceeded to fulfill her request.

Chapter 18

WITHIN THE NEXT FOUR DAYS, THE NEWS OF COREY Randall's arrest for the old crime had spread all over town and up into the rural countryside.

When Moe received the call from the chief that he would not be charged and that the story was going to be released as Aidan had requested, he thanked Lon profusely, then cried all the way out to the cemetery to tell Roberta the news.

The first person who patted his back and shook his hand for what he'd done made him feel guilty. But as the news spread and the days wore on, he accepted the praise.

Myra Franklin made another call to her cousin, Sonja, but Sonja didn't answer. Myra suspected she was screening her calls because she never went anywhere without that phone. Myra left a voicemail. "It's me, and I suggest you get over yourself and call me back. The mystery of Marty's death has just been solved."

And then she hung up, glanced up at the second hand on the clock over the cooler where they put fresh flowers, and began counting how long it would take for the snot to call her back.

Myra's cell phone rang. Thirteen seconds. It had taken her thirteen seconds. "I thought that would be of interest," Myra said.

"Oh my God, Myra, I can hear you smirk. I have the

call on speaker so Joe can hear, too, so spill it! Who set the fire?"

"It wasn't set on purpose. An eighteen-year-old kid was trying to rob the auto supply store by blowing up the safe. Instead, he set the place on fire."

"Who was it, and how did they find out? Was it Aidan instead of George? I never thought of him, but I should have," Joe said.

"The Paynes had nothing to do with it, and you're an ass," Myra said. "It was Corey Randall."

"Who?" Sonja asked.

"Moe Randall's son. The one who was always in trouble all through high school. Somehow Moe recently found out and went straight to the police, and, with Moe's help, they tricked Corey into coming to the station. They arrested him on the spot. I heard Moe was there to witness it, too. Moe has cancer and is dying, by the way. He only has a few weeks left to live."

Joe Ritter stared at Sonja until a muscle began to jerk near his right eye, and then he looked away.

Sonja's head was spinning. "It's a sure thing?"

Myra snorted so loudly over the phone it startled Sonja. "Of course it's a sure thing. What father would turn in his own son for a crime like that without good reason? I've delivered my last message to you. If you care enough to keep in touch, this phone works both ways."

Sonja heard her disconnect, then laid the phone back on the kitchen counter. Joe wouldn't meet her gaze, and she didn't know what to say. It was hell when the guilt sat equally on their shoulders.

But then she pulled herself together, dropped the phone back in her pocket, and went to find her purse.

"There's a sale on summer shoes downtown. I'll be back later."

She didn't give him time to speak, which was just as well because for the first time in Joe Ritter's life, he had nothing to say.

———◊———

Aidan and Lee finally had all of the empty rentals painted, and most of the renters' plumbing and electrical problems had been addressed. Aidan listed the three empty rentals for sale. The sale of the fourth rental, the one Lee had mentioned, was in escrow to one of the teachers from Blessings High School.

The insurance adjustor had come and gone at Phoebe's house. The ruined living room and dining room furniture had been hauled away, the beds had been stripped down to the frames, and the dressers were sitting empty. Yesterday the work crew had gutted the kitchen, and today a mold remediation crew was at work.

Aidan was going between the work at Phoebe's house and the work on the rentals and was finally on his way back to Preston's house, but not before stopping off at the jewelry store in town.

He went into the house looking for Phoebe and found her in the living room with the photo album Preston had made for him in her lap. She was crying. When he walked in, she looked up.

"Aidan, what a precious gift. I didn't know he'd done this. It breaks my heart all over again for what I kept from you."

Aidan sat down beside her, put the book on the coffee

table, and handed her a handful of tissues. "We're not doing the past anymore, remember?"

She nodded as she wiped her face.

"Good. So no more crying for me, okay?"

"Okay."

He ran a finger down the side of her face, eyeing the fading bruises and healing cuts. "I have something for you, and I have a question to ask. Which do you want first?"

He watched her eyes widen. "The surprise…then the question, please," she said.

He took the little black box out of his pocket and opened the lid, revealing the emerald-cut solitaire diamond ring inside.

Phoebe gasped. "Oh, Aidan, it's beautiful. I've never had anything so elegant." Then she looked at her ring finger—still taped to her little finger. "Oh no."

"That's not a problem, Bee," he said, and he carefully unwound the tape, slipped the ring onto the proper finger, then rewrapped the tape, leaving the diamond shining.

Phoebe lifted it to the light, watching the sunlight catch in the facets. "I love it…and I love you," she whispered, then leaned into his embrace.

Her lips were soft and yielding. It was slow, sweet torture for Aidan not to take her straight to bed. But it was ten o'clock in the morning, and he had an appointment with the real estate agent in thirty minutes.

For Phoebe, it was the thought of that unanswered question that made her reluctantly end the kiss. "You gave me a son, and now you are giving me a jewel fit for a queen. I'm almost afraid to ask, but what's the question?"

"When do you want to get married, and where?"

She shivered. "Oh, this is a good question! This is really happening, isn't it?"

He laughed. "Lord, I hope so."

She reached for his hand, needing to hold it in hopes he understood. "The thing is…I don't need all the pomp and circumstance, and I don't have much of anybody who's a close friend. Just mostly the people I work with and Lee. I learned a long time ago that things don't make you happy. People do, and you and I are running out of family, so unless you want a big event, I'd be just as happy with you, me, and Lee and a justice of the peace."

"That's perfect," Aidan said. "Want to get married here or in New Orleans?"

She didn't hesitate. "In New Orleans. That's where everything will be fresh and new."

"That's great. It won't be long before we can leave now. As soon as I can get a good manager in place for the rental properties, we're going home."

——~~——

Betty Purejoy was home now, and even though she was still healing, every time she fell asleep she relived the wreck. Sometimes she lived through the wreck, and a couple times she'd dreamed she died. The last time she woke up in tears telling Jack she wasn't taking another pain pill. They made her have crazy dreams.

She had yet to meet the temp, but they talked every day. He was such a good replacement that she couldn't believe that's what he did for a living. If she hadn't known better, she would have thought he was a lawyer himself. As for what he looked like, Jack had told her he had all the girls at Granny's buzzing and fussing every

day at noon over who got to wait on him, so she guessed
he was a looker.

———⁓———

Dan Amos was falling in love with Blessings. It was
the slower pace of life he appreciated most. Every day
after work, he drove the neighborhoods, looking at the
houses and the neat green yards and the massive trees
that had been here long before anyone had even thought
of building a town. It was the kind of life he and Holly
had dreamed of. The kind of place where they'd wanted
to raise their kids. But his dreams for the future had died
with her and their son.

Yesterday after work, he'd driven to the north side of
town past the Blue Ivy Bar, then circled back through a
less prosperous neighborhood just to get a feel for the
town as a whole.

As he did, he saw a little blond-haired girl in shorts
and a T-shirt running barefoot in the back yard, squeal-
ing in high-pitched shrieks as only children can do,
while an older boy stood under a shade tree squirting
both her and the huge bloodhound behind her with a
water hose.

The boy saw him and waved.

Dan waved back. He couldn't help but compare it to
the trailer park where he lived in Savannah. Just good
people doing the best they could with what they had.

He was still watching them when he saw a young
woman emerge from the house—likely the mother. She
looked tired, but that look wasn't there long when the
boy turned the hose on his mother's bare legs and feet.

She squealed just like the little girl had, and then the

race was on. Dan braked, wanting to see the outcome, and watched the woman chase the boy down, take the hose away from him, and soak him to the skin.

Dan's heart hurt. This was what he'd lost. This was what he missed. He looked away and drove toward his residence, wishing there was someone waiting for him to come home.

He fingered the scar on his face, tempering the rage that came with the memory. All of a sudden, the thought of returning to Savannah turned his stomach. After what had happened to his family, he had quit his career and run as far east as he could go. But why was he still there?

The next morning at breakfast, Aidan paid Lee for the week's work.

"You did a great job, Son. We're not going to start any new projects unless there's a problem at one of the rentals. And there's a little something extra in your pay for selling the first house to one of your old teachers."

"Thanks," Lee said, but when he pulled the check out of the envelope, he nearly fell out of his chair. "Dad! A thousand dollars?"

"You earned it. We're getting a hundred thousand for the house…thanks to you."

"This is amazing! I have thought about following in Granddad's footsteps many times…owning rentals, flipping houses. This is a good beginning." Lee put the check in his wallet and picked his fork back up. "Hey, Mom, how soon before another stack of pancakes is ready?"

Phoebe lifted one of the pancakes on the griddle to check. "Right about now," she said, scooped them onto the serving platter, and carried them to the table for Lee. "Another short stack coming up in about two minutes. Do you want more, Aidan?"

"I've already had two stacks and sausage. You eat those," he said, then glanced back at his son. "What are you going to do with your money?"

"Bank it," Lee said. "I'll be that much ahead when I go back to school in the fall."

"You can work in Mimosa if you want when we go back to New Orleans. Ever waited tables?" Aidan asked.

Lee laughed. "Are you kidding? That's the standard job for college students. I bussed tables at a pizza joint and waited tables at a steak house."

"Perfect," Aidan said. "You're hired for the summer until you go back to college. So after you bank your money this morning, why don't you just take it easy for the next couple days? We're going to be leaving Blessings soon. If you have goodbyes you want to say, now's the time to do it, and when we get to New Orleans, I'll have one more job for you."

"Okay, what's that?" Lee asked.

"We've decided to get married in New Orleans, and I want you to be my best man."

"And I want you to walk me down the aisle," Phoebe said. "Neither one of us has family left to invite. I just want you and Aidan and a justice of the peace."

Lee grinned. He was watching his best dream coming true. "That's awesome, Mom. It would be my honor to stand in for the both of you. But if we're leaving that soon, I do want to go tell a couple of my friends goodbye. See you at noon."

Phoebe felt like she was walking on air as Lee left.

"You know, what I thought was going to be a hard summer has turned into the best summer of my life."

Aidan was sitting beside her. When he leaned over and kissed her, the faint taste of syrup was on her lips.

"God, how I love you, Bee. I have to confess that I dreaded coming back and finding you happily married. I know how utterly selfish that sounds, but it's the truth."

Phoebe leaned into another kiss and ended it with a whisper in his ear that made him ache. But the sound of Lee's footsteps overhead cooled their ardor.

Adam sighed. "And hold that thought. I have another suggestion. Don't plan on cooking tonight. We're going to have to clean out the refrigerator before we leave. We can go to Granny's instead."

"That sounds wonderful."

"And we'll need to clean the house as well," Aidan said.

Phoebe nodded. "Yes, Preston had a cleaning service. It's owned by a woman named Laurel Lorde. She's building up quite a business in Blessings. Someone told me she now has two other women working for her."

"I have her number. I'll have her come after we leave."

"What are you going to do about this house?" Phoebe asked.

"I don't know yet," Aidan said. "I think I'll just leave it as is and see what plays out with the other properties."

"That sounds like a good idea."

Dan Amos literally had nothing to do and decided to give Betty another call.

"Hello," Betty said.

"Betty, Dan Amos here. I was wondering if you had

any more work you needed done. Maybe something that isn't urgent but would keep me busy?"

Betty didn't bother to hide her surprise. "You are already finished with all the work that was on that agenda I gave you?"

"Yes, ma'am. I type pretty fast, so..."

Betty sighed. "That's amazing. Do me a favor and don't tell Mr. Butterman what a whiz you are when he returns, or he'll likely offer you a job full time."

"Oh, I doubt that, ma'am. From what he told our director, you mean the world to him."

Betty smiled, then winced a bit from the pain. "Really?"

"Yes, ma'am. I'm sure your job is safe."

"Well then... Why don't you take a couple of hours for lunch, and I'll get back to you?"

"Okay, thanks. I have some errands I could run after lunch. I'll put a sign on the door and be back at two."

They disconnected, and Dan made himself a sign, fastened it to the office door, and left the building. Since he had all this time, he decided he was going to pick up what he needed from the hardware store and then go home to eat.

It was ten minutes to twelve when he pulled up in front of Bloomer's Hardware. His mind was already on the items he needed. He walked in and had paused a moment to orient himself to the layout when he heard a woman's voice.

"Hello. Can I help you find something?"

He glanced toward the register, then saw a slender woman with the biggest blue eyes he'd ever seen. She looked vaguely familiar, but he couldn't place where he'd seen her.

"Uh…yes. I have a door with squeaky hinges and need some WD-40. Also an air filter for a 2016 Dodge Ram and some superglue."

She smiled. "Yes, sir. Follow me," she said and led him three aisles over and then about halfway down. "WD-40 just to your right. Top shelf."

"Got it," Dan said.

"The air filters are back here," she said and shifted one aisle over. "You said a 2016 Dodge Ram, right?"

"Yes, ma'am," Dan said.

She looked up at him. "Please call me Alice."

Lost in those eyes again, all he managed was a nod as she searched a couple of minutes before finding the right one.

"Got it." She pulled it down and then kept it as she led him up another aisle with a dozen different kinds of glue. "Take your pick."

He grabbed a smaller tube.

"Anything else?" she asked. "How about I take everything to the register so you can look around? You might see something else you need."

"I don't think I need—"

"Take your time," Alice said, took the glue he was holding, and left him standing.

Dan wasn't sure what had just happened, but she seemed so sincere that he felt like he should find at least one more item to please her. So he strolled up and down a couple more aisles without choosing and then was on his way back to the front when he saw work gloves. He actually needed a pair of those at home and picked up cotton ones as he went up to the register.

She smiled sweetly as she added them to his gathering assortment and began ringing up his purchases.

As he was watching, it suddenly dawned on him where he'd seen her. She was the woman with the garden hose! The one who'd chased the boy down and soaked him from head to toe.

When she gave him the total, she handed her a credit card, signed the slip, and thanked her before he left. He was still thinking about her as he drove toward home, and then he shifted to what he was going to eat for lunch and let it go. He wasn't interested in other women or another relationship.

———

Lee was standing at the foot of the stairs, fidgeting.

"Hey!" he yelled. "How much longer until you guys are ready to go? It's already after six, and I'm starving."

Aidan was putting on his shoes and Phoebe was trying to find a lipstick in her purse when they heard Lee yell.

Aidan grinned. "The kid is starving."

Phoebe rolled her eyes. "I heard him, and Elliot Graham from across the street probably heard him too."

He watched her pull a lipstick from her purse and give her lips a couple of swipes.

"I'm ready," she said.

They left the bedroom and started down the stairs, only Lee was no longer there. They got all the way to the front door before he caught up, chewing.

"Are you eating?" Phoebe asked.

"They're just cookies. You know they won't ruin my appetite."

"Nothing ruins your appetite," Phoebe said and then hugged him. "It's a good thing I love you so much."

Lee wiggled his eyebrows at his dad and grinned.

Aidan laughed all the way to the car, and they arrived at Granny's shortly afterward. As usual, the place was busy, but they didn't have to wait to be seated. Their waitress had already come with iced tea and hot biscuits, when Aidan noticed a man come inside. He looked familiar, but he couldn't place him.

"Who's the guy who just came in?" he asked.

Phoebe and Lee looked and then shrugged. "I have no idea."

"Really?" Aidan said. "I know him from—"

And then the man looked up and saw Aidan staring, and both of them froze.

Aidan was the first to look away. "Son of a…"

"What?" Phoebe said.

"That's Danner Amos."

"Who's Danner Amos?" Lee asked.

"Biggest hotshot lawyer that Dallas County, Texas, ever had until one of the perps he put in prison put out a hit on him. But his wife and kid got in the car he usually drove, and when she started it, it blew up with them in it."

"Oh my God," Phoebe whispered.

Then to Aidan's surprise, Amos was coming to their table and stopped beside where Aidan was sitting.

"We've met, haven't we?" he asked.

Aidan nodded. "I'm Aidan Payne. You were at my restaurant a few years back. Mimosa, in New Orleans."

Dan flinched inwardly. That was when Holly and Blake were still alive. "Yes, I remember now."

"Are you here on your own?" Aidan asked.

Dan nodded.

"Why don't you join me and my family? This is Phoebe, and our son Lee. We're leaving town in a couple of days, heading home," Aidan said.

Dan thought about home. These days it was the trailer house he rented. It would be wonderful to have a place that really felt like home again. He glanced at Phoebe, who was already smiling and moving things on the table to accommodate another diner.

"Please do join us," Phoebe said.

Lee grinned. "You're very welcome to the seat, but I'll fight you for the biscuits."

Dan laughed. "They're worth fighting for, aren't they? If you guys are sure, I'd love company. Been eating on my own since I got here."

"We're sure, have a seat," Aidan said, and flagged their waitress down to let her know they'd added a fourth for dinner.

As the meal progressed, Aidan hid his shock in finding out what Danner Amos was doing in Blessings, but he certainly understood the reason he'd quit practicing law.

And as the evening went by, not only did Aidan and Phoebe share a bit of their story, but people were coming by to congratulate Aidan and Phoebe on their engagement or talk about her dance with death.

As they did, Dan came to realize how remarkable Phoebe Ritter was. She'd been knocked down at every turn in life and not only kept getting back up but hadn't lost faith in the man who'd left her, while raising their son alone.

What hurt Dan most was knowing if Holly and Blake hadn't died, Blake would be about the same age as Lee.

Dan was still lost in thought when he suddenly keyed in on what Aidan was saying.

"…so I need to either find someone to buy the properties as a whole or find a manager."

Dan frowned. "Wait! What? You have the whole rental business for sale? How many rentals are you talking about?"

"We have fifteen rental properties and three empty rentals that have been put up for sale. Lee and I just remodeled and repainted those, and we're current with rental repairs. Granddad's house would sell with the business, and the house is amazing. It's a big two-story built right after the Civil War. It has a little over 3,500 square feet and all the updates. In a way, I hate to see it go out of the family, but on the other hand, we have no intentions of living in Blessings again."

"If you sold everything, including the three houses you have up for sale, what would your asking price be?" Dan asked.

"A million three," Aidan said. "Although the likelihood of anyone in Blessings having that kind of money is slim to none, which is why I'm looking for a manager. I'd already reassured the renters that I wasn't going to raise their rent and anyone late with rent wasn't in danger of being evicted. It was Granddad's policy, and I felt it only right to honor it, too."

"I might be interested," Dan said.

Phoebe gasped. "Seriously?"

Aidan was surprised. "You'd be content to live in a place this small?"

"I was born and raised on a ranch in West Texas. Nearest town was fifteen miles away, and it had a population of about five thousand people. I miss that slower way of life."

"Like I said earlier, we're leaving in a couple days, so I'll take you on a tour of the properties tomorrow if you want."

Dan knew this notion to stay was knee-jerk, but the more he thought about it, the more enticing it seemed. "Yes, I want."

"I'll pick you up," Aidan said. "Just tell me where you're staying."

"I'm staying in Mrs. Butterman's prior home."

Phoebe smiled. "You're staying in Ruby's house? I love that place. I'll show Aidan where it is when we go home," Phoebe said.

"How about nine a.m.?" Aidan asked.

"That's good for me."

Their waitress came by with the check, which Aidan promptly picked up.

"Thank you again for the food and the company. I'll see you in the morning then," Dan said and then left.

———

Long after Aidan had fallen asleep beside her, Phoebe was still awake watching him sleep. The night shadows had stripped the past twenty years from his face, but not even the darkness could hide the breadth of his shoulders or the firm cut of his jaw.

No longer the boy.

So very much the man.

He murmured something in his sleep and then turned over on his side. Even as he slept, he reached out and pulled her close.

"Love you," Phoebe whispered and then finally closed her eyes. She was thinking about a big two-story house full of windows and light in a place called the Garden District. And in the front yard standing sentinel were ancient live oaks, heavily bearded with Spanish moss. She fell asleep with Cajun music in her head.

The next time she woke it was daylight and she was alone in bed. She lay there for a few moments, remembering she'd been dreaming about the day Preston Williams moved her into her little house rent-free. It was the first time since she'd been abandoned that she had felt hope.

And now her house was being repaired. One day soon it would be as good as new, and she'd been debating whether to sell it or rent it until last night. The dream had been the answer, and she knew exactly what she was going to do.

She could hear the shower running in the bathroom as she got out of bed and remembered Aidan was giving Dan Amos a tour of the rental properties later that morning. Amos was going to do this. She could feel it. The release of that responsibility would rid Aidan of his last tie to Blessings and leave them all free to leave.

A few minutes later, Aidan came out showered and shaved and in a pair of briefs. Phoebe tried not to stare, but he was too delicious to ignore.

Aidan grinned. "I saw that look, Bee. Don't let go of that thought," he said as he wrapped her up in his arms and kissed her soundly, then gave her a quick pat on the backside as she headed for the bathroom.

"Hey!" Phoebe said. "I haven't been near naughty enough for all that. And as soon as I get out of the shower, we need to talk about my little house."

He gave her a thumbs-up and then grabbed a pair of Levi's and a clean polo shirt. He dressed in haste then hurried down to the kitchen to jump-start breakfast, only to find Lee already at the stove.

"Hi, Dad. I'm cooking the last of the bacon and sausage. Mom said we need to use up what's here before we leave."

"That's right," he said and snatched a piece of warm, crispy bacon as he went to pour himself a cup of coffee.

A few minutes later, Aidan was scrambling eggs and Lee was making toast when Phoebe came in.

"My two favorite men cooking my favorite breakfast, bacon and eggs."

"And it's ready, Mom," Lee said. "You sit. I'm the breakfast chef today."

"I guess that makes me the sous chef," Aidan said as he began portioning out the eggs onto the three plates, making sure Lee got the lion's share.

As soon as they were seated, Phoebe took a sip of her coffee and then set it aside to cool as she buttered a piece of toast.

"I have an announcement to make," she said. "You know how we talked about just selling my house and leaving the car at the bank parking lot with a For Sale sign on it? So, that's not happening."

"Then what are you going to do, turn the house into a rental?" Aidan asked.

"And what are you going to do with your car? Dad says you'll have your choice of one of his two cars in New Orleans, and he is giving me his Jeep, which is the coolest thing ever. I'm selling my truck to one of the renters before we leave."

She shook her head. "When Preston moved me into that house rent-free, it was the first time in months that I'd felt hope. I'm keeping the house as an honor to Preston and calling it Hope House. I'm going to share it with people in dire need, just like he shared it with me."

Aidan reached across the table and clasped her hand. "Ah, Bee…again you warm my heart. That's an amazing legacy."

"That is so cool, Mom. Who's going to be the first family to live in it?"

"Remember that woman and her two kids who moved here with nothing because their house burned up with her husband in it?"

"Is that the kid with the bloodhound? The one you told me about who found a missing lady from the nursing home?"

Phoebe nodded. "Yes. Right now they're living behind the Blue Ivy Bar…and they don't have a car. I know this because she comes into the Piggly Wiggly with her kids every Saturday that it's not raining, and whatever they buy, they have to carry it all the way home."

"That's freaking awesome, Mom!" Lee said.

Aidan smiled. "Yeah, Mom! That's freaking awesome."

"It feels freaking awesome to be doing this, too," Phoebe said.

And then Aidan being Aidan reminded her of the business end of that project. "You don't have a lot of time to get all of the legal end of this done, but I'll mention it to Dan Amos. He can get the ball rolling on paperwork, and when the lawyer gets back from his honeymoon, he can finalize."

"What I can't finish here I'll finish by phone in New Orleans," Phoebe said. "But today I am going to tell Alice that while she's waiting for the house to be finished and new furniture to replace what was ruined, she has a car. I'll need one of you to pick me up from Bloomer's Hardware afterward."

"I'll do it, Mom," Lee said. "Dad's doing the tour."

Phoebe picked up her fork and started eating. "This is delicious. Thanks for cooking."

Alice Conroy was pricing a shipment of grease guns when she heard a customer entering the store. Her boss was at the bank, so she dropped what she was doing to hurry up front, then saw it was Phoebe, one of the nicest people at the Piggly Wiggly.

"Hi, Phoebe! Can I help you?"

"No, today I came to help you."

Alice was taken aback. The people in Blessings had already helped her and her family with a food and clothing drive when they'd first come to town. "I don't understand," Alice said.

"Do you know anything about my story?" Phoebe asked.

"No, ma'am," Alice said.

"Then I'll make it quick before a customer comes in," Phoebe said, and proceeded to explain everything, right down to the storybook ending of going to New Orleans with Aidan to begin a new life, and what she intended to do with her little house. "I just want you to know that you and your children will be the first family to live in Hope House rent-free and for as long as you need the

help. One day your life will take a good turn, and when
it does, Hope House will be empty again, waiting for the
next person to come along needing a hand up."

Alice was in tears. She kept hugging Phoebe over and
over, telling her she was an angel.

"There's one more thing, and it's not a loan. It is a
gift," Phoebe said and handed Alice a set of keys and
an envelope.

"What's this?" Alice asked.

"The keys to my car and a signed and notarized title,
with enough money to pay for a couple months of insurance and the title transfer into your name. All you have
to do is sign it and go from there."

Alice gasped. "You are giving me your car?"

"I'm paying it forward," Phoebe said. "Maybe one
day you can do the same for someone else. It's the blue
Ford Focus parked a couple doors down. My son, Lee,
even detailed it for you."

Alice ran to the door and looked out, the keys clutched
beneath her chin in disbelief. "That's mine?"

Phoebe laughed. The rush of joy from this was intoxi-
cating. Now she understood some of what Preston had
done all his life.

"It's yours. I'll be leaving Blessings in a couple of
days, but I'll be thinking of you driving to the store for
groceries instead of walking, and I wish you a long and
happy life," Phoebe said.

Alice threw her arms around Phoebe's neck, shaking
so hard she could barely stand.

"Everyone in Blessings has been so wonderful.
They've given us food and clothes, paid utilities, and
brought medicine and toys that were so appreciated.

But you have given me much more than a home and a car, Phoebe Ritter. You gave me back my dignity. I will never be able to thank you enough."

Now Phoebe was in tears. "Oh, I know exactly how you feel. Remember my story? Have a good life, Alice."

"We will, oh dear lord, we will. God bless you," Alice said as Phoebe walked out the door.

———

Aidan carried the last box from the house to the U-Haul, then went back to shut and lock the doors.

Lee was standing in the yard visiting with old classmates, and when he saw his dad was about ready, they left, wishing him well.

Phoebe was coming out of the house, talking on the phone, when Elliot Graham came flying across the street, waving his arms. She quickly disconnected and hurried to where Aidan was standing. Lee came rushing up behind the two of them.

Aidan grinned and waved back. Did that old man ever just walk? It seemed like he was always hurrying from place to place.

"I'm so glad I caught you all," Elliot said. "The first time you left, it was under a cloud of disgrace. Unfounded, but nevertheless humiliating. This time that will not be the case. Be ready."

He grasped Lee's hand. "Your heart already knows the path you will follow. Don't change who you are for anybody."

Then he reached for Phoebe. "Valiant little warrior that you are, your new life will bring all kinds of surprises. Be ready to enjoy them. Preston says to tell you

how proud he is of all of you. He also says don't look
back because he's not there. He's in your hearts. Safe
journey, and God bless."

"It's been a pleasure being your friend," Phoebe said.

Lee shook Elliot's hand. "Thank you for many things,
not the least of which was teaching me a mean game of
poker."

Elliot's eyebrows rose, and then he smiled. "Yes,
there was that, wasn't there, boy?"

Moments later he was gone, and Aidan was still shaking his head. "I still don't know what to think about his
ability to 'know things' as he puts it, but I like him."

"Let's get this show on the road," Lee said. "I call
dibs on the whole back seat. Mom gets to ride shotgun."

Aidan checked the hookup one last time, making sure
everything was secure, and then got into the truck with
his family. Without planning it, all three of them turned
and looked at Preston's house one last time, then looked
away without comment.

Aidan started up the truck and eased out of the driveway with the U-Haul, then out into the street. But when
they turned onto Main Street and saw every police car
in town lined up at the curb and the chief standing in the
street, Aidan braked.

"What the hell?" he muttered and rolled down his
window as Chief Pittman approached. "What's wrong?"

"Not a thing. Speaking on behalf of the citizens of
Blessings, they deeply regret the way you and your
father first left Blessings and want you to know how
highly you all are regarded, how much they are going
to miss you, and that they send their wishes for a long
and happy life. You and your family are about to leave

town in our best version of a blaze of glory. Me and two of my officers will lead, then you fall in line behind us. The remaining officers will be behind you all the way to the county line. We're sorry to see you go, but we're sending you off in style." Then he tipped his hat and jogged toward his cruiser.

"I don't believe this is happening," Aidan said and felt Phoebe's hand on his arm.

Moments later, every cop car in town started, and lights began to flash followed by the warning scream of sirens. People came out of businesses while others got out of their cars to watch.

By leaving together, they'd put an end to the feud between the Ritters and the Paynes. And with the real arsonist behind bars and awaiting trial, it was also the end of a twenty-year mystery.

"Look!" Lee said, pointing to the old man holding onto the streetlight beside the bank. "It's Mr. Randall."

When Moe lifted a hand to wave, they all waved back at him as the convoy of police cars escorted them out of town.

It was a far cry from the last time Aidan had left, and this time they weren't quitting Blessings in anger. They were just driving to their happy ever after.

Epilogue

New Orleans, Louisiana

I T ONLY TOOK TWO WEEKS BEFORE P HOEBE FELT LIKE SHE'D lived in this house all her life. The housekeeper and the gardener called her Miss Bee, while Lee was basking in the joy of being his father's son.

Everywhere they went, their look-alike appearances were remarked upon. As for Phoebe, she was already becoming known as the Southern beauty and childhood sweetheart of one of New Orleans' most eligible bachelors and the woman he'd fallen in love with all over again. In an old city full of drama and loss, their story was a familiar one. But this time it was going to have a happy ending.

They'd been married exactly one week when Aidan threw the biggest reception Mimosa had ever seen. His best and oldest customers, including the mayor and the governor, had personal invitations. The best blues musicians played two-hour sets in a sea of rotating celebration and chaos—or, as Aidan had put it, as much fun as Mardi Gras on a hot Saturday night.

All night long, Phoebe heard people calling her name.

"Miss Bee, smile for the camera! Miss Bee, look at that! Miss Bee, taste this."

Aidan was never farther away from her than his arm could reach, and the security at the doors made sure the party stayed "invited guests only" and free of party crashers.

Phoebe was overwhelmed by Aidan's status in the city. It wasn't something she had expected, and accepting her part in it might have been daunting had she not put it into the Blessings perspective to which they all adhered.

The size of your jewelry and the cost of your clothes do not prevent you from farting in public.

She'd heard that all her life and continued to remind herself of it tonight as she was constantly being introduced to people with pedigrees longer than this city was old.

She snagged a glass of sparkling water from a tray and passed on another canapé at the same time Aidan leaned down and whispered in her ear, "You are stunning in the white silk and lace. Makes your hair look darker and your beautiful eyes greener. Are you having fun?"

Phoebe spun around to face him. "I feel like a queen. I am living a dream."

He lifted her hand to his lips, gently kissing the tender knuckles, then ran his thumb over the emerald-cut diamond and the delicate band of diamonds below it. "You have given my life here new meaning. Thank you, my darling, for giving me a second chance."

Phoebe smiled. "Oh, Aidan, if you only knew. You are most welcome, and I have one more gift to give you, but not until we are home."

"Good. I love surprises," he said. "Oh. Lee is waving at us. It must be time for the toast."

"I'd rather keep my sparkling water. I'll pretend it's champagne, okay? I'm not much of a drinker, and I don't want to ruin this beautiful night by making myself sick."

"Absolutely," he said, "but we'll get you a fresh glass. Just come with me."

He whispered an order to one of the waiters as they

began to move toward the stage. The musicians were between sets, and the piped-in music playing softly in the background was something to keep the mood of the partygoers upbeat.

When the introduction began, a waiter appeared at Phoebe's elbow with a tray bearing a single flute of sparkling water, while another waiter appeared at Aidan's elbow with a flute filled with the finest Dom Pérignon. Lee was standing beside his dad with a smile on his face, offering no excuses for the glass of Pepsi in his hand.

Aidan lifted his glass. "Ladies and gentlemen, you are here because I value your presence in my life. But there are two other people I want you to meet who beat all of you to the table."

Soft laughter, a couple of wolf whistles, and a few calls of "Hear! Hear!" drifted across the room.

"It is with great pride that I introduce you to my son, Lee, a student at Savannah State University, in the fine state of Georgia."

A round of cheers went up for the state of Georgia.

Then Aidan turned to Phoebe and lifted his glass. "And it is with so much love in my heart that I introduce you to my wife, Phoebe Ann, who most of you already know as Miss Bee. She was my childhood sweetheart. She is the mother of my son and the woman I will love until the day I die. Welcome to New Orleans, Bee. Welcome to the rest of our lives."

Confetti and gold and silver streamers fell from the ceiling as music began to play. A trio of Cajun musicians came into the room with their concertinas and accordions, playing toe-tapping, boot-stomping music with a zydeco beat.

Aidan took the glass from Phoebe's hand, set it aside, and swung her up into his arms, joining others on the dance floor, and the music played on.

———~~~———

It was nearing two in the morning when Aidan and his family got home. They were tired and sleepy but swore it was the best time they'd ever had.

Lee paused to give his dad a hug and his mom a quick kiss on the top of her head. "I'm beat. Can we sleep in tomorrow? Oh wait…it already is tomorrow," he said and groaned.

Aidan laughed. "Yes, sleep in. You're not on the schedule anyway."

"Thank you," he said and headed upstairs to bed.

Phoebe was tired but in a good way. "Are you ready to go up?" she asked as Aidan reset the security panel.

"Yes, ma'am. Bed never sounded so good."

They climbed the stairs together, still talking about the events of the evening and sharing opinions about the people she'd met. By the time they reached their bedroom at the far end of the long hallway, Phoebe was carrying her shoes. She dropped them inside the walk-in closet and began stripping out of her clothes.

"I'm going to take a really quick shower," she said and took her nightgown with her into the bathroom.

"Good idea. You'll sleep better," Aidan said and turned on the television as he began to change.

As she'd promised, Phoebe returned less than ten minutes later, devoid of makeup with her hair down and loose around her face. She walked up behind Aidan and slipped her arms around his waist.

"Thank you for the most wonderful party ever and for making me feel so special," she said.

Aidan pulled her into his arms. "It's nothing more than you deserve. You have given me all that matters in life—love and family. As I said earlier, I will never be able to thank you enough for giving me that second chance."

Phoebe smiled. "You're proving yourself to be the master of second chances. I told you I had a wedding present for you, remember?"

Aidan hugged her. "You've already given me the world."

She held his hands against the thud of her heartbeat. "What do you regret most about our separation?" she asked.

He sighed. "That's easy. Not getting to watch Lee grow up."

She pushed his hands down onto her belly. "I'm giving you a second chance at being a father. We're going to have another baby."

Aidan froze, letting the news wash through him in wave after healing wave. "Oh, Bee…oh, sweetheart! I'll take that second chance, and I swear on my life I will not let you down ever again." He kissed her, then swung her off her feet into his arms and started laughing. "Oh my God…thank you! I can't believe this is real."

Phoebe was laughing and crying all at the same time. "Yes, a father…through teething and earaches and poopy diapers. Through temper fits and boo-boos, through tears and hugs worth the world."

"I don't care! I don't care! I see Lee and already know what I missed. I won't let that happen again. Does he know?"

"Of course not!" Phoebe said. "This is your news to tell."

"Let's go tell him now!" Aidan said.

Phoebe laughed. "You want to give him babysitting nightmares?"

"This isn't a nightmare, honey. It's a dream come true."

He took off out the door, dragging Phoebe with him and yelling up the hall as they went. "Lee! Lee! Wake up!"

Lee came staggering out into the hall carrying his baseball bat from high school like he was ready to swing. "What's wrong?"

Aidan grabbed Lee by the shoulders. "Guess what! You're going to be a big brother."

Lee looked startled, and then he looked at his mother and then his dad while the grin on his face got wider and wider.

"Dang! Way to go, y'all. You weren't just whistlin' Dixie when you told Mom you had more to offer than your sexy body! Hot damn! I am going to be a big brother."

He hugged Phoebe, high-fived Aidan, and went back into his room and closed the door.

Aidan looked at Phoebe, then burst into laughter.

Phoebe was blushing just the tiniest bit, but she was as happy in that moment as she'd ever been in her whole life.

Aidan hugged her, kissed her again, and then danced her all the way down the hall to their room and closed the door behind them. Still beaming, he couldn't stop touching her very flat belly, unable to fully grasp the miracle she sheltered.

"Thank you, Phoebe. You have made me a very happy man."

Phoebe put her arms around him. "I believed in you. I waited for you. Do not ever doubt your part in this joy, because none of this would be happening if you had not come back to me."

Here's a sneak peek at

Forever My Hero

SHARON SALA

Elliot Graham had had a dream last night about Gray Goose Lake, which made him remember the overlook where he and his wife, Helena, always picnicked. Today he was going back to that overlook and painting the scene. It would be a wonderful reminder of happier times that he could frame, and he had the perfect place to hang it.

His drive out to the lake was relaxing, and when he parked and got out, he put on his painting hat—an old paint-stained Panama hat with a wide, floppy brim—then began to gather up what he wanted to take with him.

It had been years since he'd been to the lake, and the hiking trail was a bit overgrown. The old man stumbled once and dropped his paint box, then had to gather up the tubes of oil paint that fell out. Even after all that, he reached his destination only slightly out of breath. Once he set up his folding easel and the little portable folding stool, he opened his box of paints, prepared his brushes, and then sat for a few moments, just enjoying the view and talking to his long-deceased wife.

"Look, Helena! There is an eagle perched at the top of that big pine straight across the lake. Oh, how magnificent. I must remember to put him in the painting… just for you."

He felt a slight breeze against the back of his neck and smiled. There was no wind today. Only his love.

Without any further delay, he picked up a piece of charcoal pencil and began to rough-in the scene, delineating the horizon, then where the tree line would be. He sketched in the shape of the shoreline, and then the boat ramp just to the left, and tossed the charcoal back into the box.

His first choice of paint was to mix what would be the darkest colors in the lake. Dark was depth, and a painting was nothing without depth—like a person was nothing without depth of character—and he applied it to the canvas with a palette knife, giving contour and texture. The lighter colors would come in later on top of the darker, and then the lightest color, which would be glints of sunlight on the ripples, would be added last.

The sun rose higher, but Elliot's hat kept the sun from his face. He was totally into the work, oblivious of everything around him.

—∞—

Alice Conroy woke up in a cold sweat with the echo of Marty's screams still in her head.

Nightmares! Would they be with her for the rest of her

life? God, she hoped not. But she still had secrets from the day her husband died and never intended to share them.

To this day, no one knew her side of what happened—that Marty was in their house, high on the same meth he was making in the old shed down by the barn. She'd known it since daylight. He kept muttering about starting over, and needing to wipe the slate clean. He kept saying he was going to set everything on fire and walk away from that life. He kept promising and promising he would fix things. But she'd ignored him because he always talked crazy when he was high, and went outside to the garden she was working, getting it ready to plant in a couple of months when it warmed up. And that's why she was in the garden when her house exploded behind her, knocking her facedown into the freshly tilled earth.

She sat up in bed and covered her face. When she did, the whole nightmare came back in detail.

Burning debris was still drifting down around where Alice was lying. Thrown several feet forward, she was facedown in the garden, unaware it was their house that had exploded until she heard Marty screaming. She rolled over, saw the blaze and the smoke, and in seconds, was up and running toward the house, shrieking for help.

But it was too late for Marty. She watched him stumble out the back door, on fire from head to toe. He swayed forward, then fell backward just as the roof of the porch collapsed on top of him.

She needed her cell phone, but it was in the car parked under the blazing carport. And the car was on fire.

They still had a landline.

But it was inside a burning house.

The only saving grace about the whole day was that her children were at school.

She turned around and ran the three miles to her mother-in-law's house, screaming all the way.

Thank God for alarm clocks, Alice thought as she threw back the covers and headed to the bathroom. She made a face at herself in the mirror as she washed away the last of the bad dream. She needed no reminder of how much she had to be grateful for now. Waking up in Hope House every day, and knowing she and her family were living here rent-free for as long as they needed was nothing short of a miracle.

The last five months since Marty's death were behind them, and there were no tears left to cry for his absence in their lives. She had grieved his loss three years ago when he started making and selling meth, and kept the relief of his death to herself.

Today was Monday, and the beginning of the second week of September. She had a job to go to, for which she was grateful, and school for the kids. It was time to wake them up. She turned the heat up a bit after she came out of her bathroom, and crossed the hall to her son's door.

Charlie had just turned thirteen, and was now in seventh grade. Not only was he a head taller than she was, but the last year of their life had turned him into a man far too young.

Her seven-year-old daughter, Patricia, who went by Pitty-Pat, was still young enough that she would forget the hell her daddy had put them through before he died—but Charlie never would.

Alice knocked on Charlie's door.

"I'm up, Mama," Charlie said, and came out into the hall smiling. "It's gonna be a good day," he said, and hurried to the bathroom.

"Thank you for him, Lord," Alice murmured, then went next door to wake her baby. Pitty-Pat always slept with her head under the covers, so she had to unwrap her first.

"Good morning, Pitty-Pat. Time to get up."

"Not now," she whined.

Alice pulled the covers back. "Yes, now. Charlie is in the bathroom, so you can come to my room and use mine."

Pitty-Pat rolled over, yawning. Magic words. Mama's bathroom was so shiny and beautiful.

"Brush my teeth in there, too?" she asked.

"Yes, but bring your toothbrush this time. You may not use mine."

Pitty-Pat swung her legs off the side of the bed and got up. "Mama, I'm too big to be Pitty-Pat now. I am just Patty, okay?"

Alice blinked. It actually hurt to hear her daughter say this, although raising children to be independent and think for themselves was what Alice's parenting style was all about.

"Of course, it's okay…Patty."

The little girl nodded. "Gettin' my toothbrush now."

"I'm going to start breakfast. Don't dawdle getting dressed or Charlie will eat all of your eggs and toast."

"No! Don't let him!" Patty cried, and dashed out of her room with her toothbrush in her hand.

Alice grinned. It worked every time.

—⁓—

Lovey Cooper was already at Granny's Country Kitchen feeding the early risers in town. Mercy Pittman, the police chief's wife, was in the kitchen at Granny's, baking biscuits by the dozens.

Mercy's sister, Hope, who was a nurse at Blessings Hospital, was going off duty after a long night spent in the ER. Hope thought of her husband and brother-in-law out on the farm, already up and feeding cattle by daybreak. She was so tired, the thought of getting home and then making a big farmhouse breakfast before she got to go to bed was overwhelming.

But there were always Mercy's awesome biscuits, so she stopped by Granny's long enough to say hello and take a dozen sausage biscuits home. She thought to herself, as she headed for the farm, that she might have just enough energy left to scramble some eggs for the guys to go with them before she crawled into bed.

—◈—

While Blessings was readying for the new day, Danner Amos was still asleep, lost in the never-ending nightmare of his past, and it always started in the same place.

He turned away from the sink as Holly came hurrying into the kitchen. "I thought you and Blake were already gone," he said.

"My car won't start and Blake is going to be late to school."

"Take mine," Dan said. "I'll call the garage to pick yours up, then take a cab to the office."

"You're the best," Holly said, and blew him a kiss.

Dan followed her to the front door and then stood in

the doorway waving as she buckled their seven-year-old son into the back seat, then jumped into the car.

Dan's heart was beginning to pound. He knew what came next and was trying so hard to wake up, but it would never turn him loose until he rode it all the way to the end.

The early-morning sunlight reflected on the hood of his Lexus as he watched her check her makeup in the rearview mirror. He smiled. She always looked good to him. Then he saw her reach toward the ignition. Blake was waving at him from the back seat.

He stepped out of the doorway and into the sunlight, his hand lifted to wave back, when the world exploded before his eyes.

Pieces of the Lexus went airborne. All of the windows in the front of their home shattered. Something hit the side of his face as the car burst into flames.

He screamed.

And then he was sitting up in bed, awake and shaking. He touched the scar on the right side of his face and felt tears.

Nothing ever changed.

He threw back the covers and got out of bed. After a quick shower, he dressed for the day and went to the kitchen. Discovering he was out of milk ended the idea of another bowl of cereal at home, so he opted to go to Granny's for breakfast.

The food there reminded him of home. From the chicken and dumplings on the Sunday menu, to the biscuits and sausage gravy on their breakfast menu.

He did not regret taking on the manager duties for Aidan Payne's rental properties and was seriously considering buying him out. Right now, he was still learning the routine and building a relationship with the renters. He sent Aidan a monthly statement of repairs, including names of the people moving in and out, and the running total of received income, along with paying himself. There was no pressure, no worries, and was as low-key as he wanted to be.

He was wearing a long-sleeved shirt, Levi's, and boots as he left the house. He jammed his old cowboy hat on his head before he got in the truck and headed uptown. It was a little after eight a.m., and he was thinking about the biscuits and gravy as he drove. He braked at a stop sign, waved at the woman walking her dog, then accelerated through the intersection.

The parking lot at Granny's was more than half-full as he parked and got out.

Lovey was at the register, and she still hadn't gotten used to seeing a cowboy in Blessings, but it was beginning to grow on her. The man was seriously good-looking, even with that scar.

"Morning, Dan. Are you joining anyone?"

"No, just me today," he said, and took off his hat.

She picked up a menu and led him toward a small booth. "Your waitress will be with you shortly," Lovey said. "Enjoy!"

"Yes, ma'am. Thank you," Dan said, and laid his hat on the seat beside him. But before he could open the menu, Shelly Mayberry, the newest waitress, was at his table with a pot of coffee and a glass of water.

"Welcome," she said as she filled the cup. "Do you

need to study the menu a little longer, or do you know what you want?"

"I know what I want. Biscuits and sausage gravy with a couple of scrambled eggs on the side."

"Coming up," Shelly said, and left to turn in the order.

Dan was waiting for his food when Lon Pittman came in. Dan could tell by the look on the police chief's face that something was wrong. He watched, curious as to who he was looking for, then saw the chief make eye contact with him and head his way.

"Morning, Dan. Sorry to disturb you, but I'm doing a welfare check on your neighbor, Elliot Graham. He isn't answering his phone, some of his landscaping has been damaged, and his car is missing. I was wondering if you remember when you saw him last?"

Dan frowned. "I saw him early yesterday morning, and I actually witnessed the shrubs going down. Elliot did it. He took one out the first time he tried to back out of his drive, then took the other one out when he tried it again. But he made a joke about it as he drove away. I haven't seen him since."

"Was he going toward Main?" Lon asked.

"Uh…no, toward the park."

"Okay, sorry about interrupting you. If you happen to see him, give me a call."

"Sure thing," Dan said.

Lon wasn't really worried about Elliot—yet. What was odd was how the old man had flown under the radar in Blessings for as long as he had. He'd lived across the street from Preston Williams for years, and had spent a lot of time traveling. But after Elliot's wife, Helena, passed away, he'd given up everything and turned into something of a hermit.

It wasn't until Mercy Dane had come to Blessings that he'd come out from under the shadow of loss. When Mercy became the renter of the apartment over Elliot's garage, it was her indomitable spirit that, once again, pulled him into the flow of life.

Even though Mercy and Lon were married now and living in Lon's home on the other side of Blessings, she'd stayed in touch with her old landlord, and it was Mercy who'd called attention to the damaged shrubs, and then to his absence yesterday evening when she stopped to check on his welfare. When she went by again this morning and he still wasn't there, she alerted Lon to the fact.

He'd started out thinking this welfare check would amount to nothing, but he wasn't so sure now. The longer he looked and the more people he talked to, the more concerned he became.

Elliot Graham was no longer in Blessings, of that he was certain. But where did he go? When was he coming back? Or had something happened? Was he lost? Had he become the victim of a crime? The possibilities were endless, and the longer he stayed gone, the less chance Lon felt he had for a positive resolution.

He was cruising the perimeters of the park when his cell phone rang. It was the police dispatcher.

"What's up, Avery?" Lon asked.

"Just got a phone call from Millie Powers. Said there's a car parked out at Gray Goose Lake that's been there for two days now. She saw it yesterday and didn't think anything of it, but when she went back today and saw it was still there, she felt something was wrong. It was unlocked, so she checked inside and found mail in the passenger seat addressed to Elliot Graham. That's why she called us instead of the sheriff."

"Did she give a location of the car?"

"Do you know where Millie lives?" Avery asked.

"Yes," Lon said.

"So, she said take the first turn west past her place and it's parked near boat ramp number two."

"Notify County what's going on and let them know I'm already en route. I'll stay in touch."

"Will do, Chief."

Lon hit the lights and siren, then made a U-turn before heading out of Blessings. He was already planning to get Charlie Conroy and that bloodhound again if he couldn't locate the old man in a timely fashion.

The closer Lon got to the lake, the more anxious he became. By the time he passed Millie Powers's home, he was sick to his stomach from thinking about what might await him. He braked as he arrived at the turn, and took the gravel road.

He saw Elliott's car just after he pulled up. Thinking of what wild animals might be around the lake, the most dangerous ones that came to mind were snakes, big cats, an occasional black bear. It wasn't likely, but it was a possibility.

He grabbed a hand-held radio and popped the trunk to get a rifle. After checking to see if it was loaded, he pocketed some extra rounds, shouldered his backpack, and headed toward the car. He knew Millie Powers had been inside it looking for a clue as to who owned it, but he looked inside to satisfy himself before setting out. After circling the car a couple of times, he finally found a set of tracks leading along the shore and followed them.

He was about two hundred yards from the car when he found his first clue. It was a tube of oil paint—burnt umber. That's when he remembered that Elliot was an accomplished artist.

He took a picture of the tube of paint, then dropped it in an evidence bag and kept moving.

Lon paused a moment along the shore to look around and slowly became aware of what might have led Elliot out here—the views from any direction were stunning. Then he turned back to the footprints and kept walking. About fifty yards farther, the land began to slope upward, forming a cliff about thirty feet from the water below. It was the high point at the lake, and the place people referred to as the overlook.

He started up the slope in long strides, and only seconds after breaching the crest, saw a folding easel on its side, a canvas lying in the grass, and a little folding chair still sitting in its upright position. Elliot was flat on his back on the ground beside the chair.

"Oh no," Lon muttered, and started running. The moment he reached the body, he dropped to his knees, all but certain he was dead.

Also by Sharon Sala